A Pride & Prejudice Reimagining

Kitty Bennet's Adventure
Book Nine

NEY MITCH

EXPLORATION & ENDEAVORS

ISBN: 979-8-88653-496-2

Published by Satin Romance
An Imprint of Melange Books, LLC
White Bear Lake, MN 55110
www.satinromance.com

Published in the United States of America.

Cover Design by Caroline Andrus

Dedication & Author's Note

Readers, welcome to Book Nine, nearing the end—oh, but who are we joking? Each time I get near a finale, there is always so much more story to tell, and I look as if I have egg on my face.

This next entry is a little different than previous ones in that it is more of an ensemble tale where half of the book is from Kitty's perspective and the other half focuses on other characters, to give it a more fleshed out narrative. I hope this will be satisfying for the reader. Also, I wish to inform you all that there are a couple of sensuous scenes in this chapter of the saga, and hope that you are not averse to it.

And yes, it's been quite a while since this series has left off. I swear, this was not done out of laziness on my part, but simply that, with us humans, there will always be other conflicts that get in the way of finishing things as soon as we wish to. If you are still here, and still follow Miss Kitty Bennet to the very end of this tale, I am...well, there is no words for it, now is there? But believe me, I appreciate it immensely. You make this lowly writer feel special.

I also wish to give a special thanks to my family, my publisher and all who helped to get this book published.

And lastly to Helyn-Roberts Vickers, A. Madison, and Ms. Novo, thank you for standing with me.

Friends, let us go forth, and have fun once more!

Chapter One
SCRIBBLINGS

Doing my best to not spill my ink, I tried to steady my diary as it was propped up on my knees. Due to the travels on The Lilia, our living quarters were quite sparse, and we were unable to have a desk.

Since Georgiana was wise enough to bring a writing desk with her, she always allowed me to borrow it when I needed to write in my journal. I had removed all the contents from the desk, always closed the ink pot after dipping my quill into it and attempted to make any progress.

Writing on a ship is always problematic at best, but to write on a merchant vessel during a storm is even more of a trial.

Yet, I had to write. Every instinct within me cried out to do so, and Georgiana, knowing that when the impulse struck me, I was an unstoppable force.

And the storm...was an immovable object.

Let us see how we would get on together...

It's been two days since Georgiana, the Rileys, Miss Emma Watson, and Mr. Blake and I set sail from London. When I refer to Mr. Blake, his true name is Mr. Howard. However, since being onboard, he told us that he has never really preferred his last name. As such, he often asks us to call him by his middle name: Blake. I find that I prefer that name as well. How ironically interesting that his middle name is the same name as his sister's married name.

Between the odds and evens of walking away from everything that one is familiar with, I was prepared not to see what was behind me, but of the world ahead.

However, the one thing that a person cannot ever prepare for, or predict, is the weather.

The captain and crew could foresee a storm, but not always. This tempest decided to appear on us, in a very unexpected fashion.

While rain and clouds can be somewhat uncongenial on land, it's hazardous on water.

I don't hide in here, for fear of the drink. On the contrary, I am curious to see how the crew handle themselves during such an ordeal. Yet I dare say that they would wish to be free of my presence—especially since my fascination with them must be a little overwhelming.

Enara was right!

This crew is one of the most fascinating crews that a person could ever encounter. While my experience with voyages is severely limited, I doubt that my ignorance was working against me. On the contrary, sometimes, I think there can be something redeeming about ignorance on certain matters. After all, to me, the world looks prettier—even its ugliness takes on an interesting shade, because it gives me something to gasp at.

Oh, I am starting in a foolish way.

I had to write. For the freedom of unleashing the fire of my inner voices.

That's the only problem with being on a ship—one cannot talk to oneself. I am not one to pretend that I am not a little mad, for I am. However, I flatter myself that I am not the only one, who when alone, does sometimes shout many words at themselves, be it to express ideas that you wonder how it will sound out loud, or merely wishing to say all the things that you wanted to say the entire day, but you were afraid to. After all, freedom of speech does not mean that you ought to say everything that's on your mind in a public setting. Even I understand that etiquette has its uses in the world.

But a diary is different. It does not judge you. And that's what makes it the most charming friend of all. You need some place to reveal your evil.

And evil is what I write. Being shut up here, I can finally say that I have been both selfish and selfless.

These have been both the most entertaining, as well as longest days of my life.

When it became evident that Georgiana was eager to regain her long past friendship with Emma Watson, I decided to do well by her and give them time together.

After all, I have the Rileys for company. I would say that Mr. Blake is charming, but two days is not enough to gain a wider acquaintance with him, or to know his character yet. In truth, I still cannot fully make him out.

But Emma Watson is a different matter entirely.

There are some people that a person can know for a day, and you know, instantly, that you both will never be on intimate terms.

And that is the selfish reason that I do remove myself from them all.

I fear that I don't like Emma Watson very much at all. It is not hatred, of course, but it is discomfort. Every time that I am around her, I am reminded of things that I wanted to leave behind.

Her nature is very fine. It was evident, from her history, that she was raised to be very refined and genteel. There is a striking elegance to her as well, but I knew that from the very first time that I met her.

Everything about her is superior to me, but it is not jealousy that I feel. I speak in truth; at this point in my life, I have seen the evils of envy, and I don't wish to be like that.

But when she looks at me, I can see it: there is a coldness, and a hidden judgment to everything that I do. When I speak, she sometimes does not respond and can be politely disagreeable.

It is not wrong to have opinions. We all have them. But she seems to be on the wrong side of our youth: the side that has one image of what us ladies ought to be, and that is all. I am not of that image. Georgiana is, but not me.

Also, I feel unwanted. As if I am the odd one out, as it were. And as if I am intruding. Never before have I experienced such a thing. It is almost as if I feel hollow inside, and worthless. Is this natural? And so, when I am around them, I try to overcompensate and speak more than usual, but I can tell that it looks forced. And it must feel so.

I do not understand. What has happened to me?

I was never popular. I was not Lydia.

I was never accomplished: I was not Mary or Elizabeth.

I was not universally loved: I was not Jane.

But the one thing that I always had to my name, that I could boast was my own virtue, and I coveted it, was my power to be approachable. To be amenable to company, to be comfortable to be around, to having someone in the room who cared to be near me.

And now I did not have that. We all have that one thing that makes us special, and it ought not to be taken from us. My skill was taken from me.

When looking at Emma Watson, I cannot help but view her as the source behind it all. She never smiles when near me, never seeks me out, or is happy when I seek her out. And opinions can be contagious things.

How long will it be until Georgiana realizes that I was never a proper companion for her? And that women like Emma Watson will always be better than I?

That is what I fear. That opinions are, and always will be, contagious.

And this time, the contagion will fall hardest on me.

One cannot help but be selfish.

I should tell Georgiana, shouldn't I?

No! That would make me pathetic.

But I am at a pathetic state.

Yes, I should tell her.

If Finlay and Colonel Fitzwilliam were here, I would not feel worthless.

Oh, I must stop writing about them! Spite it all! I must stop focusing on them so...for what good would it do? Mistakes and I are old friends. I have made quite a few of them. But I will not dwell on such a mistake of always remembering affections long past. I will not spend my days thinking of them all the time, rather than moving forward.

I do them and myself no service by that.

BOOM!

~

The sound above me made me drop my quill. Seeing that it was fruitless to continue, I placed all my items on Georgiana's desk, placed it under my bed, and looked up at the sound of it.

Above me were the scurrying feet of sailors who were doing their best to handle the sails and expel as much water from the ship as possible.

How I wanted to go up and see how they handled the helm! Even when one knows how not to behave, curiosity will always be curiosity. And the short and the long of it is that I would not be satisfied until I saw a little.

Therefore, placing my cloak over my head, I tiptoed out of my cabin, walked past all the other cabins down below and walked to the stairs that led to the top deck. The water was coming down hard, and I knew that I would get wet all over, but Nature never frightened me. After all, could Nature help herself?

When I reached the steps, diligently, I walked up the stairs, only going so far, that my face scanned over what was happening above board.

Scurrying back and forth were not only the sailors, but at the wheel was the captain. Or to be more accurate, the Master. With it being a merchant vessel, Master was the most appropriate title, but he was accustomed to people calling him Captain Archer.

James Archer was his name, and he looked every much like his position. As he stood at the wheel, as opposed to another sailor doing so, he presented a majestically masculine image. Some men age remarkably well and take their beauty into their elderly age. The Master, Captain Archer, was in his late sixties, had blue eyes, had gray hair that was turning white in some patches, he kept it cut short and refused to wear a wig, for any reason. His skin was peach and a little brown, which naturally came from being somewhat weather-beaten. Then again, he never struck me as the sort of man who was pale at all but was born looking healthy. When he was younger, he must have been a beautiful man, because in his older age, his form was still handsome, his face was a little long and quite thin, he was well-made, and he was quite tall.

He was a leader. That was to be expected. Next to him on the landing was his Chief Officer, Mr. Kenneth Turner the Third, so he was often called Trip by everyone, because being the third made him the triple... the triple meant Trip. Like Captain Archer, Trip was also an elderly man who's face clung to the beauties of earlier days. He too had gray hair, but unlike Captain Archer, he did not fear going a few days being unshaven.

Also, unlike Captain Archer, Mr. Trip's American accent was distinctly Southern, since he had been from North Carolina, our one-time Colonies.

The first surprising crewmate was the Second Officer. It was only natural that the post was always a male because it naturally ought to be. But here, on the Lilia, it was not so. The Second Officer was a handsome middle-aged woman, named Miss Tepree, from Maryland. Due to never having children, she maintained a strong figure, had a striking face, peach skin, short brown hair, similar to the captain's hair, and she was moving back and forth on the deck, her face wet all the way through as she conveyed the captain's orders to the entire crew, even assisting in swabbing the deck to keep water from dripping down below.

My eyes were fixed on her. From the first time that she had set out to plan her life, how did she do it? Between her intention to be a bosun and officer, and actually committing to the deed—a deed that it was impossible for her to ever fill...what happened? Every now and again, there will always be that character in your life, that person who defied convention and overcame a perpetual standard that they served under. Tepree was that sort of person in my life. She did everything that a lady ought not to do.

Due to her striking character, often she found me staring at her, very blankly, as if in wonder. Between her ability to rise above the standards of her time, as well as her striking figure and face, I found myself too intimidated to approach her very much.

I suppose—that I admired her.

And she could not help but find it hard to stand me. I could not blame her. There must be something so very vexing about being wondered about and adored. It must be a daunting concept.

The wind and cold from the rain whipped across my face, and I was almost prepared to return to my cabin, when I caught sight of the Watch Leader, an Indian named White Wolf, of the Dakota Tribe, as he marched around the ship, also making sure that everything was running smoothly. He caught sight of me and winked.

I smiled and waved.

To my happiness, he understood my fascination with him and did not shy under the notice. Perhaps, it was because he was accustomed to it, especially since he still wore some of the familiar items that Indians were known for wearing. His hair was long and black, which he kept tied up, but it swayed behind him, and so did the beads that dangled from his neck. He didn't fear the harsh winds and the water that sloshed against his face but always seemed to welcome it.

He was fascinating, to be sure, especially since he had a certain regality about him.

"Kitty!" I heard from behind me.

Turning around, I saw Emma Watson standing in her cabin's doorway.

"Whatever do you do there?"

"I was watching the sailors."

"You will fall ill. That is unwise."

"Perhaps, I will. But the sailors have it worse."

I looked at her face and saw that she was grieved in some sort of manner.

"What is that look for?" I asked her, coming down the stairs.

"It's Miss Darcy."

"She is not averse to you calling her Georgiana, you know."

"It's not proper." Her tone was imperious.

"It's friendship; it does not have to be proper. Now what is it?"

"She's ill again."

"Oh!" I gasped, rushing up to her. When I reached her, she looked squarely at me.

"Why do you always do that?" she asked me.

"Do what?"

"Look at me as if I am about to be cross."

"Because you often are, if you must know," I replied. "You are telling me that you are not always being critical of me when we speak?"

For a second, she did not answer the question. Oh, very well. For *ten* seconds, she didn't answer the question.

"See?" I asked her. "Told you."

"It is just that some things you say and do are a little spirited—"

I groaned, moving past her.

"I don't have time for this now."

When I went into her room, I saw Georgiana hurling up her breakfast into a wastebin.

"Oh, Georgie." I said, going to her and helping her to hold her hair so that it did not get in the way of her purging.

When she finished, I quickly closed the bag, tied it up, and went above deck. As I did so, the wind and rain crashed against my face viciously, and I almost fell over, since the deck was so slippery. Racing to the edge, I threw the bag into the sea.

Out of my peripheral vision, I saw a figure standing there. Turning, I saw the Third Officer, Charles Reedus, watching what I had just done. Being the Third Officer, he was quite like a bosun. Another term for bosun is boatswain, who has charge of the anchor and anchor gear, cargo-handling, boats, and instruction of the crew in practical seamanship. With a rope in his hand, Lieutenant Reedus was watching my actions as I had dumped the bag overboard.

Reedus was a fellow British citizen. He was from Wales, and like the master and Commander Trip, he was middle-aged, with gray hairs mingled with his dark brown locks. His face was distinct, and he spoke with such an elegant manner, that he brought an element of class to the rest of the crew. Not only that, but he didn't sound like he was born to the life of a sailor, but of a gentleman. I always wanted to ask him why his life took the turn that it did, but that would have to be at another time.

Meanwhile, he was still staring at me, quizzically.

"My friend," I said, gesturing to the water, "she was ill."

"Ah," he said, the look of familiarity filling his eyes. "Seasickness claims another victim. Have Phineas look at her. Of course, he'll say what I said before, but nothing bests a confirmation."

"Right."

"Now get down below, or you will be soaked all the way through."

"Righty ho, sailor!" I said, saluting him. He laughed as he moved past me, answering to an order that Tepree cried out to him. Giving her a quick look, where she avoided my gaze, I went down below again, to see Georgiana.

When I went to the cabin, I saw that she was not there. Coming to an assumption, I went to Doctor Phineas' room, and I found Georgiana and Emma Watson there, with Doctor Phineas inspecting Georgiana. When seeing me, Georgiana's eyes lit up.

"Did you tell anyone that it was my purging?"

"No," I assured her, "I told no one it was you."

She sighed, her face still a little green. Looking everywhere else but at Emma Watson, I held Georgiana's hand. I knew that it was only a matter of time before Emma would inform me that this was all her idea, and I was not left to wait for long.

"I thought it would be best to have Doctor Phineas see her," Emma observed.

"Yes," I replied. "Mr. Reedus confirmed your decision."

We didn't say it, but we knew it; despite how juvenile a tendency it is, it is no less human, and quite the ageless habit, of now being in competition for who could be the best sort of friend to Georgiana.

Well, if that's how she would like to play it...

"This is her third time purging, Doctor," I said. "Is there anything else that might help her?"

"Yes," Doctor Phineas said, going to his briefcase and pulling out some tonics. "I think that I do. Of course, Miss Darcy, this seasickness is customary, and there is nothing to be ashamed of. The insecurities of youth have no claims on a ship. Seasickness is seasickness."

Georgiana looked at Emma and me.

"And yet my friends have not suffered the effects."

"Different bodies are set up in different ways."

He handed her a tonic.

"Drink one spoonful of this every two hours. If it does not work, do not overdose. You simply must accept that it might take your stomach a little longer to grow accustomed to the fact that your home likes to rock from side to side."

He smiled amiably at her.

"Give your body time, Miss Darcy, and time will prefer you."

Emma Watson offered Georgiana her arm to help lead her to her room, and I didn't even try to best her efforts. After all, I knew Georgie; she wouldn't want anyone's help.

I was proven correct when Georgiana thanked her but insisted that she could walk on her own. They both left the doctor's quarters, and I remained behind, curious.

"What was in the tonic that you gave her?" I asked.

Doctor Phineas raised an eyebrow.

"Don't worry." I brushed my hand through the air. "I do not ask you that because I doubt your abilities. But what happens if one of my friends grow ill again and you are not around?"

"Oh," Phineas responded. "You wish to take matters into your own hands."

"Is that so wrong?"

"Not at all. I use a blend of ginger and peppermint, liquidized. The only difficulty is measurements. 550 milligrams of ginger with a teaspoon of peppermint often works. Mind you, these sort of tonics are not an exact science."

"Meaning that they can work for some, but not everyone."

"Precisely."

"Thank you."

Looking over my shoulder, his eyes focused on Emma Watson's room.

"You three, if I don't mind me asking, are friends?"

"Oh," I replied, a little curious at how I was to describe us. "I am friends with Miss Darcy, and Emma is friends with her. What I refer to is that she shares us as mutual friends between, but Miss Watson and I are acquaintances."

"I see. Now it all makes sense."

I looked at him, interested in what he meant.

"What makes sense, I wonder?"

"The dynamic between you three. Forgive me for noticing such things, but when you are a surgeon on a ship, where no one needs you to repair anything, you become a creature of observation."

"Naturally. What do you see when you see the three of us?"

"I have offended you."

"Don't worry about hurting my feelings. I am tougher than I appear as. I stopped fearing observations long ago."

"It is all a matter of analyzing one's body language. You speak with Miss Darcy, Miss Watson speaks with her—and then you and Miss Watson engage in conversation sparingly. And the tension is so thick that it can cut a beam."

"And I thought I was being careful," I noted, rolling my eyes.

"Some things cannot always be hidden. I cannot claim to know everything about your history, but I have undergone a similar predicament to yourself. With that known, might I make a suggestion?"

"What would that be?"

"If complete friendship between you three renders itself to be impossible, do not end in using Miss Darcy as the battleground between you both. When that occurs, no one wins."

I bit my lip.

"I was worried that it might come to that."

"Don't let it. You'll be a good friend to her if you don't ever let it reach that place."

I nodded to him and went back to my room. As I passed Enara and Arthur's cabin, my instinct was to knock on their door, barge in and tell them all my woes.

Yet my better instincts overcame that. They were returning to Australia, to a whole other side of their family. The last thing they needed was my pettiness.

Thus, going back to my room, I collapsed on my bed, digging my face into the pillow.

I wondered what was happening back in England, at Pemberley, Godfrey Park, at Meryton, and with my sisters?

Chapter Two

COINCIDENCE & CONTRAST

"Oh dear!" Elizabeth cried, clutching her stomach. She had just been laying down in her guestroom, at Godfrey Park, when she decided to get some water from a pitcher on her nightstand.

As she stood up, her knees buckled, her body shuddered, and she felt the familiar effects of her time coming. The evidence was cemented when her legs and the bottom of her gown was drenched in the water that broke from within her.

Suddenly, the pain was sharp, and she stumbled to the nightstand, grabbed the bell, and wrung it hard.

Betsy came rushing in, and when she saw Mrs. Darcy going into labor, she turned into a machine of efficiency.

"I've got you, mistress," Betsy said, helping Elizabeth to the bed. "Lay there."

"I have no choice, apparently," Elizabeth grunted. "I cannot do anything else, now can I?"

"Breathe out and in. Lucy!"

Instantly, Lucy came rushing in as well.

"It's time," Betsy ordered, "bring the midwife in, immediately, have the bath drawn, and have Daniel bring Doctor Palmer."

"It will be well, Mrs. Darcy," Lucy assured her.

"She knows that, believe me," Betsy ordered, "now get along with you, and get that sad lump of laziness in here immediately!"

"Which servant is the 'sad lump of laziness' again?" Lucy asked.

"Sarah," Betsy and Elizabeth said in unison. "Hurry about it."

"Of course," Lucy said, leaving as quickly as her feet could carry her.

"I thought she would have known who I was referring to by now," Betsy said, taking Elizabeth's hand to help her steady her breathing.

"Betsy," Elizabeth said as sweat began to trickle down her forehead, "you've gotten to the point where you've begun to call all the servants names."

"I have?"

"Yes."

"Oh," she said, wiping Elizabeth's forehead with a handkerchief. "I did not know that."

As she poured some water for Elizabeth to drink, Betsy heard footsteps down the hall.

"What took you so long?"

She was surprised when it was not Sarah but the housekeeper, Mrs. Mortenson.

"Mrs. Darcy!" Mrs. Mortenson said, "do not worry. A bath is being drawn for you at this moment."

"Mrs. Mortenson, where is the sad lump of lazy flesh?" Betsy asked.

"Oh, you mean Sarah?"

"See!" Betsy replied, triumphant. "She knows *who* I refer to."

"She is tending to the Mistress."

"Jane?" Elizabeth said, between grunts of breathing, "What is happening to my sister?"

"Mrs. Darcy," Mrs. Mortenson said, "keep breathing and prepare yourself."

Elizabeth breathed out and in.

"Two baths have to be made," Mrs. Mortenson said.

"Two?"

"Yes. Your sister just went into labor five minutes ago."

Sometimes news is so alarming that it can make one quite forget about all the pain that a person is undergoing.

Elizabeth suddenly grew silent as she and Betsy stared at Mrs. Mortenson, in shock.

"What?" Elizabeth asked.

"Yes, Mrs. Darcy. Your sister has gone into labor."

"They are both in labor at the same time?" Betsy asked.

"Yes."

Betsy looked at Elizabeth, incredulous.

"What is with you two always doing everything together?"

"Betsy, Jane and I have no control over our biological functions."

"It does not change the reality of the present situation."

Elizabeth thought on this. "No, I suppose it does not."

A sharp pain surged through her stomach, and she cried out again.

"Oh, the memories," Mrs. Mortenson said as they held her.

"Is this what it was like for you?" Elizabeth asked, shrieking afterwards.

"Every time. I would say that it gets easier, but...well, perhaps you don't need to hear that now."

"As long as this agony—argh!—is natural!"

"Oh, it's natural as the driven snow."

"Where is Mr. Darcy? I need him!"

"Never fear," Mrs. Mortenson informed her, "I sent a servant to tell Mr. Bingley and Mr. Darcy that you have begun your laying in. They will be here presently."

"We cannot let him in here," Betsy said.

"Why not?" Elizabeth cried. "He's the one responsible for doing this to me!"

"Ah, hatred towards the husband," Mrs. Mortenson observed. "That is the next natural sign."

Mr. Darcy burst into the room.

"Where is my wife!"

"On the bed, you fool," Elizabeth cried. "Don't you have eyes?"

When hearing himself being insulted, Mr. Darcy halted for a minute.

"Does she hate me now?" Mr. Darcy asked Betsy.

"No," Betsy responded.

"Casting aspersions at your character is natural in her state," Mrs. Mortenson urged him, "because you put her in this predicament."

"Oh."

Mr. Darcy dashed to Elizabeth and took her hand.

"My Lizzy!" he cried.

"Oh, Fitz," she uttered, in tears, "it hurts terribly. My love..."

"You can do it," Mr. Darcy assured her, wiping down her hair. "My brave wife, you will make it through this. Just please...fight for me."

"You selfish numpty!" she hissed. "Of course, I am going to fight. I'm not leaving you."

Mr. Darcy looked at Mrs. Mortenson again.

"It feels like many knives are digging into her stomach," Mrs. Mortenson explained. "Her words are perfectly natural."

"Oh, thank you."

The midwife, Mrs. Nelson, arrived and the baths were organized for both ladies. Coming in with great authority, she had warm water placed into the baths, and the ladies were put into it.

As she was absent from the bathing room, to mash up some tree bark and other herbs for some pain relief, Doctor Palmer came in.

"Why are they in the bathtubs?" Doctor Palmer asked as Jane

and Elizabeth were breathing heavily, occasionally crying out when a contraction reached another level of agonizing.

"Because I ordered them to," Mrs. Nelson said, entering again with the tonic that she had finished mixing.

"And what reason would you have for that?" Mr. Palmer asked, removing his jacket, and rolling up his shirtsleeves.

"Hot water helps dull pain, Doctor Palmer," Nelson responded.

"It is highly unorthodox."

"Well, it is working," Jane said, between grunts. "Mrs. Nelson, this has helped me a great deal."

"And I," Elizabeth affirmed, as she gasped.

"Also," Mrs. Nelson said, "the water helps loosen their bodies when it is time to come."

"And how," Palmer ordered, "will it help? When the time comes, we cannot transport them back to their beds to help them deliver."

"We're not bringing them back to their bedrooms," Nelson insisted, "they are going to deliver, standing up in the wash bins."

"What? That is absurd."

Nelson rolled her eyes, aggravated at his refusal to embrace common sense.

"No, it's not. Experience has proven that warm water soothes pain, and that it's easier for a woman to deliver a child when she is standing. The only reason that practices changed, and women were told to lay down while they delivered their infant, was because doctors claimed it hurt their backs by sitting in such a way under the woman. Well, when a woman delivers a child, our pain is miniscule compared to theirs, so there is no contest."

Doctor Palmer looked at Mrs. Nelson, menacingly, and Elizabeth saw the resentment between them. Not in the mood to suffer through Palmer's antiquated ideas, to suit his own comfort rather than hers, Elizabeth pushed through her pain and became firm.

"Mr. Palmer! I have it upon Mr. Darcy's and Mr. Bingley's authority that this is the preferred way that they wished to deliver their children. You are paid for your services. If you wish to deny their intentions, then you may tell them so. For they are right outside of the door."

When hearing that, Doctor Palmer's face transitioned from argumentative to conformity.

"Very well," he said, going over to Mrs. Bingley while Mrs. Nelson tended to Elizabeth.

"Fool," Nelson grunted under her teeth.

"I know," Elizabeth responded, equally as aggravated that she had to bring up her husband's authority instead of Palmer naturally understanding that Mrs. Nelson's experience made sense.

As the water got colder, more warm water was brought in while the colder water was removed, to make sure that they remained warm the entire time. With each pouring of the warmer water, the women's pain was soothed, and the herbs dulled the agony a little more.

From outside of the washroom, Mr. Darcy and Mr. Bingley paced back and forth, anxious. Standing in a corner, Daniel, the servant remained sentinel.

With each shout, Bingley fidgeted relentlessly, his whole body becoming jittery, while Mr. Darcy paced slower, the tension within his body growing even more.

Elizabeth shouted in agony.

Darcy froze, worried for her.

Jane shouted from the pain.

Bingley rung his hands, in anguish and guilt of his wife being in such a state.

When hearing Jane shout once more, Mr. Bingley rested his hand against the wall, breathing out and in, as Jane was doing. Worried that he might hyperventilate, Darcy approached Bingley, to steady him. Placing his hand on his shoulder, he felt Bingley's body grow limp under the gesture.

"I'm scared, Darcy," Bingley confessed, "as if I were the little boy again, who feared being brought to his father, when he was caught out on telling a lie. My knees were shaking, and I felt as if I would die on the spot."

"You feel that now?"

"Yes, I do. If Jane dies..."

"She won't."

"We don't know that. No more than you cannot know if Elizabeth will—"

"Don't say that!" Mr. Darcy hissed savagely.

"I'm sorry."

Darcy gritted his teeth and looked away from Bingley, doing his best to calm the rage that was building up within him. Like his friend, he feared losing his wife. For a second—for a split second—Darcy realized that he was about to unleash his anguish on Bingley.

"Forgive me," Darcy apologized. "I know how I must have sounded."

"No need to apologize," Bingley said. "For we both are feeling the same thing."

"Yes, I daresay that we are."

Mr. Bingley chuckled.

"Oh, you stumbled on something funny?"

"No. Or yes. I am recalling when Jane first felt the sharp pains and her time was coming. She called me a demon and that I had destroyed her life."

Darcy turned to Bingley, astounded.

"She said that?"

"Yes."

"Jane said *that*?"

"Yes, she did."

They heard a chuckle behind them, and it was Daniel.

"Forgive me, master and Mr. Darcy," Daniel said, "however, that sort of talk is customary."

"It is?" Bingley asked.

"Oh, yes. Whenever I was near my wife during her laying in, she shouted all sorts of obscenities at me. My father always said that they get possessed at that time, and when the hardship ends, they forget they ever said those things."

"Possessed?" Darcy echoed, aghast at the phrase.

"That was the only word that my father could put to it."

From the other side of the room, Elizabeth cried out.

"Pain is a demon of its own kind, I suppose," Darcy had no choice but to reason out. "Their mother survived five pregnancies, their aunts survived theirs, and Lizzy and Jane are not sickly. They will survive this."

"But the infant?"

"Bingley, I am about to confess something horrible."

"What?"

"I want my child to live, but if I had to choose between Elizabeth living, and the child—I would choose Elizabeth."

"I understand. I would also choose Jane. After all, many parents have lost children and continued. Not everyone survived their spouse dying and knew how to continue on."

"Precisely. May they both live, of course, but if one ought to choose..."

"Yes, if one ought to choose..."

The screams on the other side reached a deafening pitch.

"Now it's time," Daniel said, "the mistress and Mrs. Darcy are about to begin."

Darcy and Bingley looked at him.

"You know?" Bingley asked.

"That's the loudest shout so far. The babies are coming. Mark my words."

~

"You are doing well, ladies," Mrs. Nelson cried as Lucy, Betsy, Sarah, and Mrs. Mortenson held their hands, as they stood up in the wash bins.

Mrs. Nelson was tending to Elizabeth, while Doctor Palmer was seeing to Jane. They raised up the ladies' chemises, tying them around their hips and placing their hands underneath, ready to cradle the child as it came out.

"The babies are properly turned," Doctor Palmer said, "there is nothing to fear. Now push downward!"

With Betsy and Mrs. Mortenson holding Elizabeth's arms, they steadied her. Sarah and Lucy were there to hold Jane. Nelson had advised the women not to hold the pregnant ladies' hands, for fear that the strength of their grip would break their fingers. Her words did not go unheeded and were very correct. The speed of pain that shot through Jane and Elizabeth as they pushed downward, willing their child to enter the world and breathe in the cup of life.

Elizabeth felt the pain take her to a new plateau of existence.

Even through her shouts, she knew that something beautiful was entering the world, and that it would change her life forever. The sounds that it would hear from the first time, the bright light that it would be met with—the whole world was laid before its feet, and they would greet the world, with new eyes. From the very first breath that it breathed; it was introduced to a whole new set of experiences and felt the magic within itself. For that is how we live and constantly survive: the magic of how our bodies work, how quickly our minds think, feel, and deduce...the magic of existence.

This child would be born! With every part of her strength, the child would be born.

With all her might, her spirit, will and courage was pushed into the infant, which was as eager to enter this new place as she was to expose them to it.

In a sudden motion, the child escaped from the womb, and with incredible surprise, Mrs. Nelson held the newborn, amazed.

"How swift!" she cried. "How swiftly she came."

True to her skill, Mrs. Nelson pulled out the rest of the afterbirth, severed the umbilical cord, took a rag, placed the baby in the water, wiped it down, put it in warm linens as Betsy and Mrs. Mortenson helped lower Elizabeth back into the water.

Overcome by the exertion, Elizabeth was determined never to move again, until her eyes opened, and she saw Mrs. Nelson cradling her child in her arms.

"How is it?" Elizabeth asked.

"Congratulations, Mrs. Darcy," Mrs. Nelson said, "you have a beautiful baby girl."

She handed the newborn to its mother, and Elizabeth easily found the strength to reach out and hold her baby.

"Oh," Elizabeth cooed, looking down on her new daughter. The baby's eyes were shut as it cried out, perhaps overpowered by the light of entering the world that it would now have to grow into. Being a mother, the world changed into a different hue. All illumination in the room dimmed except for the light that emitted from the child. All the world seemed to fall away, and all fears, all anxieties of how to be a mother and how to love this infant were entirely over. The fears that she would not want to share her husband's love with this new child were at an end. From within Elizabeth's soul, a new love was formed. A love that could not be rivaled. As great as her love for Darcy was, so was the love for this new baby girl that she had in her arms.

Elizabeth placed her finger inside of the infant's hand. The newborn's fingers closed around it, and her mother smiled.

"Never let go," Elizabeth stressed, tears filling up her eyes, "never let go. My beautiful girl."

As Elizabeth sat there, in the wash bin, holding her baby girl, she heard Jane's shouts to her left. Turning, holding her infant close to her chest, Elizabeth watched in horror as Jane had continued to struggle to release her child.

'Is that what I looked like?' Elizabeth asked herself as she watched Jane, being held up by Sarah and Lucy, crying out in agony as her body spasmed, wanting her child to be born as Mr. Palmer ordered the baby to come forth and for Jane to continue pushing. 'Is that what we will always have to endure? How did I survive this?'

"I've got the head!" Mr. Palmer cried, "now the neck is coming! Mrs. Bingley, continue pushing out! It will come!"

Jane roared out even more, her knees buckling as Elizabeth watched her, in complete horror for her sister's life. Jane was growing weaker by the second. If she pushed any more, would the exertion kill her?

No, not Jane!

"I've got the body," Mr. Palmer cried. "One more push, Mrs. Bingley. One more push!"

Jane cried.

"I cannot," she wept," "I cannot!"

"You can," Elizabeth cried out to her. "Yes, you can. Jane, just one more time."

Looking at her younger sister, and the baby in Eliza's arms, Jane gathered her courage and pushed herself onward, feeling the ultimate release.

"I've got it," Mr. Palmer declared, calmly. "It is out."

Jane breathed out, relieved as she was helped back down into the water.

Elizabeth smiled, happy to see her sister still with life within her, breathing evenly—until she looked at Doctor Palmer. Palmer held the baby in his hands, but he had not done anything to sever the umbilical cord yet. In fact, he just stared at the baby, frozen.

Despite not being told why, Elizabeth felt a coldness from that gesture. Why did he not perform the duties that he ought to perform? What halted him, but one fatal reality?

"Palmer?" Mrs. Nelson declared, "the afterbirth man, the cord and the cleaning!" She walked up to him. "What are you—"

When looking at the infant, Mrs. Nelson's face turned as blank as Palmer's. The same blank look that had a hint of horror underneath.

One look was chilling.

Two looks bearing the same expression was a horrifying confirmation.

"What is it?" Jane asked, weakly.

Mrs. Nelson and Mr. Palmer looked at her, and their blank expressions turned to subtle dread.

Jane was too delicate for her mind to reach such a conclusion, but Elizabeth, wholly immune to the evident, always aware of the outcome to nature and the way in which a coin could be tossed unevenly, did think of it. And was prepared to be sorry for her sister in ways that no apology could properly convey.

"What is it?" Jane repeated.

All eyes were on the midwife and the doctor, and they had an audience that was both unwanted and undesired. The eyes of those who had to witness a mother who was not to be.

"Mrs. Bingley," Mr. Palmer said, "I am very sorry."

"Sorry?" Jane echoed, her voice hollow and her eyes filling with dread. "Sorry?"

"Mrs. Bingley, you had a beautiful son," Mrs. Nelson said. "A very beautiful one."

"Had?" Jane repeated, her voice even more hollow.

"I am sorry," Mr. Palmer informed her, "but your son was stillborn. He was born already deceased."

Jane...well, what could be said of her? What words can explain the pain of bringing life into the world, and that life is not even being given a moment to see his mother's face, and for her to see him open his eyes and know her?

As for how to respond, to react to knowing that her child was born already taken from her, there is no proper response. There is no way that a woman can determine what they are about. Yet the body knows. The body knows that the first reaction must be nothing. All emotion must shut down, for the mother's strength is waning at that moment. Too much immediate grief could take her life as swiftly as it took the infant's. And mother and child would be lost. Taken from the father and husband before he even knew what had occurred, and what great villain of life had removed all his happiness from him.

Jane's eyes didn't move. Nor did her entire figure. She just sat there, motionless. Not one part of her showed any signs of life. At first, all thoughts of her grief had rendered her sedate. As if her entire mind had shut down and her body followed suit.

Or maybe not. Elizabeth worried of something greater—of a delicate sister, who the shocking blow of her son dying could send a sharp blade to her heart, and it had stopped breathing.

"Jane!" Elizabeth cried, then she turned to Lucy and Sarah. "Rub her chest and hands! The grief can kill her."

Sarah and Lucy obeyed, rubbing her hands and arms, but Jane was still unresponsive.

With a swiftness that came from acting on instincts and leaving thought behind, Elizabeth rose, with newfound energy, handing her girl to Betsy, rushed over to Jane, stepped into the wash bin, sat opposite Jane, and began to shake her back and forth.

"Jane, wake up!" Elizabeth cried. Then she patted her cheek. "Jane, don't fall away. Wake up!" In a final effort, Elizabeth slapped Jane. This sudden violent act forced Jane's eyes to move, her whole figure spasmed, and she woke up from her grief. She keeled forward, shaking all over as she gasped in for air.

"There you are," Elizabeth coaxed, exhausted from helping her sister return to the world of the living. "There you are."

"Lizzy?" Jane said weakly.

"Yes, Jane. I'm here. We are all here."

"Where is my son?" Jane asked, weeping. "Where is my son!"

"Oh, Jane!" Elizabeth said, holding her in the water as Jane wept into her little sister's shoulder.

"Where is my son?" Jane continued to cry. "Where is my boy? Why does he leave his poor mother?"

"He is in heaven, dearest," Elizabeth assured her, "his soul is there."

"How do we know that? How do I know? Where is my son!" she cried once more, shaking uncontrollably, then she looked at Mrs. Nelson. "Give him to me."

"Mrs. Bingley..."

"Give him to me. He might wake up if his mother calls him. He might come home."

Knowing that Jane's wish would not come true, Mrs. Nelson reluctantly handed the stillborn, wrapped in linens, to Jane. Greedily, Jane took the body and held it protectively.

"Hello there," Jane said, weakly, to her stillborn son. "Well, aren't you beautiful?"

Elizabeth remained in the tub, leaning back, and watching her sister cradle the dead. With every moment, she awaited the shock that would come when Jane fully realized that her child was lost to her.

"You're too beautiful to be sleeping," Jane uttered to her son, "too beautiful to sleep now. Won't you wake up for your mother? Won't you wake for me?"

Jane repeated it.

The tears came.

She repeated her plea.

More tears came.

With each utterance, it was answered by no miracle, no burst of life that would awaken the unfortunate boy.

"Why must you go?" Jane cried to it. "Why must you go where

I cannot follow you?" She looked up at us. "My boy is gone. My boy is gone!"

~

Suddenly, Mr. Bingley burst into the room.

"I heard Jane cry!" he declared, his face blanched. "I heard—"

He looked at Jane as she was in the water, clutching their son.

"Charles!" Jane cried. "Our boy! Our boy is gone!"

Mr. Bingley was the reverse of his wife. His reaction was immediate and swift.

"No," he uttered, overwhelmed as he limped toward his wife, and held her as he looked down at his son, lifeless in his mother's arms. "No!" Bingley cried. "No!"

Slowly, Elizabeth removed herself from the water, and Mr. Darcy walked up to her, wrapping a towel around her.

"Our baby is over there," Elizabeth whispered to Betsy.

Looking behind her, Darcy's eyes rested on their daughter.

"It's a girl," Elizabeth informed him. Following her husband, they walked to their child. Silently, Mr. Darcy raised up his arms and Betsy handed his daughter to him. Mr. Darcy looked into his daughter's face. She cried in his arms, but that was to be expected. She was in a new world, and her cries were like music to his ears. If she kept crying, it meant that she would continue to live. That was all that he asked for.

Holding her tightly to his chest, he kissed her forehead and brought Elizabeth into his embrace. Despite being exhausted and wanting sleep, Lizzy fought to remain awake as she held her child and her husband.

To their right, they had no choice but to look and see Jane and Mr. Bingley weeping over their lost son.

"What can we do for them?" Lizzy asked, her voice low.

"Be there for them," Darcy answered quietly, so only they could hear. "But the reality is bleak."

"I know."

"No, you don't. When I say bleak, I mean that there is nothing we can do to assist them, because no words can help. In fact, they will hate us."

"What?"

"If our daughter lives, she is the one who survived, while theirs did not. They will be unable to bear the sight of us."

"They would not. Bingley and Jane are too good of people."

"But they are also human. I have seen this sort of behavior before. They will be jealous of us. Any help that we give them will also hurt them. Hard times are ahead."

They watched as Bingley and Jane continued to weep over the son that would never be.

Chapter Three

SISTERS

The storm continued into nightfall.

The Lilia's cooks, a Mexican American couple named Jesus and Gloriana Nueva, had brought us all dinner in our cabins, due to the dining room being a little worse for wear. We all ate quietly, and Georgiana and I prepared for bed, having no notion of what else to do.

As we both lay in bed, under the blankets, we could not use a candle, for fear of it falling and a fire spreading.

"Do you think that Jane or Lizzy are near their laying in?" I asked Georgiana, in the darkness.

"If not already," Georgiana responded, "then they will soon be. Imagine, we will hear about being aunts through letters."

"Well, better to hear about it through letters than not at all. I cannot help but wonder, which one do you think is likely to have a girl? Of course, it's all up to fate, but still, one cannot help but surmise."

"Naturally, for what is life if we are not allowed to guess?" Georgiana pondered. "I think that they both will have boys."

"I think that one of them will have a boy, and the other a girl. I could see Bingley having the girl first—but then..."

"What?"

"I believe your brother would dote on the idea of having a daughter."

"Fitz with a girl?" Georgiana laughed. "I can see that quite easily. Imagine though, if Fitz and Lizzy had nothing but girls."

"I do not believe that fate would doom our family twice," I said with a laugh. "But it would be an interesting image."

"It would be. I think that my brother would look very amusing with four daughters."

"Or six."

"Or eight."

"Why not? Stranger things have been known to happen. But it would be best to have a son somewhere, for the sake of their peace of mind. You saw what being without a son did to my mother's nerves? Elizabeth would never let her mind get that far away from her, but still."

"Oh, there is no need to worry about that. Pemberley is not entailed to the male line."

Well now! This was a surprising turn of events.

"It's not?"

"No, it's not."

"Amazing! To live somewhere for so long, and still not know everything about it. That means that if your brother had accidentally fallen to illness before he met my sister—heaven forbid—then..."

"Yes. I would have become the mistress of Pemberley."

"Georgie, would you ever see yourself as that?"

"Never in a million years."

"I had a feeling that you would have that sort of answer. Then that means, that if Lizzy and Darcy only have daughters, then the eldest daughter will inherit Pemberley?"

"Yes."

"Well, that's a comfort and weight off their shoulders."

"Yes, it is. And since Mr. Bingley only recently owns his own house, he can make his own will, and no entailment could be attached."

"Bingley and Jane have always been blessed with good fortune. When their baby is born, I am sure that it will be healthy."

"Oh, quite sure of that."

In the darkness, I heard Georgiana shift in her bed.

"Georgie?"

"Yes?"

"Do you want to have children?"

Pause.

"Are you asleep?" I whispered.

"No, I am awake. I just— now that I think about it, I wonder if I do. You know how you dream of getting married, but you don't always think about what marriage means?"

"Yes, I do. Dreaming of something is one thing. But when it becomes a reality, it catches up with us and brings unexpected side effects to our lives."

"It's strange. You know that when you get married, the chief reason is for procreation. Of course, you are going to have children. But you still don't know what it fully means until it occurs. I would say yes that I do want children. For I do believe that, when the moment presents itself, I think I could be prepared for being a mother. But for right now, I do not know where the bell tolls. I suppose it's because I don't know where the next step is. What about you?"

Laying on my back, I looked up at the ceiling, which was low, and I could see the details of it in the dark. There was a stifling element to it all, and I felt the sense of confinement in my own mind.

"There is something so very provocative, Georgie, in knowing that your mind is a perverse one," I confessed.

"What nonsense are you talking about in the night?" Georgiana jested.

"I talk of the truth. Motherhood should come naturally to all of us, but I do not think that it can come so easily with me. I like children, and I find them often infinitely more agreeable than adults sometimes. But it is not a matter of liking them. One must have the responsibility to raise them, to be selfless enough to raise another being into the world. I do not think that I possess that sort of selflessness."

"Because we are in situations where we must think of ourselves."

"Yes, but when the time comes to think of someone else, to have the affection needed to nourish and nurture, I do not think I have it. I was born defective."

"No, you weren't. We are young. That's all. Besides, remember when Elizabeth admitted that she worried about sharing her child with my brother, and did not crave for the attention that my brother would give to it, more than her. Then she overcame that fear. Maybe what we are going through is natural, but as is the case, we are not allowed to talk about it."

"Precisely," I groaned, "we are *not* allowed to talk about it. After all, refusal to talk about what ought to be talked about is uncouth, now isn't it?"

"Ah," Georgiana said, and while I could not see her roll her eyes, her voice indicated that she did. "And now we really come down to the primary factor of everything."

"What primary factor?"

"Emma Watson."

~

And now was the popping of the postil!

"Kitty?" Georgiana asked.

"Don't worry," I relented, "I heard you and I am not against having this conversation. In fact, you have quite spared me."

"Spared you?"

"Yes. I didn't know how to approach this topic of discussion, but I knew that it was necessary. You began it for me."

"I felt that it was something that has been tearing at you for a couple of days now."

"Because it has. I know it's only been two days since Emma and I have been confined to a ship, but in that time, I cannot help but feel as if she and I are like oil and water. The qualities of our character cannot mix in a way that complements the other."

"You both are very different, and I understand that. First, I must thank you for giving her and I time alone together, to develop our older friendship. And thank you for not viewing it as me leaving you behind."

"I don't deny," I confessed, "that when I first saw you both, sitting together, and in each other's confidence again, I felt somewhat insecure. I admit it freely. However, I overcame it."

"Are you certain? Or are you only saying that to hide that you feel neglected?"

"I did feel that on the first day," I assured her, "and I did need to talk of that, at that time, however, within the last day, somehow *Sense* found me, and I have been saved from all the pettiness that would have followed from that episode of my life."

"Then you are recovered? Because any lingering envy could lead to you lashing out at Emma and overreacting to things that she says. Remember your advice to Fanny Price about Mary Crawford."

"True. I suppose that I should not write off my vices just yet and pretend as if they are dead. Give me a few days and then ask me that question again."

"Very well. But about Emma herself."

"Georgie, unless there is some miracle that occurs on the way to Australia, I do not think that she and I will ever learn to be friends."

"And I am not going to force you."

When hearing that, I breathed a sigh of relief. The rapture of being understood, of not being pressured into a bond that is inorganic, at best, is always a pleasure.

"You won't?" I inquired, fully hopeful.

"No, I will not. I'm a little wicked as well, Kitty. When we set sail, I was determined to persuade you to do all in your power to endear yourself to Emma. But that was not right of me."

"I understand why you want us to be friends. In an ideal world, it would be nice if we were. But these sorts of situations cannot be forced," I confirmed, "and must simply be played out in the only way that they can."

"And, in your defense, Emma has not shown much promise in being friendly toward you."

I closed my eyes, happy that she saw what I did.

"I am not blind about that," Georgiana furthered, "and for all her virtues, Emma does have one fault."

"Oh, Miss Watson has a fault?" I said, merrily. "How delightful!"

Pause.

"My apologies," I said smoothly, "that was too vindictive. Do continue."

"She is refined and shows all the indication of good breeding. And as such, she is reserved. Very reserved in her own habit. I am accustomed to that, but with you, she is not very forthcoming."

"And I confess," I acknowledged, "that I will never be the sort who can attach herself to a reserved person. And they cannot attach themselves to me."

"Then it is settled. I hope you both will achieve a link, someday, but I will accept that it might never occur. And that it is not your fault."

"Thank you, Georgie. You're a saint."

"And you are a London privy pit."

We both soon went to sleep.

Chapter Four

BROTHERS

Godfrey Park was in a state of unease and imbalance.

Despite that Pemberley was not far, Darcy and Elizabeth had no intention of leaving, at present, to maintain their daughter's health.

But it was not only that.

While the loss of a child is always devastating, some constitutions are stronger at fortifying themselves against such tragedy. Elizabeth and Darcy would have been somber, and lamented losing their daughter, but their tempers were more apt at surviving such an ordeal.

Unfortunately, the Master and Mistress of Godrey Park did not have the same level of emotional endurance that their sister and brother-in-law possessed.

While Darcy was in the nursery, sitting next to Elizabeth as she rocked their daughter, he was contemplating Bingley's fragility.

Being a man that was able to multitask, he leaned forward and ran his finger down his daughter's face.

"Darcy," Elizabeth uttered, "look at her. We created this."

"Yes. She is a beauty."

"She will be. No matter what, we must assure her that she is. Even if she isn't, we will believe it."

"Yes. No matter what, she is. But there is nothing to worry over. Mrs. Mortenson says that she looks like you."

"She can tell that?"

"She's seen many an infant in her time, and she declares that you both look similar. And that our daughter will be lovely."

"We must name her," Elizabeth inferred, placing her finger in her daughter's hand. "But what is worthy of her?"

"Why not your name? What is more perfect than the name Elizabeth? It's the name of queens. Of you."

Elizabeth smiled at him.

"My husband proves to be a splendid father, already."

Mr. Darcy smiled at his wife as she pinched his chin.

"But I cannot help but imagine," Elizabeth continued, "of something else. I want my daughter to have a part of me in her, the way that I want any sons we have to have a part of you, but I want her to also make her own way—have her own identity. How about her middle name be my namesake?"

"I will only agree to that if you have a brilliant idea for the first name."

"Hero."

When hearing this suggestion, Mr. Darcy's eyes widened.

"Hero?"

"Like the character from Shakespeare's *Much Ado About Nothing*."

"Yes, of course, I remember."

"Of course, I tend to favor the character of Beatrice, but Hero is..."

"A name for the ages."

"Yes. And, also, she lived. Darcy, our daughter is the girl who lived."

"Yes, she is. And saved us in the process."

Together, they looked at the girl, with her large eyes and determination to bring her world into focus and greet this new life with an open mind and a willing heart.

"Hero Elizabeth Darcy," Mr. Darcy said, fondly. "A name for the ages."

"Yes," Elizabeth said, and then her expression grew wistful, which did not escape her husband's notice.

"Lizzy?"

"We cannot tell Jane or Bingley anything about this. Not right now. We cannot even tell them her name just yet."

The pain of it!

To not be able to talk with one's closest friend about the naming of your daughter was agonizing.

But Darcy was not surprised.

The burial of their stillborn son took place the very next day after his delivery. They had attended the burial and Jane stood there, as a shell of her old self. Bingley was quiet and held his arm around her the entire time.

Darcy and Elizabeth gave them time alone afterwards, for they knew that company would only be antagonizing them both.

"When do you think we should speak with them?" Darcy asked.

"We've given them time. Now is as good as any."

"Too right. Bingley is scared. And I don't know what to say to that."

"It will come to you in time."

Elizabeth handed the baby to Sarah.

"Sarah," Elizabeth demonstrated, "you know the routine."

"I do, ma'am," Sarah assured her, "when I finish my shift, I will retrieve Lucy, and her shift will begin."

"Shift?" Darcy asked Elizabeth as they walked out of the room.

"It's something that Mrs. Nelson advised us. From her experience, she declared that sometimes babies suffocate in their sleep. They occasionally forget to breathe. By having a servant around her, at all times, we can oversee if Hero stops breathing. When that happens, Sarah or Lucy know to push air into her mouth by breathing into it."

"Mrs. Nelson made that suggestion?"

"Yes, she did. It's quite clever of her."

"Ah. Doctor Palmer must despise her."

"Yes. With every fiber of his figure."

Mrs. Mortenson told Mr. Darcy that Mr. Bingley was in the field, bird hunting.

Surprised that Bingley chose to do it alone, Darcy went out to the trees and walked in the direction of where he heard gunshots.

When he did, he stood there, and watched Bingley as he was in the woods, his satchel bag at his feet, and without any servant to tend to him.

While he wore the traditional clothing and habit that one wore when shooting, his face was pale, and his eyes were a little red.

Bingley had been crying as he hunted.

All questions for why he was alone had been answered. He did not want anyone to see him like that. Darcy especially.

Well, Darcy concluded, *sadly, I cannot give him what he wishes.*

"Bag any birds?" Darcy called out to him.

When hearing that, Bingley fired randomly, surprised. It only led to him hitting a tree branch.

"Forgive me," Darcy apologized, "I alarmed you."

"I am not upset, nor will it break my heart," Bingley said, cleaning his musket.

"I fear nothing else could, since your heart is broken already."

Although he heard Darcy's announcement, Bingley was resolved not to react. Instead, he continued to clean out his musket.

"No," Bingley answered. "I have not bagged any birds."

"I suspected as much. Bingley, tell me truly, you are not even trying to aim at anything."

Bingley still did not respond.

"Bingley—"

"Go away! I don't want you to see me like this."

"We are friends."

"And I am ashamed."

Mr. Darcy squinted, confused by this confession.

"Why are you ashamed?"

"Darcy, forgive me," Bingley uttered, breathy.

"What have you done against me?"

"We are friends, as you say, and friends ought to be happy for each other."

Darcy was a man of deductions; he was able to foresee what Bingley was going to say next.

"But you are not happy for me, are you?" Darcy asked. "You are angry that my child lives, and yours is gone."

"Yes," Bingley responded, whispering. "I do feel that."

Darcy neither flinched nor was upset about this.

"I assure you," Bingley promised, "I do not want your daughter to be gone. I just want my son to be here, with us, as well."

"I know. You are not evil, Bingley."

"But I feel as if I am."

"It is only natural to be upset at being struck with such misfortune, when the reverse happens for a friend. As long as you are aware of this, I know you will recover."

"But can I? Darcy, I feel so hollow right now. And Jane is heartbroken. She keeps blaming herself for the baby being dead."

"It is not her fault. Death during infancy is common."

"I know. She knows, but there is no telling her. When I feel as if she is done crying, she continues again. Nothing I can say can remove the pain that is inside of her, and it makes me feel more helpless than ever. I could not protect my child, and I cannot protect my wife."

"You protected your child. These things simply occur."

"And I don't care!" he cried, throwing his musket down, raising up his arms and crying out to the woods. "I just don't care! I don't care that logic shows that there is nothing that I could have done. I was going to be a father, and that was taken from me. When a man cannot protect his child, he feels helpless. Even against the tides of nature."

"Mrs. Mortenson told Elizabeth that Jane's behavior is natural. She gave birth and is suffering from a depression that befalls ladies at their first child loss. But she will rally and take comfort in you both together. This is not the end, but a mere step backwards that can be succeeded by many more steps forward. You ought to feel pain now, but when you and Jane have your next child, these wounds will heal."

"And if we lose our next child?"

"You must not think that way, or have Jane think that way. She does not deserve that."

"She does not deserve this now. She does not deserve any of this. Have you ever met a more maternal woman than my Jane? She deserved to be a mother—more so than E..."

Mr. Darcy looked up, anger replacing the sympathy.

"More so than who?"

"I didn't intend to—"

"More so than who, Bingley!"

Bingley bit his lip.

"Than Elizabeth?" Darcy pressed. "Is that what you were about to say!"

Darcy grabbed Bingley's shoulders and drew him close, with the instinct to throttle him.

"Say no ill of Lizzy!" he roared.

"I'm sorry!" Bingley cried, and Darcy saw the true grief in Bingley's face as the almost-father burst into tears. "I'm sorry. I don't know why I said that. I just—it hurts so much, Darcy. It hurts so much."

Realizing that Bingley was speaking from a place of heartbreak, Darcy's temper deflated as he found himself returning to sympathizing for his friend.

As Bingley fell into Darcy, Darcy held Bingley's arms to steady him.

"I cannot help it," Bingley cried, "this hurts so much, and I cannot bear it."

"I know it does," Darcy assured him. "I may not know what the pain is that you are feeling, but I can imagine. You have a right to feel improperly. After all, this is not a proper moment. Nothing about this moment makes sense. It is well to fall apart for a while. But Bingley, you must promise me that you will rally from this."

"I don't know if I can."

"You will. I have faith in you, brother."

When hearing him being called thus, Bingley's weeping subsided.

"Yes. We are brothers, aren't we?"

"Yes, we are. And I tell you this now, and I need you to listen. Jane is broken. When our wives break, we can break a little, but we soon must patch ourselves up, put on a strong demeanor, and be their support. I'm sorry, because I know you are cracking from within, but soon, you must repair yourself quicker than you would like. You must be strong for her. That is what we husbands are meant for."

"Yes, you are right. Just give me this one last day. Tomorrow, I will do right by her."

"Of course. Of course."

And for one more day, Bingley contemplated everything that was shattered within him. Then the next day, he had to abandon all pity and be the fortress to shield his wife.

Chapter Five

FRANCE!

"Cherbourg, France, ahead!" Tepree shouted as she was on the top rigging. Like a spider, she wove her way around the mast, grabbed a rope and swung down to the starboard.

When she had done that, Georgiana, Enara, and I ran to the deck and watched her with amazement.

"Arthur always misses the spectacle, doesn't he?" I asked Enara.

"Yes, he does have that habit. Which reminds me, I really should fetch him. Being married to him and all."

Enara dashed below deck, back to their cabin, just as Emma Watson emerged, with Mr. Blake coming behind her. He was talking to her about his time at university and Emma was listening to him, very interested. Standing next to me on the ship's larboard, Georgiana gave me a look.

"Do you think that she favors him?" I asked Georgiana, "or am I seeing things that are not there?"

"I am not at liberty to say," Georgiana answered, "but she does find him amiable."

"Whenever someone says, 'I am not at liberty to say', that means 'yes'."

Georgiana groaned.

"I walked into that, didn't I?"

"Like a moth to a flame. Never fear, I understand how to keep someone's confidence, even when they didn't ask me to keep it. And Emma never would have asked me."

"Kitty..."

"I will behave. But if she sets her sight on him, I hope she will be sensible."

"Sensible?"

"At Emma's age, a person is so eager to be in love, that they can always mistake 'the idea of being in love' for the real thing."

"Well, they are on a ship, and that will be long enough to learn of each of their character."

"Yes, for there is not enough competition to compare each other with. Whatever differences that Emma and I have, I do not wish for her to rush into anything. Or Mr. Blake for that matter."

Soon, Mr. Blake and Emma Watson joined us.

"I heard that France is ahead."

"Yes, it is," I responded. "I do so hope that I do not sound unpatriotic, but I am excited to step on French shores and meet some of them."

"Well," Emma answered, "you will not see a great deal of France, for we land there merely for a couple of hours, and that is not nearly enough time to go on any sort of holiday."

"Would you believe that I go to other lands as much to say that I was there, and that I am interested in knowing that I moved amongst the people? Or do they not count?"

Mr. Blake looked between us, as Emma glanced away from me, and Georgiana covered her mouth, to hide her expression. I recalled the promise that I told Georgiana of behaving myself; and how that didn't even last more than three minutes. But honestly, Emma Watson started it! She was so bent on sounding clever that it always seemed to end in her just finding the pleasure in being contrary.

To do my best to try and return to a place of diplomacy, I calmed my voice.

"It is merely the reaction of a provincial girl who is happy to see another part of the world, be the architecture beautiful or plain."

"Understandable," Mr. Blake answered, "after all, there is a charm to caring as much about seeing a new world, for the sake of knowing one was there, and merely that."

"I agree," Georgiana confirmed, smiling at him in a friendly manner.

"I prefer to go to a place and absorb as much culture as I can," Emma added, "oh, to see every aspect of every society and feel the deep secrets possessing it."

"It is a fascination that is in its proper place, Emma. What do you say to that, Mr. Blake?"

"I say amen to it, Miss Darcy," Mr. Blake said. "And that you phrase it wonderfully. Well, I have three ladies here who are eager to see new sights and experience new worlds," Mr. Blake said, charmingly, "I hope that I am a chaperone that is worthy of you."

"I believe that you will be, Mr. Blake," Georgiana confirmed.

"Yes, I believe so," Emma replied, gently and demurely.

Was her demure tone real or false? I still was not certain.

"Never fear, Mr. Blake," Arthur Philips added, approaching us with Enara at her side, "when it comes to chaperones, we will be two in number."

Taking his wife's arm in his, he looked out over the water and saw the land ahead.

"France, we meet again," Arthur said.

"You've been to France, Mr. Philips?" Emma Watson asked.

"Yes, I have. Being a sailor, it might be easier to list the places that I have not been to. In fact, I spent so much of my time on ships, that whenever I would go ashore, I wobbled when I would set foot on dry land, for I was so used to the ground rocking underneath me."

We all laughed.

"France," Arthur commented, "England's constant enemy."

"And I don't care," I inferred. "A person can admire their enemies, as long as both sides are honorable."

"That is a good maxim," Arthur said, "you propose that there can be honor amongst adversaries."

"There is sense to that," Emma submitted.

"Thank you," I replied, surprised that she was kind to me.

"Of course, when we will inevitably be at war with them, I presume that you will rally to your patriotism."

"Yes," I responded, "I will. But maybe, in the course of my life, war between England and France will end. It once reached such a point that our American Colonies became a battleground between us with them. I wonder if we even remember why we are still fighting. Sometimes, I think it all has to do with simply because it has become so much of a habit."

"It's more than that," Emma responded.

"I cannot help but agree with Kitty," Georgiana said, "we've been fighting for too long, and too many French and British have died because of it. When national prowess becomes more important than people's lives, then one should reflect."

"Oh, I do like how *you* phrase it," Emma said. "It was properly explained that way."

And, with that last sentence, Emma and I were back to where we started—again.

This was growing very monotonous. Even for us ladies who were raised to sit in a drawing room and suffer the same scenes day in and day out. Now that was saying a great deal, coming from me.

The Deck Cadet was the next phenomenon. It was a handsome Japanese woman named Miyoshi. At this point, The Lilia was now fully defined as being the most eccentric crew in the history of merchant vessels. And, for those who did not comprehend or were adaptable to difference of any kind, was also the most notorious. And naturally, that's what made them so popular. I also marveled at her, especially since she spoke over eight different languages, and I had yet to know what they all were. As she moved among the line, relaying the Chief Officer's and Second Officer's orders, Reedus arranged for the anchor to be dropped over the edge of the ship.

Watching the massive weight plunge over the edge, I moved away from my group and saw it as it splashed into the water. Subsequently, I was standing right next to Miyoshi when it happened.

"You ever wonder," I said to her, "if an anchor had eyes, all that it saw when it sinks to the bottom of water?"

Miyoshi smirked at me.

"Every single time."

"Miyoshi!" The Master, Captain Archer, declared, "arrange the ramp."

"Aye, Master," Miyoshi called, "White Wolf and Merriweather!"

"Coming, sir," Merriweather said, with White Wolf following behind her. Since the sun was shining, White Wolf had a certain feather woven into his long black hair.

"What bird did that come from?" I asked him.

"Falcon," White Wolf responded. "Don't worry, I never hurt it. It fell off the bird when it was flying, and I happened to find it before anyone else did."

He followed Merriweather as they organized the ramp to be lowered on the Cherbourg docks. Even though we were along the river, I still was able to look out and see the magnificence of the Cherbourg embankments and the immediate edges of the city. Even on the outskirts, it was obviously a lovely city.

"First time in France?" Trip asked me.

"Very much so," I answered. "Do you go ashore?"

"I've got two hours to collect more food for our next part of the voyage and arrange for more supplies to see us get to Portugal in time."

"We go ashore," Reedus said, "but it's all duties and no pleasure."

"I am sorry," I said.

"Don't worry," Trip said, eyeing Georgiana, Emma, and I with interest, "we have some more pleasures on board that will suit us nicely."

"Sirs, you are being a little too forward," Mr. Blake said.

"We beg your pardon," Reedus said, but there was no hint of remorse in his eye. "The charms before us were just a little too overpowering."

Emma, Georgiana, and I blushed. There is something to be said for innocent charm.

Looking between Trip and Reedus, while one was American and the other was British, and their looks were different, they felt like two heads to the same man. It was as if they had developed such a deep friendship that at some point, their souls fused together in a way that they were separate, but still united.

As the ramp was lowered, we secured ourselves against the cold, and I looked at the larboard, where the Master, Captain Archer stood, talking with Tepree.

As I secured my bonnet, he spied me out of the side of his eye. Though he didn't smile at me, his eyes twinkled. We had never spoken, but I decided to be brave.

"Does the Master and Second Officer not get the chance to enjoy shore leave?" I called to him and Tepree.

Captain Archer laughed.

"When you are the Master of a ship," he called back to me, "your life is not your own."

I looked at Tepree and she nodded at me but did not say anything. I still could not fully make her out, or her impression of me.

"Miss Bennet," Emma Watson whispered to me, but it might as well have been a hiss.

Groaning inwardly, I turned to her, knowing precisely what she was about to say.

"You must not shout at gentlemen across a deck," she advised, "or anywhere for that matter."

I was about to open my mouth, in protest, but over her shoulder, Georgiana gave me the 'please, Kitty, you promised', look. I ought to comply, for her, if for no one else.

"Miss Watson," I replied, attempting to be diplomatic, "I thank you for your advice. If we were in Britain, in society, then I would agree. But I doubt that a naval Master from Massachusetts would be alarmed and overpowered by a woman calling out to him on his own ship."

"Yes, but just because we are not in England does not mean that you should abandon your principles. You would not want to be viewed as..."

"As what?"

"As a bit crass."

While I was determined to be civil in my response, it did not signify that I was going to submit to her criticism.

From behind Emma, Enara looked on her with quiet alarm, and she rushed between us, to save me from any form of retaliation.

"Come, Kitty," Enara said, "we have Cherbourg to enjoy in two hours. Let's not waste one moment."

"Yes," Arthur said, coming next to me, for support. "We have not a moment to lose."

I fell into step with them easily, and we had walked down the ramp, with Georgiana and Emma behind us.

"You saved me," I said to them both.

"That is what family is for," Enara said.

"Never mind her, Kitty," Arthur assured me. "The truth is that you are simply two very different sorts of women, and women like

Miss Watson have a tendency to still contain the prejudices of a young mind who was raised to a high society."

"I know," I said, "that does not make seeking revenge any easier to overcome."

"I understand," Enara said, "but try to rise above it. I know it's difficult, and I can understand why it affects you. But if you ever feel as if she is trying your nerves, just ignore her. It is just as effective as retaliation of any sort."

"I confess that I am not used to not speaking up," I admitted. "I do not think that I know how to suppress that side of myself anymore."

Truly, the last time I did that, it was with Lady Catherine de Bourgh, and I had done that at Elizabeth's request, and that resulted in her regretting ever offering me that advice.

"Oh, spite," I sighed, under my breath. "Oh, hell."

"Will you ever let go of that phrase?" Arthur asked me, amused.

"How can I release it? When it never actually releases me?"

As we walked along the docks, we came to one street that was full of houses and shops.

A real French Street, and it was beautiful. There was nothing altogether noteworthy about it, and yet, it was spellbinding.

"Oh my!" I said, smiling.

"Yes," Enara said, "isn't it splendid?"

"Yes, it is."

"That is the magic of France," Arthur said, "you can walk down a street, and it was as worthy as walking along Versailles. Even in the very simple, it is beautiful."

And the way that the street was angled, you saw a significant portion of the city, and in a picturesque manner. Emma Watson, Mr. Blake, and Georgiana eventually caught up with us and they stood with us, seeing the scene in the precise same manner.

They too were speechless. In my opinion, nothing was superior to Britain in its appearance and the feel of the land, but my preferences for my own country would not suppress my instincts to admire other scenes that did not belong to us.

"I can see why Henry V wanted to take France," I uttered, "even though he had no right to do so."

"No, he did not," Georgiana confirmed. "But I understand the impulse. He wanted it because it is breathtaking."

"Yes, it is," Enara said. "Sometimes we resent things because of its differences, but in truth, we resent it because we want its beauty, and we won't be happy until we have it."

For one moment, we all were united in our rapture. Even Emma Watson and I felt no animosity toward each other. Because when you stand in the face of perfection, all tension falls away.

"Come now," Mr. Blake ushered us onward, "we cannot stand in one place, or the locals will start gossiping at us, and I can't blame them."

We walked along the docks and saw glimpses of the rest of the city through open streetways.

With every view that we saw, I was drawn to the idea that I had to return to France one day and commit much of it to memory. I knew that I might be faced with discomfort. After all, my motherland was their old and constant enemy, but I doubted that I would spend my life not being given the opportunity to see every aspect of this land. I must know it. I must experience it.

As I walked along one street, an officer crossed our paths, without even looking at us.

But with a swish of his uniform, my mind played tricks on me. His uniform turned into a redcoat, his face disappeared, and it was replaced by Colonel Fitzwilliam's.

I halted.

I wanted to follow him. Instinctively, every voice within me wished to shout his name. For why did he not tell us that he was here, amongst us, and that he ought to join us along our journey?

However, the mirage disappeared as soon as it had come upon me. Shaking my head, I saw the reality for what it was, and not as my emotions wished for them to be. Driven from my own imagination, the French soldier was returned to the man that he was.

Of course, I knew my nature. This wouldn't be the last time that my heart played a trick upon me. Our minds and imagination, often, cannot leave us well enough alone. They play upon us, and prey upon us, and we must remain as we are: going somewhere, and still looking back, or staying put, and still wishing to go somewhere else.

Eventually, it was time to return to the ship. We discovered that two French travelers had bought passage on the Lilia.

As we set sail once more, I looked at Trip and Reedus, who had been shouting orders as Tepree stood by Master Archer along the top deck, turning the captains' wheel.

"Got what you needed?" I asked Reedus.

Reedus smirked.

"I'm alive. That's the main thing any British man wants when he returns from French soil."

"I can imagine so."

Deck Cadet, Miyoshi, ordered the sailors to raise the anchor and the Lilia was off once more.

I watched France grow smaller and smaller in the distance.

"Now we have been on the shore of our frequent enemy," I said to my company, "and what do we all think of them?"

"It's as simple and as complicated as it always is," Mr. Blake said, "they look just like us."

"Precisely, that is the problem. They always *look* like us."

"While it is always easier to imagine one's enemies to have demonic horns on their heads," Enara said, "we have to always accept the reality."

"We are always going to be odds with people that are just another part of ourselves," I summed up.

"The way of the world," Arthur responded.

France grew smaller in the distance.

Chapter Six

BROTHERLY LOVE, FATHERLY AFFECTION

"Well now," Elizabeth said to Hero as she began to feed her from under a shawl, "aren't you just the hungriest little bear cub in the world?"

In the nursery at Godfrey Park, Elizabeth was sitting in a new rocking chair that Mr. Darcy had purchased for her. Despite the rain, Elizabeth still had the chair placed by the window, so that she could look out of it. Even with the bleak prospect from outside, the effects of motherhood had led to a shine over everything she saw now. Despite the tradition of handing her child off to a wetnurse to nurse Hero, Elizabeth was adamant about performing the duty herself.

In the background, Betsy stood there, as a sentinel.

"Sit down, Betsy," Elizabeth advised her. "Standing too long can hurt the feet."

"Thank you," Betsy replied, relieved as she sat down in a chair. "And I am pleased to deliver a happy report."

"I am all ears," Elizabeth responded.

"Sarah, Lucy and I are making certain to look after Hero in shifts."

Elizabeth looked over her shoulder, smirking.

"Promise me that you all are not dozing during it?"

"Never," Betsy assured her. "We are smart. We know to either knit or sew while we are sitting with Hero. And if we do find our eyes growing heavy, we learn to either pace around the room, or chew on some mint root. The constant chewing keeps us awake."

"Mrs. Nelson is right. Sometimes babies have been known to not breathe in their sleep."

"We know what to do when the time comes, madam," Betsy assured her. "Nelson told us to open the baby's mouth and breathe into it. Unless illness were to suddenly come into this room, Hero is going to live. We'll make sure of it."

"We must keep ailment at bay," Elizabeth stressed, looking fondly down on her new daughter. "We will fight for you, Hero. Yes, we will."

"How strange," Betsy said.

"What?"

"I remember when you were thirteen, and you swore that you would never marry anyone."

Elizabeth chuckled.

"I did say that, didn't I?"

"Yes, you did."

"I was still in the phase of finding romance to be a repulsive sort of thing, and I still thought boys were... like little gnomes. Also, I was going through my rebellious phase and would do anything to thwart Mama."

"Yes, you did. I do not think that she ever grew past seeing you as anything else but that contrary creature. And what's more, I don't think she ever connected that creature you once were to the means through which it led to you being the mistress of Pemberley."

"You noticed?" Elizabeth asked. "I am glad that someone has, for I was afraid that the irony would be lost on the world."

"Well, it wasn't. Not with the hired help, for we see everything. We knew where it all began. If you had not been adamant to walk to Netherfield Park when Jane was ill, then it would not have thrown you into the company of Mr. Darcy as much as it would have. That's when he began to fall in love with you, wasn't it?"

Elizabeth looked at Betsy, astounded.

"How did you become aware of that?"

Betsy smirked. "Hired help, Madam. Netherfield Park had them as well, and they work here now."

"Ah," Elizabeth responded, rolling her eyes. "Servants were always there, in the background, seeing everything."

"And now I live with those servants," Betsy confirmed. "I do so love being in the *know*."

The nursery door opened, and Mr. Darcy entered.

When seeing him, Betsy stood up and folded her hands in front of her, to appear proper.

"You're excused, Betsy," Elizabeth offered, "but if you will go to Jane and tend to her, that would be best."

"Of course, Madam. Very good."

Betsy greeted Mr. Darcy as she was leaving.

"I must inform you, Betsy," Mr. Darcy said, still looking at Elizabeth, "Sarah is with her now."

Betsy's reaction was precisely what he was looking for. Sometimes, we humans cannot deny enjoying a delicious scene of disagreeable habits and taciturn manner. Despite being a man of elevated education, Mr. Darcy was as mortal as the rest of humanity.

When hearing this, Betsy's eyes practically flashed between aggravation and anger.

"That sour-talking wench!" Betsy spat, leaving the room. "What does she know about coaxing heartbroken mothers?"

When Darcy closed the door behind her, he leaned against it, amused.

"I love those two," Darcy commented.

"Of course, you do," Elizabeth inferred. "Some characters are invaluable to a person's existence. Their vulgar and colloquial manners are cathartic to our kind. They get to speak the crass and crude obscenities that we ladies and gentlemen are not allowed to say. In a strange way, they are catalysts for our ruder sides."

"My wife is wise, even when nursing her infant."

"I think my wisdom flows from her," Elizabeth replied, gesturing to their daughter. "But either way, a woman ought not to lose her wisdom just because she's been elevated to the title of mother."

Smiling, Mr. Darcy pulled up the chair and sat down next to her.

"How is our Hero today?" he asked.

"As alive and eager as ever. You understand why I wish to nurse her myself, don't you? As opposed to another woman doing the deed?"

"Yes, I do. You want her near you, at all times."

"And, in case something was to happen and befall her in the dead of night or of illness, I can declare that I spent as much time with her as I could."

"Lizzy, can I hold her?"

Elizabeth did not have to reply, because her actions were words enough. She removed the girl from under the shawl, wrapped Hero even more securely, and then handed their daughter to her father.

Cradling Hero in his arms, Mr. Darcy leaned back as she began to cry.

"Do not be offended by her cries," Elizabeth said, over the wails. "That is merely what babies do."

"Of course," Mr. Darcy said, "perhaps though..."

He stood up and began to pace, rocking the baby as he carried her. All the while, he spoke to her as she wailed on, then he placed his finger over her face, and wiggled it.

Soon, she calmed down and began to try and close her hands around his finger.

While watching him, Elizabeth felt a serenity wash over her. Light is lovely when washing down in front of a person's countenance and waving its blessing amongst those who feel its presence.

Elizabeth knew, even if Mr. Darcy did not. She felt the halo envelop him, making him even brighter and more elegant in her estimation than he had ever been before. When you meet someone first, they possess an illumination. The second time you meet them, then the light remains. But for others, over time, the light fades. In Elizabeth's eyes, Mr. Darcy was the opposite. Over time, he continued to shine in his wife's esteem, and she could not account for such a thing to behold.

When seeing her watching him with his daughter, Mr. Darcy smiled.

"What?" he asked her.

"You will never know," Elizabeth declared, "and I am very sorry for it."

"Sorry?"

"That you will never see how lovely you are, thus."

Unable to refrain from his humanness, Mr. Darcy's cheeks turned quite red.

"And he blushes," Elizabeth mocked. "I never knew that it was a man's province as well."

"Goodness me! What can a husband say in response to that?"

"What can the Master of Pemberley say back to that?" Elizabeth furthered. "No reply will do for the present. I would not want you to think that you must feel pressured to perform."

"Thank you. I am a poor actor."

"And I prefer to be married to a man who lacks pretense. There is something to be said for transparency."

"Lizzy, I am sorry that we cannot go to Pemberley just now."

"As am I. Yet, while it is a delight to be home, we're still needed here."

"Has Jane spoken to you very much on the matter?" Darcy asked.

"That is the very problem," Elizabeth furthered, somber. "She often is tired, does not confide in me, and she always says that she prefers more time to herself. Of course, I wish it, for I do not wish to press my curiosity on her, or to be imposing."

"Bingley is doing the same."

Elizabeth leaned forward, wholly engaged.

"The same? Darcy, he is your friend and I understand that friends say things in confidence. But since she is my sister, I feel that it is still within my interest to know."

"Of course. He tries to speak to Jane, but he is..."

"What?"

"Afraid."

'What a word to use regarding my sister,' Elizabeth pondered, alarmed at such a description.

"Afraid?" Elizabeth questioned. "Of Jane?"

"Yes. I have not seen her myself for the last couple of days."

"She prefers to eat in her bedroom," Elizabeth said, "her spirits are still low."

"More than low, in Bingley's estimation. When he entered her room, he felt as if she was half the woman that she was, as if the darkness in the room was consuming her. Lizzy, he was genuinely afraid to approach her, for fear of breaking her heart even more. He does not know how to talk to her."

Leaning back against the rocking chair, Elizabeth let its powers wash over her as she rocked back and forth. Outside, the rain sloshed against the windowpanes with fervor, almost tauntingly. The clouds in the sky felt ominous, as if it marked her sister's mood, and Bingley's fear of what to do.

"I swore that I would not press her," Elizabeth acknowledged, "for what can you say in such a time? What words can there be to ease the heart of a hurting mother? Jane is so gentle, and for the first time, she has experienced something that has shocked her gentleness to the very core. When a spirit like hers is so overturned, it is like a tree breaking in the wilderness, and nothing to nurse it whole again."

Mr. Darcy looked at her, his eyes serious.

"Do you think this tragedy might really consume Jane?"

"At first, I thought she would feel the tragedy and then recover. Especially since she bore Bingley's initial deserting her with such fortitude and disinterest. But I have been wrong before. What if this is one of those moments?"

"I don't like seeing Bingley like this. He's already heartbroken from the death of his son." Mr. Darcy rubbed his cheek, nervously. "He cannot lose his wife as well."

Lose his wife? Elizabeth was altogether horrified of the possibility and did not expect that Jane's low spirits would drive her to the point where she would do unconscious harm to herself. But when in a maternal state, one's mind is not wholly in its proper place. Especially when a mother has just lost a son. There is no end to the feeling of grief, and how it affects someone with delicate health—a constitution as fragile as Jane's could be susceptible.

And what if it were so? If it was, and Elizabeth had allowed her to go to waste, all because she did not bother to attempt to reach her, then what could be said of being Jane's sister?

"You make me quite ashamed of myself," Elizabeth determined, standing up decidedly.

"Ashamed?" Mr. Darcy asked. "Between sitting down and my last sentence, when did I begin to reign shame over you?"

"Not with your declarations, but with your observations. I must go to Jane soon, once Betsy returns."

~

The wait.

The waiting of Betsy to return. In faith, Elizabeth had not wrung the bell for anyone else to come and assist her, because she also marveled at seeing Mr. Darcy still sitting there, doting on Hero.

As if she had been transfixed to the spot, Elizabeth remained standing there, watching her husband and daughter as if they were a mirage that left her spellbound. There were no false realities to this image, however, but real and tangible joy achieved... while her sister had lost so much.

It rendered Elizabeth grateful, feeling as if her fate had been judged with mercy, as opposed to sorrow.

"You look at her," Elizabeth noted, referring to Darcy and Hero, "as she is: a great wonder."

"It's because she is. But it is more than that."

"What?"

"Lizzy, does your mind ever wonder over hill, mountain, and water, and think of what our sisters are doing now?"

"Oh. Kitty and Georgie."

"Yes."

"I acknowledge that I do. Quite often. Since France is still our enemy, we know that they can't send us a letter until they reach Portugal. But it still does not stop one from worrying."

"Precisely. It does not. Do you know a reason that us men always wish to place you ladies in drawing rooms?"

"I thought there were many reasons, and some of them to be quite constrictive."

"This reason has well-meaning inclinations behind it. It's because, when you are in the house, you are safe. We know where you are, we see you, and we know that we are properly protecting you. But now, Georgie and Kitty are off, going toward the uncertain." Mr. Darcy looked up and out of the window, as if looking outside he would summon his sister and sister-in-law back to Derbyshire, well within his sight and supervision.

But they would not come. And until they were safely returned, where he could follow them, he would always be torn with concern.

"You are still afraid for them," Elizabeth determined.

"Yes. Very much so."

Elizabeth stood up, walked over to where he was, and sat down on the floor, resting her head on his lap as she held Hero's hand.

"So am I," she added. "Until now, I did not know what you men felt when you are stricken with worry."

"And we cannot always put words to it," Mr. Darcy said, gravely. "I regret it now. Anything can happen to them. Every time that someone goes to a new climate, they risk disease. Every time that someone chooses to travel by sea, a tempest or whirlpool can seize them. I tire of thinking the worst!"

Elizabeth held his hand, to soothe him.

"And I wish that I never let them go," Darcy furthered. "I should have stopped them."

"We could not. Kitty needed to go, and Georgie would follow her into Hell, if need be. Their friendship is real. It will not break until a greater bond comes along to bind either of them even tighter to someone else."

"Georgiana is delicate."

"She only looks so because of her figure. But her character is robust."

"But what if she goes to New South Wales and she likes it? If she finds that she does not ever wish to return home?"

"She will. It is Kitty that you have to worry about, on that score."

"Kitty? You think so?"

Elizabeth tapped her fingers against his thigh, in contemplation.

"At first, I wondered why Kitty was so adamant about going to Australia," Elizabeth theorized. "After all, her family, her world, her comforts and the men she loves are here. What more could she want? And then I realized, now more than ever, how much Kitty is not like the rest of us. Jane, Mary, Lydia, and me. We are happy to be wed, to have our domestic felicity, be mothers, happily married to men we love. But with Kitty... perhaps I will expound on topics that will seem wholly foreign to our way of life. I don't think that Kitty really wants this."

Elizabeth gestured around her, indicating the house, wealth, and style of living.

"I think Kitty wants freedom," Elizabeth summed up.

"Freedom?" Mr. Darcy repeated, perplexed. "She has freedom. All of this, is liberty."

"For us, yes, it is. This is the precise sort of liberty that we desire. But liberty is not a singular thing. Her vision of liberty, I think, stretches beyond this sort of life. I think she wants the ability to stretch over and beyond Pemberley, Longbourn, and Godfrey Park. Maybe even England itself."

She paused briefly. "I don't think she fears adversity, or the harsh realities that comes from having to face the habits, hindrances, and dangers that the world presents. I think she believes in humanity and is not afraid of it. The world that revolves in a provincial town might not be able to contain her spirit. I think Georgiana can always make the transition back to our ways. But Kitty, I think she wants to be part of everything. I think she can no longer be anything else other than...involved."

"Involved? In what, pray?"

"I don't know. In fact, I don't even think that she knows. But I do believe that she is chasing after something. For her, it's just a matter of discovering what that is."

"And what if she never finds it?"

"Then that is where the great unwinding might take place." Elizabeth reached a delightful conclusion. "You have grown to admire Kitty, haven't you?"

"I realize that I spoke so hastily when I first met her," Mr. Darcy said. "I mistook her spiritedness for crassness, and her lively youth for lack of propriety. She was happy, that was all. And I did not understand until I gathered a wider acquaintance with her. She was a young woman who did not want to wait around until old age and use took her over. She wanted to enjoy life, in a way that I did not expect.

"And between Lady Catherine, Frederick and Colonel Fitzwilliam, my family has done nothing but confuse her, present difficulty after difficulty, and complicate her life. For normalcy, she never stood a chance. I cannot judge her now, for my family has driven her to such distraction that she had to leave Britain to give my cousin his best chance. That is admirable. I feel sorry that I didn't fully know her when first making her acquaintance, and I've been trying to make this up to her for a while. I suppose—that I am sorry. And I never told her that I was. It has eaten away at me for quite some time."

When hearing this, Elizabeth took Darcy's hand, covering it even firmer.

"Well, this is a changed way of thinking indeed," Elizabeth finalized. "You have been dwelling on this a great deal?"

"Yes, but with every moment, it has come to my attention. No doubt, there can be no surprise to what inspired it."

"On the contrary, dearest, you have me entirely at a loss. What drove you to these conclusions?"

Mr. Darcy gestured to Hero.

"Her. It is true, Lizzy. Parenthood changes a person. I love you, more than my life."

"And I feel the same. But you love Hero more. I am not afraid, Fitzwilliam. Not in the slightest. Always have we been told that you will never feel a deeper love than that of the love for your child. Now I understand, more than ever."

Mr. Darcy placed his hand on Elizabeth's cheek.

"Does my Lizzy understand me that well?"

"Yes," Elizabeth said, smiling. "I just might."

"Well," Darcy said, looking back down at Hero. "I have a little girl now. And now I know, more than ever, the world that we have brought her into. I feel that no matter what I do, I will not always be there to protect her from everything, no matter how I would try. And if I dictate every move she makes, I will be a tyrant of a father. I want to give her the world, Lizzy, but I don't want the world to hurt her. And when I let Kitty and Georgie go, what does that say of me? Will I know how to be a proper father? Out of an impulse to protect Hero, will I shackle her down and hold onto her too tightly, or will I give her too much liberty, and she will be lost to us? What do I do, Lizzy? What is the right thing to do?"

Seeing her husband growing more unsettled, Elizabeth stood up and held him from behind, as well as closing her arms around Hero.

"It is well, dearest," Elizabeth coaxed him, "it is well. The right thing to do is obvious. It is to take one day at a time, and we will win. We will persevere. Remember, my love, you do not do this alone. I will be here with you, and I shall never leave your side."

"Do so, Lizzy," Darcy urged harshly, "never leave me. Love me always and never leave. I cannot do this without you. Please."

"I am here," Elizabeth promised. "I will always be here."

Chapter Seven

CONVERSATIONS WITH THE CREW

As I sat on deck writing in my journal, I watched the Lilia crew around me walk to and fro', either from just completing a task, or about to begin another one.

The life aboard a vessel seemed to be a whirlwind activity that I could not fathom. Between the rigging, the maintenance, and the success of upholding sanitation onboard seemed to be never-ending.

"Miss Bennet?" White Wolf called from nearby. I looked to my left and saw that he had a unique necklace on. It must have been tribal. "Do you draw there?"

"Oh, no," I said, closing my journal, standing up and approaching him. "I couldn't even draw a flower if I tried. If you assumed I did because of my background, then I would hate to disappoint you."

"I don't assume anything of you. In fact, I never grasped the notion of you all having to learn the same skills to be, as you all phrase it, accomplished."

I laughed.

"Come now, I may be ignorant of many things, but I know that your people paint and do cave drawings."

"We do, no doubt," White Wolf said, picking up some twain and taking it to the larboard. Eagerly, I followed him, for he was quite approachable.

"But when we do it, we don't criticize the artist for lack of execution or to be regarded as masters. Artwork is not merely artwork for us, but it must follow a function. For us, art is history."

"Your history?"

"Yes. Whenever another tribe is destroyed in America, their art dies with them. When our art dies, our history dies along with it."

I was silenced. Due to our need for constant documentation, my country's history would never be forgotten. We made certain of it, but even as such, it would be very unlikely that Britain would fall. We had done everything to maintain our permanence in the world, for the better of ourselves. However, what of where we landed and colonized?

White Wolf didn't notice my melancholy, because he had just ordered some sailors that their shift was over, and he organized a rotation. When he turned back to me, he looked at my journal.

"I was writing down all your names in my diary," I explained, "so I don't forget you and to remember the sort of people that you were."

"You know that you get more of our history if you speak to us," he said, smirking. "Looks can only go so far."

"Then you are not afraid of me asking you things?" I asked.

"No more than you are evidently not afraid of me," he observed. "Why aren't you?"

I squinted.

"What do you mean?"

"Why aren't you afraid of me? Your kind usually are."

"What I don't know about the world is a lot, mark my words. But I do know something."

"What?"

"You have more reason to be afraid of me than the reverse."

White Wolf chuckled.

"Start with the feather," I asked, pointing to his hair. "Where did you get that?"

"From an owl. If you are about to have a romantic notion of how I came to have it, there is nothing incredible about it. It fell from the owl when it was bathing itself, and I had the ability to be there to pick it up."

"And your necklace?"

He touched it.

"My mother made it for me."

"It's beautiful. Did she look like you?"

"No, I look like my father. My sisters looked like our mother."

"Where are they?"

"They died. Smallpox."

I felt immediate sympathy. "I'm sorry."

"Everyone is. I'm the last of my side of the family."

"But if you don't have children and something happens to you..."

"There is nothing to fear. While one cannot predict what the future will hold for my tribe, I have many aunts and uncles. With any luck, our family will continue. And if it ever gets frightful, our tribe knows parts of Canada that is still not inhabited."

"What tribe are you from?"

"The Santee Dakota. When last I was home, our tribe was still there. We were wise. When the States and you lot went to war again, my side of the tribe did not partake in assisting your side, in case you lost. We learned our lesson when we sided with the French during the Seven Years War, and the French lost, which worsened the relationship between us and the colonists."

"You wanted us all out of the Colonies, didn't you?"

"We had no choice. We were caught between a rock and..."

"A hard place."

"Precisely. To keep our home and preserve our future, we made alliances, and it was always with the losing side. This time, my tribe decided to remain neutral to the fight, and we were right. Some tribes joined the British during the second war you both had with the Americans, and they lost more when the war was over. We didn't, and that was when we decided to remain completely outside of your colonies' society. Forgive me, but every connection we had with anything connected to your lot, left us losing a great deal."

"I know."

And I wasn't afraid to know. That was another wonder to it.

When I looked at his arm, I saw a long scar.

"Did our colonists give you that?"

"Others in my tribe have faced your colonists in battle, but not me, actually. I've been told that I look harmless, and I was taught your education, so that helped. No, on the contrary, this scar came from a battle that my tribe encountered with another tribe, the Sioux."

"Really? You were in a battle."

"Yes. And, fortunately, they had failed to trade with your lot, as of yet, so they didn't have that many muskets to overtake us."

"You had to fight hand to hand, mostly."

"Yes, we did. This scar came from when another Brave sliced me down my arm."

"And you survived."

"At the expense of killing him."

My eyes widened, but not from the shock of this knowledge. On the contrary, when you meet officers, and you fall in love with them, you know that they face danger. You know that they sacrifice much for king and country. And yet, you never imagine them killing anyone.

But that's precisely what they must do.

Suddenly, in a quick succession, a series of tableaus passed along my thoughts, dancing across my imagination.

I saw Lieutenant Finlay, alongside Denny, Captain Carter and others charging into battle, expressly under Colonel Forster's authority.

Then I saw Colonel Fitzwilliam, on a horse as he led his army against the French.

Then I imagined the Dakotan Braves rushing toward the Sioux, with some muskets, but mostly bows, arrows, and action.

Three battles, all colliding into one across the lightning that was filling up my mind.

The armies came closer, and they clashed against the other.

Suddenly, I saw a quick image of Finlay colliding into a French soldier and getting stabbed in the stomach.

Then I saw Colonel Fitzwilliam getting shot from his horse and falling into the earth.

Of White Wolf getting sliced across the arm and falling as he raised up his pickaxe to defend himself.

Of Finlay falling.

Of Colonel Fitzwilliam dying.

Of White Wolf getting hurt.

Enough!

My disturbing reflections had overcome me so much that I grimaced, my face evidently distorted as I covered my eyes.

"Miss Bennet?" White Wolf asked me.

"Forgive me," I said, steadying my breath.

"I have upset you."

"No, you have not. I was just remembering."

"Remembering what, pray tell?"

"Two men. Two warriors, like you."

"Ah. Are they family or do you love these men?"

A person should never unfold their hearts too much to anyone they have so small an acquaintance with. However, who was he going to tell? What did I risk by telling a Brave what was in my heart?

"I loved them."

"Why did they not choose you?"

"Because I have no money."

White Wolf moved his face very little, but his eyes twinkled.

"Another defect to your way of living. Money is too much a calculation of your happiness."

"It is," I admitted. "I do not deny it, and yet, this is my world, and I will make the most of it."

"Did neither of them understand that they could make their fortune?"

"They are both soldiers, White Wolf. Soldiers need a wife who will save them from that."

"If they are brave, it shouldn't matter. If they can face a death on a battlefield, then what is there to fear in life?"

I chuckled.

"It's more than that."

"No, it's not. It never is. It's very simple. We humans are merely in a hurry to always complicate the mind and how we live. I never understand that tendency of ours."

"Me neither. It is the way that we have been built."

Archer called for White Wolf to bring him his report.

"You must excuse me."

"Before you go, I have one more thing to ask."

"What?"

"Why did you choose this life? To be a sailor on the Lilia? Most Indians do not do that, from what I have seen."

"It was simple. On this ship, I feel free. Can you say that you are free all the time?"

I flinched. How did he know that?

"No," I admitted, "I cannot."

~

"I've been on a ship since I was eleven years old," First Officer, Trip, said as he and Third Officer, Reedus, were down below, taking their shift to eat a brief meal while Tepree oversaw both larboard and starboard. "So, my whole life has been on a ship."

"And you?" I asked Reedus.

"Actually," Reedus said, "my life took an unlikely turn than the Reedus family expected. I'm from Swansea, and came from a respectable family, attended Cambridge, with every intention of wishing to be a tutor, and even gaining a fellowship."

"Did you?"

"I lost every chance I aimed for—I had no great name to connect me and endear me to anyone's good opinion, and therefore, there was very little chance of advancement. That is often the story that one meets in life: you are given an education, and then what do you do with it? For, the world renders itself not as much onto what you know, but rather whom do you know."

"I'm sorry."

"When I was sixteen years old, the reality of my situation was finally thrown upon me as if I were pushed into a rude awakening. I was not to be in the way of educating anyone. You see, some of us are born into a world where no one wishes to see an upstart, and I was not to be fortunate. So, through some mates that I had befriended at Cambridge, one of them was to go into the Navy. I asked him for some assistance, and I entered the service."

"Did either of you look back and wonder what else you could have done with your life?" I asked.

"There was nothing really to look back to," Reedus responded.

"Everyone wishes to be a perfect gentleman," Trip said, biting into a biscuit, "but, in life, you learn it's just as important to be a simple kind of man. I think there's a certain charm to us."

"There is. And you're from North Carolina?"

"Yes, ma'am, it's one of the best places on earth. Rugged land, mixed with the best and worst of humanity. No place like home," he chuckled.

"Really?" I laughed. "That is North Carolina."

"That's the United States in a nutshell, and out of a nutshell. We Americans are brilliant... until we get stupid and violent."

I couldn't help but laugh even more at that, because I got the impression that Trip was telling me the truth.

"Ah, you barbarians!" Reedus commented.

"It takes one to know one, is what I say," Trip retaliated, "and you can quote me on that. Don't forget, we come from you. Like father, like son, is what I have to say."

"How did you both learn to become friends?" I asked. "The contrast between you is extreme, to say the least."

And it was.

Trip's deep Southern American accent indicated that of the roguish charming frontiersman, who lived his life by the edge of his seat. Reedus had the immediate level of aristocratic magnetism that came from a sophisticated education from the highest circles in London. Only their pale peach skin was identical, and that neither of them was very tall.

"The contrast is what it was all about, if you believe in that Goddess called 'Irony'," Reedus informed me.

"And also a matter of finding the pleasure in disagreements," Trip acknowledged. "For example, I think that our War of Independence was the greatest thing that could have happened and that we are about to greet the world, greater than ever."

"And I think that those traitorous Americans were completely erroneous and horrendously ungrateful for rising against us," Reedus countered, "and not remaining alongside the nation that spawned them."

"*Father*," Trip called Reedus, mockingly. "All children grow up and leave the nest."

"And in Britain, the son also inherits the estate and does what the father says." Reedus smacked Trip across the head. "Ungrateful boy."

"And this is why we rebelled, you tyrant!" Trip nudged Reedus.

"And you both really talk like that to each other?" I said, amused.

"Oh, yes," Trip said, "and we mean every word of it."

"Personally, I believe this sort of confrontation is healthy to friendship," Reedus explained. "We confront the matter, and by so doing, we reconcile ourselves to the fact. Then we assimilate to each other's point of view and learn the ability to adapt to another mindset without having to feel as if we must make them conform to ours."

I looked between them both and made a deduction.

"Neither of you like conformity, do you?" I asked.

"Not precisely," Trip said, "but whoever does like always being told what to do? Mind you, I can follow orders, provided those orders are logical. I can't serve under a madman."

"I believe in drawing order from out of chaos," Reedus acknowledged, "but conformity of thought? No, I refuse to ever surrender or sacrifice my intellect."

"Always remember, we all have to serve someone eventually," Trip said, tapping my forehead, "but never let anyone take that from you."

'Trip, you touched my forehead without asking me first. You've got courage.'

"Well," I said, "this is lovely. Two real friends in the world. Outside of myself and Georgiana, I began to wonder if it actually existed."

"Oh, you and Miss Darcy," Reedus said. "You both are a handsome set of friends."

"But I get a little curious about the third one," Trip observed, "that Miss Watson."

"Oh," I said, groaning. "Yes, her."

"Knew it!" Trip declared, turning to Reedus. "Told you there was trouble there."

I grimaced.

"Really? How could you even notice that?"

"Miss Bennet," Reedus commented, "we're on a ship. Since human nature is thrust on us very often, we have no choice but to theorize."

"This is our world, isn't it?" Trip said. "A wandering island in the middle of a large body of water."

"Here, we can be philosophers."

"Well, I prefer just to call us observers, but philosophers sound more sophisticated. I'll take it."

"How in the world did your uneducated kind ever win the revolution?" Reedus declared.

"Because fate loved us more than you all and wanted to knock you down off your high horses. And she still loves us more than you all."

"Falsities and fallacies. We should have won."

"No, you were right to lose."

"Not true."

"Very true."

They continued arguing like this for a while, and I just marveled at them.

As I looked at them, I wondered if that was how Finlay and Colonel Fitzwilliam would have felt if it had not been for them falling in love with the same woman. Perhaps. Two men, with the same heart.

The argument didn't last long, however. Both men were called back to their duties by the Deck Cadet, Miyoshi.

Before they left me, I had a sudden thought.

"I just realized something," I observed.

"What?" they both said in unison.

"You both know you are beautiful, don't you?"

"Oh, yes," Trip commented.

"Very much so," Reedus confirmed. "If you had seen us when we were young, you would have thought we were the most stunning things that you had seen in creation."

"Just wondering, but what made you realize that?" Trip asked.

"The way that you both talk to each other," I theorized, "usually older men and women only speak with that level of confidence when they were aware that they were once handsome."

"Oh, you have no idea," Trip said, winking at me, "the Greek Gods had nothing on us."

They followed Miyoshi out.

"So," I heard someone say behind me, "enjoying your analysis of our crew?"

I turned around and it was the cooks, Jesus and Gloriana Nueva.

They laughed at me.

I didn't take it personally.

~

"Forgive me," Gloriana said, as I sat in the doorway of the kitchens as they cooked, "but most of you Europeans cannot cook to save your lives."

"What?" I said, offended. "That is nonsense. You're prejudiced."

"Who isn't, in this world?" Gloriana asked me.

I honestly could not think of an answer to that, because she had a point.

"What my wife means," Jesus said, (and I had to remind myself that his name was pronounced *Hey-Zeus*) "is that your food is somewhat bland. It is as if you are against the idea of seasoning things."

"And you boil everything," Gloriana continued. "Why do you do that? It removes the taste from things that need to satisfy your tastebuds."

"Tastebuds?" I asked, confused. "Forgive me, but that cannot be a word."

"Yes, it is," Jesus responded, "it's a word. It refers to your taste palate. The tastier food is, the more it becomes a pleasure in life.

However, if you drain the flavor from an item of food, you lose your love for eating."

"Well, we do regard eating as a necessity," I admitted.

"Because you don't believe in sugar or salt at the right times," Gloriana continued, "your biscuits have no flavor. Your meat is bland, and you cannot make a cake for your lives."

"Our food is fine," I replied defensively. Truly, I think I was now learning what it meant to be offended. While I admit that I did enjoy Gloriana's and Jesus's cooking—breakfast especially—I still was willing to come to Britain's culinary aid any day of the week. "And no, I do not see anything wrong with it."

"Like what you like, dearie," Gloriana said, removing some strange contraption from a pantry. The cupboards were covered in chipped paint, the kitchen was ghastly, and smoke hung about the air, where the door had to remain open, for the sake of them not suffocating under the denseness. "Now open your mouth."

In front of my mouth, she held up something that I was wholly foreign to and almost made me want to purge up what I ate.

"What is that!" I asked.

"It's called a quesadilla."

"It looks horrid. It looks like some random foods shoved into a thin bit of paper."

"That paper is bread, just like what you make," Jesus replied, "we lay ours flat, and roll our food in it."

"I cannot," I said, grimacing at the prospect. "You cannot make me!"

Gloriana lifted an eyebrow. In her eye was a challenge that taunted me, bringing out every competitive aspect to my character. In fact, I had no notion that I even had a *competitive aspect to my character* until this moment. Usually, I found competition to be a complete waste of my own time and efforts, which easily could be distributed to other areas of my life. In fact, in my opinion, competition was meant for other individuals who were desirous to be the best in life. When you are told, at a young age, that you were never the best at anything, you walked away from the race a long time ago. More and more, I was beginning to wonder how it made even more sense that I am the last Bennet sister to marry. If I ever do. I never was competitive.

"Are you afraid?" Gloriana asked, the challenge still in her eyes.

"I refuse to let that work," I declared, resisting the temptation to be baited by her.

"You certain? Because I think you are afraid."

Grumbling, I opened my mouth. Oh, it looked so gruesome. The last time that I was perplexed at eating something was when I first saw black pudding... oh dear! While I have been told that it is actually delicious, I still could not venture forth.

But I did not want to look like a coward.

Curses!

With one final burst of courage, I bit into the quesadilla.

Oh, dear lord, it tasted heavenly!

A burst of different flavors rushed into my mouth, and I experienced many different taste sensations. Never before had I eaten anything that incredible.

I had another bite of it.

"You like it, don't you?" Jesus asked.

When I opened my mouth, for I had shut it, as a reaction to enjoy the meat, rice, and beans that were in the *wrap*, I opened them again and saw the couple looking at me, triumphantly.

I opened my mouth, about to do just that. They were right; it tasted better than anything that I had ever experienced.

"Bah, bah, bah!" Gloriana said, placing a finger near my mouth, like a mother reprimanding her child. "Like we said, do not lie. Don't make this a matter of patriotic pride."

"I cannot help it," I declared. "Our food is good."

"That is neither here nor there. Did you like it?"

I sighed.

"Oh, very well! I loved it."

Gloriana and Jesus cheered.

"Mexico wins the day!" Jesus cried.

I had a strong impulse to go to my room, raise our Union flag and run with it, along the deck.

I resisted the urge.

Diplomacy was something that I was determined to learn how to be.

Besides, I didn't have our Union flag with me.

As I left the kitchen, I passed by Doctor Phineas. Of all the men on the crew, Phineas was the least handsome. And, also, was the most comfortable to be around.

Phineas was from Canada. He had curly gray hair, was hefty in girth, and he had a very warm face, as well as an animated voice. He was one of those men, who when he spoke to you, he always appeared to be happy, and you trusted him.

"Coming from the kitchens?"

"Yes. And I learned something."

"What?"

"We're all proud of the country we come from."

"Naturally. We all ought to be, in my opinion."

"Well, it hurts to learn when another country does something better."

He smiled.

"Yes, I suppose that it would be difficult. That takes a great deal of courage. Surely, that must help in some way."

"Thank you."

"You are welcome. Gloriana and Jesus made you taste their food, didn't they?"

Well, this was quite the surprise.

"How did you know?"

"They make us all eat their food to display their superior cooking. With your curiosity to learn about them, it was only a matter of time."

I looked down.

"If you ever feel like your national pride is being affected, here's my advice."

"As a doctor, you have to deliver a great deal of that, don't you?"

"Usually, us doctors and surgeons result in being the person that everyone expects to know the meanings of life. We are the closest things to Socrates, Plato, and Aristotle all wrapped up into one distorted amalgamation. My advice is this: insecurity over another nation's good ideas, should never overwhelm you too much. It usually results in getting angry at that other nation. And secondly, each nation does not do something better: we just do it differently. Once you enjoy that notion, insecurities won't affect you at all."

"Oh," I replied, not overwhelmed by his wisdom. After all, he didn't say anything too profound that I had not tried to learn myself. But it was nice for it to be reaffirmed. "Well, that is very pleasant to hear. I think I can adopt that way of thinking."

Doctor Phineas smiled, rubbing his hands on his apron.

"Did you ever feel that way?" I asked. "Insecure when another nation might do something superior to yours."

"Never," he replied, confident. "But it's natural. I'm from Canada; no one does anything better than us."

"Oh," I groaned, walking away. "You are no help at all."

"I am so sorry to hear that," he yelled to my retreating figure.

Chapter Eight

ASKING ARCHER

As I went aboard deck, I passed by Emma Watson and Mr. Blake, as they were walking alone together.

Instinctively, my impulse was to turn and walk in the other direction. However, they had already spotted me, and nothing was left to do, except approach them and pretend to be comfortable.

"Miss Bennet!" Mr. Blake greeted me merrily, while exchanging a side glance at Emma. While I may not have been the best judge of expressions, I did not need to be. Rather, the language that was spoken silently between them was speaking as loud as my thoughts in my brain: he knew that Emma and I were uncomfortable around each other. At best.

"Mr. Blake and Emma," I replied, falsely appearing pleasant. I had no intention of always wearing my emotions on my sleeve, but nor was I going to pretend to a camaraderie that I did not feel. "Taking a turnabout on the deck?"

"Exercise is always beneficial," Emma said, "and Mr. Reedus informed us that ten walks around the deck indicates that we have been walking almost a mile."

"Well, if Mr. Reedus knows, then I would not doubt it."

"He is a refined man. I am surprised that he is a sailor."

"A sailor can be refined," I responded, "qualities of gentility are not confined to gentlemen. After all, Mr. Blake is congenial, and he is a tutor and past clergyman."

"You flatter me, Miss Bennet," Mr. Blake said.

"I speak as I find. If you were not, I would not say so."

"Honest? How different than the rest of the world. I like that."

I nodded, flattered.

Turning to Emma, I saw a subtle apprehensiveness as she looked between Mr. Blake and me. I do not believe that she preferred that Mr. Blake and I were pleasant to each other. And I knew why. While Emma Watson would never confide in me, she didn't need to. I know little, but I know the look of love when I see it.

Emma Watson had been struck with a lightning bolt of affection. And there was no going back.

Whatever she was raised to be, no matter how refined, the heart cannot be dictated so. And she had no choice but to experience all the looks that one suffers under when under love's influence.

As such, I was doing both of us a favor when I decided to untangle myself from their company.

"Where is Georgie?" I asked them.

"She wanted to finish the book she was reading," Emma answered, "and of course, she ought not to be disturbed by our company."

"Ah. She is a great reader."

"It's one of her virtues."

"And speaking of writing," Mr. Blake said, pointing to my diary, "I see you are still at work, chronicling our adventure."

"You are keener than I, and more dedicated," Emma said, before I could form any response. "To write your experiences every day, especially when confined to a ship."

"I like to write down what the crew are like," I said, "when it comes to studying people's characters, there is always something. I should not delay your walk with my scribblings. I know when three is not the company, but quite the crowd."

"Miss Bennet!"

I looked above me, and coming down the steps from the starboard side, was Second Officer Tepree.

~

Without even knowing what I was about, I began to shake in my boots.

As she came down the steps, in the second officer's uniform, I quaked under the intimidation that comes when you admire someone, and they might not enjoy your company.

"Yes, sir," I said, standing there, my face blanched with slight alarm.

"I have been making many observations as you have been walking around the ship," Tepree said. "You have been interviewing the crew."

"Have I been a nuisance?"

"It has distracted the sailors, somewhat," she said, her voice as flat as always. Truly, her way of speaking had a monotone base, that sent shivers down my spine. Always it made it impossible to decipher what she felt, because she never displayed any emotion that could betray her. And her beauty did not make it any easier. "But nothing to cause any alarm. It has merely raised the Master's attention, and he requests your presence at the wheel."

My eyes widened in surprise.

"The captain wishes to speak with me? To what point and purpose?"

"That is for him to tell you."

Since we were standing on the other side of the deck, near the foremast and the forward hatch, I saw the Master, Captain Archer, standing near the wheel while another sailor was handling it.

He looked every bit the powerhouse of a man that I imagined him to be. For so long, I had looked on him, in the same manner that I had looked on Tepree: in wonder. But now, I was to meet the man who I had made into a legend in my mind.

"Very well," I said, both uneasy as well as happy to leave Emma and Mr. Blake to their own conversation. "You both must excuse me."

"Of course," Emma said, her eyes filled with a subtle delight. I think she found amusement in this ordeal.

And no wonder why. From all outward appearances, it felt as if I was walking to my doom, or at most the equivalent to being called to the front of the room by a very caustic governess who wanted to punish you in front of the classroom. Oh, very well, in some ways, that *is* the equivalent of walking to one's doom.

Following Tepree, we walked past the scrap-hopper and chimney and flue.

"How did he look when he asked you to summon me?" I asked Tepree, attempting to sound as disinterested as I could. I did not want her to know that her presence awed me. It might make her dislike me even more. "Did he sound pleased or disgruntled?"

"I cannot tell you. Though, I would recommend that you look on him in a more amiable eye than you look at myself."

My thoughts were as sharp as my head was when I turned toward her.

"I beg your pardon?"

~

Tepree did not initially respond to my outburst but only kept walking.

"Sir," I said to her, decidedly moving slower to make her slow down as well, so that she would be forced to explain. "Forgive me, but I think that you owe me an explanation for judging me so erroneously."

Having no choice, she turned to me. Her moves were elegant and graceful, but decided, precise, and striking. The woman was a living Greek goddess.

"Do I?"

"Yes, you do. Whoever told you that I do not look on you in a favorable light has done me a great injustice. Who told you that I look on you cruelly?"

"No one tells me anything. It is your demeanor and the shift in countenance when you look on me. It's horror. Believe me, Miss Bennet, you are not the first woman to look on me with a sense of being ashamed. But it affects me, not at all."

"That's what my face indicates?" I asked, utterly astounded at how an expression can quite betray you.

"It came to my attention."

"Well, this is perhaps another of the most humbling moments of my life," I assented, resigned to the fact that there were still things about myself that I was unaware of. "Then, I suppose, I ought to add that to my collection."

"You are being metaphoric," she observed, stoic. "Explain."

"Sir," I said, "if my expressions gave me the appearance of looking on you with dismay, then I am mortified. I assumed that you did not like me."

"How could I not? After all, we hardly know each other."

"Because that is usually how one reacts to when one admires you," I said. "I admire you, sir. You, Miyoshi, and Gloriana. You work professions that us ladies do not do."

"You do not consider us oddities?"

"Only in the sense that you have overcome what I do not understand how to."

When hearing it, she looked on me, curiously.

"That is what you felt?"

"Yes. I did not know how to approach you, because everything that I said felt wrong. And, perhaps, that led to me appearing as apprehensive around you. I apologize. I just did not know how to approach you about it."

"Then I am sorry," Tepree replied, "I misjudged you."

"Perhaps, I helped you make that misconception."

"No, it could also be my own misconceptions. When you are a woman who has chosen to do something that ladies rarely do, you eventually are forced to grow cold to overcompensate, to forearm yourself at the reaction that you traditionally receive."

"People judge you."

"Everyone judges everyone. When it comes to individuals such as myself, everyone misjudges us. So, you look on me with reverence?"

"Yes, I do. I wish that I had your courage."

"And that is the first thing to accept. Courage. Truth is, Miss Bennet, you have to begin to understand."

"What?"

"When you are a woman who dares to do something that is wholly untraditional, that only men do, you are not a heroine. There will be no one who cheers for you, who says that you are helping them see that there is more to life for us all. You will feel rejected from every single aspect of the world, man, and woman. It requires the courage to know that no one might be there to support you."

The reality that she presented made me grow cold inside. That could not be true? Surely, it couldn't...but it could.

"I just realized that it would be better if you would know me," Tepree explained, "so you can understand why I am the way that I am."

I squinted, discerning what she meant.

"You are warning me."

"Yes, I am." Her eyes were keen, her focus intense as it was directed solely at me. Despite that there was nothing supernatural about her appearance, I knew it: she was reading into my soul. "If you have it in you to enjoy the life you already have, cherish it. But if you admire me because your impulses are pulling you in a certain direction, then I am telling you now, you will always be living in an inferno. Unless you are fortunate."

"Fortunate?"

"Unless you find a place that you fit within, and it envelops you."

"Like you do here?"

"Yes. The Lilia is my only home. And Archer is the only master that I can have."

She led me to the other side of the deck. We were silent for the rest of the way because there seemed to be nothing more to say.

But much to consider.

This whole time, she had been looking on me as another person who found her to be an embarrassment and had willfully misunderstood me.

With me, I had to consider that I was somewhat of a coward. I wanted her liberty, her right to choose her life, but I did not have the ability to face the world shouting at me. I did not want to risk shaming my family.

I suppose that is what so much of life resorted to: shame. Also, this miscommunication would have ended if I had been brave enough to have spoken with her earlier.

At last, we reached the wheel, and I stood in front of the master.

Captain Archer was standing before me, in all his glory.

What a strange sensation.

One would expect that I would be intimidated now that the moment came to it. After all, I had only seen the master of the Lilia from short distances, but I never actually spoke more than one sentence to him.

And now that the situation had presented itself, in so sudden a manner, all that I could assume was that I did not have sufficient time to be scared.

In fact, now that I was close to him, I was not frightened at all. Perhaps it was because of his eyes. They were kind.

"The Master of the Lilia," I announced, deciding to be charming.

"Miss Bennet," he said, though he didn't smile, his eyes were twinkling. "And if I am not mistaken, Miss Catherine Bennet."

"You are correct. Though, from the traditional habit of things, I go by the name Kitty. Of course, I understand if we never reach such terms where you can call me such. Decorum rules us all, does it not?"

"Very true."

"I am surprised you know my name at all, to be candid."

"Well, when a young lady is walking around the ship, with a journal in her hand, I do make it a habit to learn of her intentions."

I laughed.

"Do you think I am a spy of some sort?"

"No, but I am curious about your purpose for it. After all, what is a master and commander of his ship if he does not worry for his crew?"

"You care for them."

"They are my sailors. I am their master. I had better do so, do you not think?"

"I do. And I appreciate that. They like you."

Captain Archer raised an eyebrow.

"That's always a pleasure to know. But are you distracting me?"

I handed him my journal, without any hesitation. My diary was my private business, and yet I was not inclined to conceal anything from him. Perhaps, it was because I very well understood that he was correct to worry, and maybe, I did answer to him in some way.

"You can read it," I offered. "I don't mind."

He looked at my journal, not with suspicion, but wonder.

"You give it to me freely?"

"I trust you," I realized. "I do not know you, but I do trust you. Yet I suppose that it is more than that."

The light hit his eyes and augmented the blue in them, which matched the color of the sky.

"What else would it be?" he asked.

"I think that I would prefer it if you also trusted me. After all, trust cannot be done in one direction, can it?"

"Not if it's done correctly." He took my journal and opened it. "What page number should I be looking at?"

"Fifty-one is where I begin to write about your crew."

He flipped to the number and began to read my first entry. After he quickly looked through the sentences, he closed it.

"It will suffice," he determined, handing it back to me.

"Suffice?" I repeated.

"Yes. You really are just writing about us, to simply be writing about us."

"What else did you expect?"

"You will be offended, and it would be inadmissible to offend a lady such as yourself."

"I don't fear the truth, Captain. Forgive the erroneous title. I know that the correct term is master."

He swiped the air, dismissively.

"Every passenger we get calls me captain. The true title is implied, and I respond to both. Well, the truth is that I do not want people writing fallacious reports of my crew, for the sake of exploitation. Most of my crew thrive on the reputation of being exotic, but it is also only a matter of time before the outside world decides that it has to push its way into our lives."

"And tries to destroy the little bit of life that is within your control," I theorized.

My remark surprised him, and I was equally amazed at the words that were coming from out of my mouth. Everything that I said was organically delivered and spoken more from instinct rather than through deliberation.

Captain Archer turned more toward me, and I was able to analyze the beauty of his countenance even more.

He was a great deal taller than me. His figure and face still clung to the beauties of his youth. His gray hair was combed and clean. When he was younger, he must have had a figure that was like the statue of David, by Michelangelo.

Finlay's figure was such.

So was Colonel Fitzwilliam's.

~

Finlay and Fitzwilliam.

The beautiful who were not regarded as beautiful. But they were to me.

Their images not only flashed across the streams of my mind, but I imagined them standing there, where Archer was. I blinked, trying to banish their image from the present scene.

In that moment, I had to accept the reality that maybe I could not forget them, because I didn't have the right to. Maybe the point was that no matter where I went, I ought to remember them. After all, if I did not, then what would it say about my heart?

The heart of a woman!

All of fiction and literature was against us, determining that our affections were like a puff of smoke, that was very changeable. In that moment, I wished that my feelings were. There is something to be said for individuals who could move on from one romance to another. They possess a carefree element that others of us, who feel deeper and longer, can never experience.

Yet I was not that way. And I must resign myself to the fact that I was always going to look to the past, even when I was racing to another future. People such as us are forlorn, hurled into a constant state of indecision, and aware that while we are looking forward, we are also looking back. And while we are looking back, we are willing ourselves to move forward, to another tomorrow, where we expect new horizons that will always be tarnished by recollections of yesterdays.

Torn from my thoughts, I directed my attention back at Archer.

"Yes," he confirmed, "that is precisely it. Miss Bennet, when you are on this ship, it is a means of transport to you. A way of getting from one place to another. Yet when you are the master of a sloop, she becomes as real to you, and as cherished as any home. But the outside world loves to invade, as you would say, and control what it has no right or reason to."

"And that's what it all culminates to," I said. "The right to life, liberty, and the pursuit of happiness. It's the God-given right that everyone ought to have but is so difficult to maintain. Because the outside world will always be obsessed with controlling that little piece of life that you have. It already has everything, and yet it wants to take more from you."

"And it won't be happy until it takes everything," Archer continued. "Yes, quite right. I would say that I am surprised that you know that, but you are a woman; you are accustomed to life taking everything from you."

To hear a master of a ship speak so! I could hardly believe my ears, as I beheld the man who I had just met, and yet here we were, not pushing ourselves to understand the other. Yet we merely did.

"You know that?" I asked.

"Yes, I do. Why do you think that I have women crew, when it is quite impossible to do so?"

"That is the main thing that I really wished to ask you about. Why did you allow women to be on your crew? Especially as a second officer and the deck cadet."

"Because they are good at what they do. And, also, there is the matter of chances for themselves."

"Because they have nowhere else to go," I confirmed.

"True, they don't," he answered gently.

"If something happens to you, or your ship, they might have nothing. No master would take them on."

"Never fear, I have made promises. If I die, Trip will take my place, and if something happens to him, then Reedus will. Tepree, Miyoshi and Gloriana will always have a ship to call home. That's the delight of being a master of a vessel. As long as you have a ship, an able crew, and money, this is one part of life that the rest of the world cannot touch. Out here, in the sea, how can life and its double dealings, its underhanded behavior, and its prejudices touch us? It cannot."

"What made you interested in having a crew of this level of diversity?" I asked casually. "I do not ask it to be censorious."

"I know you don't. Your diary said as much. Well, first, there is security in it."

"Security?"

"When you have a crew of such difference, and the world fears that difference, your crew clings to those who don't fear it. I don't fear it. I love the dynamics of our world. I love Canada and Massachusetts, but I joined a ship at a young age because I knew that I would never be happy in one place. I would not be content until I saw the whole world. And I wanted it on my ship."

"Oh, yes. You are from Massachusetts."

"Partly. Yes. I was born in Quebec, Canada. But when I was growing up, my parents moved us to Nantucket, Massachusetts, where I was raised. My mother was from Boston."

"Birthplace of Benjamin Franklin and John Adams?"

His eyes sparkled.

"You know a bit of our history?"

"A mere little. It's impossible not to know about the Colonies. You may be independent of us, but we are still your mother. Even when your child is an ocean away, it's impossible not to know what your child is doing. You have no choice but to know such things."

"Then again, I should not be surprised. After all, you referenced the Declaration of Independence a moment ago."

I smirked.

"Make no mistake, I am a proud British lady, and I expect you to always treat me with respect. Do not misunderstand me, I admit that the Impressment is wrong, but that's as far as it goes."

"Thank you. Stealing sailors is never right to do, so I appreciate that. But as long as you return the compliment of respecting me, no one will disrespect you here, or on land. As long as you are my passenger, I will see to it."

"Thank you. I quote your Declaration because it is a good quote. Didn't President Jefferson write it?"

"Yes, he did. For a tall man, he certainly speaks quietly."

"He does?"

"Yes, I saw him speak one time, when he visited New York. I could barely understand him. He spoke clearly, just low."

"How did he become president?"

"I've been told that he understands diplomacy, and when he is around his peers, he is said to be very agreeable. His party is also more congenial to immigrants, which helped his cause. Charm will get you far in life. But make no mistake, he is as flawed as any other politician. Government will always be a necessary evil. The trick is to choose the least evil option. Sadly, humans often can't see the forest for the trees."

"Ah, now it makes sense."

"Yes. He was regarded as the lesser of the two evils. That's the way of the world. Do you wish to talk about something else other than politics?"

"Yes, I would," I said, laughing, "in truth, I don't even prefer talking about it too much."

"Neither do I," he said, his face looking as if he sniffed something that he didn't like. "Why did we even begin to speak about it?"

"Stream of conversation," I said. "We started talking about one thing and accidentally found ourselves drifting."

"Yes, that's what happened. But let us talk of other things."

"Agreed. We can begin."

We looked at each other, entirely at a loss.

"Now we don't even know what we are about," I determined.

"No, we don't know what to say to each other at all now. The pressure of performance, as it were."

"Yes, I know."

We both laughed.

~

"Oh, I do have one good thing to report that can spark your interest," he said.

"What?"

"In two days, we are going to have a ball on the ship."

Immediately, I became animated.

"A ball? On a ship?"

"Yes. There have been balls on ships before."

"I know, but I have never partaken in one. This would be my first."

"Then I give you a new experience. That is the delight of being on a ship. If the weather is disagreeable, we can always steer away from it."

I laughed again.

"Captain Archer, that would be delightful."

"Yes, it will be after we make berth at Spain and Portugal. Once we depart there, gathering more passengers, we will celebrate as we continue our voyage. Also, it's good for my men. Sailors always need a little bit of dancing to keep their sanity about them."

"I can't wait to tell Georgie."

"Georgie?"

"My friend, Miss Darcy. I call her Georgie. She will love it. Do you have a pianoforte or a violinist?"

"Yes, we do. The pianoforte is below deck, and it will be

brought up for the duration. Gloriana is proficient at playing, and Merriweather is a great violinist."

"He is?"

"It runs in his family. They all learned to play. It's how his grandfather bought his freedom and his wife's freedom. Their owner always let them keep their wages from when they played outside events. Merriweather was born a Free Man, however."

"Really?"

"Yes."

"Another piece to the puzzle is now coming together."

"Yes, I suppose that it is," he continued, "so, that only leaves me to ask."

"Ask what, sir?"

"Might I secure you hand for the first two dances?"

I pointed to myself, amused.

"Me?"

"Yes. Why not? And, from what I understand from your English customs, you cannot refuse me. For if a woman rejects one offer of dancing, she cannot dance for the entire evening."

I bit my lip.

"I hate that rule," I said.

"Naturally."

"Well, even if I did have the power, I accept."

He smiled.

"You do?"

"Yes. You like me."

He chuckled, nervously.

"Never fear," I said, "I do not mean romantically. I mean from a transient sort of admiration. A sort of affection that is passing through."

"Yes, that is it," he said. "I am not here to oppress you with intimidating words of love. However, yes, I do like you. You are the precise sort of British woman that men such as myself enjoy. Also, when you get my age, you arrive at a romantic stage of life. When you are young, you are serious, and you spend so much time proving yourself, in hopes of being taken seriously. Then when you get older, when it's too late, only then do you properly learn to enjoy the company of the opposite sex. You are safe from me, but I will always expect your company."

"As long as you ask me by way of request and not command, then I will accept. I would hate to think you would think to order my life."

"I will not. I only admire beauty. But I do not abuse it."

"I shall have a ball and dance with a master from the Colonies. Now that is a story worth writing down."

"You all still call us the Colonies, don't you?"

"Of course, we do. And we're always going to. Good God, man. That's a reality that you must embrace."

I walked away from him, to go and tell Georgiana.

"We are the States, you know?" he called after me.

"Doesn't matter," I called over my shoulder. "We may not be able to control you all anymore, but we can control what we call you."

"That only means that you secretly miss us."

"Why would we?" I laughed, completely in jest and not serious at all. "You're all savages."

"Liar!"

"Possibly," I admitted, for it was obviously a joke.

I took comfort in being right; Captain Archer was truly a superior man. Thank goodness his age and my state of being was entirely to my advantage. He was too old for me, and I was too preoccupied with still being in love with two other men. But in another life, if we were the same age and I did not know what it was like to already be in love, my heart would have betrayed me. I would have fallen hard.

~

Rushing along the deck, I went down below, and I knocked on our door.

"Georgie," I said, "can I come in or are you not decent?"

"Come in, Kitty," Georgiana said.

When I entered, she was sitting on her bed, closing the book.

I dashed up to her and plopped on her bed, merrily.

"Guess what we shall experience in two days?"

"What?"

"Prepare yourself. There's going to be a ball!"

"A ball?" she repeated.

"Yes. A ball on The Lilia."

Georgiana laughed, we jumped up and began to dance around the room together.

"A ball!" she cried.

"A ball," I echoed. "Captain Archer said so! A ball, a ball!"

We stopped when we heard knocking on the door.

"Come in, Enara," I said.

Enara entered.

"What's this brouhaha about?" she asked. "You look happy."

"Because I come with glad tidings," I said. "We have a ball to attend."

"A ball?" Enara said.

"Yes. And we have no choice but to have the time of our lives."

Enara laughed and began to dance with us.

"I must tell Arthur."

She went to leave, and then she turned back to me.

"And who taught you to know people through their knocking again?"

"A trick I learned from Maria Lucas," I answered. "I wonder how she is, back home."

Chapter Nine

ANOTHER GRAVE MATTER… ANOTHER GRAVE

"Aunt Philips!" Mary Atkins called from her room, in Meryton.

Since her aunt ordered her to remain indoors after she declared that she was not feeling entirely well, Mary had been confined upstairs.

Soon, Aunt Philips entered, eager to dote on her niece.

"What is it, Mary? Do you need to eat something?"

"Aunt…"

"You didn't eat enough at breakfast," Aunt Philips insisted, sitting down on the bottom of the bed. "You have to remember that you are eating for two now."

"Aunt," Mary declared, "I can assure you, I am well. And I ate as much as I could, to the point where I despise the sight of food right now. I only called you to get permission to leave my room."

"You are in a fragile state. You think you are strong now, but your condition is not stable. Believe me."

"I just wish to do a little bit of walking about," Mary pressed. "Being so couped up, as it were, is affecting me. And wouldn't it help the child if I could have some fresh air? Being confined to one room all day surely cannot be as conducive as one would expect."

"I know that you think that I am being tyrannical," Aunt Philips said, "but believe me, one can never be too careful. And—"

Aunt Philips stopped talking when they heard commotion coming from downstairs.

When hearing some very frantic footsteps below, Aunt Philips rushed to the door, opened it, and looked down the staircase.

"Atkins?" Aunt Philips called. "What do you think you are about?"

"A grave matter!" Mr. Atkins cried from downstairs.

"Good God, what is wrong?"

"It's Maria! Maria Lucas."

Mary stood up from the bed, eager to meet Mr. Atkins as he dashed up the steps and faced his wife and her aunt.

"What is it?" Mary asked him, worried. "Has something happened to Maria?"

"Yes," Mr. Atkins said, his tone anxious and his expression heavy with concern while his eyes were on fire. "She has had an accident."

"An accident? What sort of accident?"

"She was visiting the Long sisters, and she fell down the steps, knocking her head as she did so."

"What?" Mary gasped. "Dearest, please don't tell me. Maria isn't..."

"Please," Aunt Philips uttered, saying what Mary feared to voice. "Is Maria Lucas dead?"

Dead.

The word hung in the air like that of a dense fog on everyone's vision.

Mary could not fathom the concept. For a young woman to be alive, and so very much full of vigor, and then to be cut down in her youth.

No, it could not be true. It could not be so!

"Never fear," Mr. Atkins assured them both. "She lives. Maria Lucas still lives. It is merely that she was rendered unconscious from the fall, was transported to her home and they still have not managed to get her to wake."

"I helped her," Mary uttered.

"Mary?" Aunt Philips questioned.

"I helped her learn to play the pianoforte," Mary finished, speaking in the way that people often do when they encounter a great shock. "I helped her." With a burst of energy, she rushed to get her cloak. "We must go. We must go to Lucas Lodge."

"Mary, do not make any sudden movements," Aunt Philips advised.

"I must see her," Mary insisted. "If we waste any time, it might be too late."

She pressed her hand against Mr. Atkins' cheek.

"My love, can you have the carriage drawn? Things like this ought to be done quickly."

"Yes, dear," Mr. Atkins said, not wishing to argue. "I must tell your uncle where I am going first, but I am certain that he will let me forsake my duties."

"You are coming with me?" Mary asked, hopeful.

"Of course, Mary."

She smiled.

"I'll be down soon."

Mary put on her bonnet, and Aunt Philips tied Mary's ribbons for her.

"Thank you."

"Find hope," Aunt Philips said, "and try not to let your emotions get too roused."

"Too roused? Aunt, Maria might be dying."

They looked at each other, heavily.

"I know."

"The coach is ready!" Mr. Atkins called from down below. "Ladies, we are prepared."

~

When they arrived at Lucas Lodge, Liam Lucas greeted them immediately.

"Mary, Atkins, and Mrs. Philips!" he said, desperation in his eyes. "Thank you so much for coming."

"How is Maria?" Mary hurried up the steps. "I must see her."

"She is still breathing," Liam Lucas explained, ushering them inside. "Thank God for that! But still, she will not wake."

When they entered, Sir William greeted them, his face filled with agony.

"Mr. and Mrs. Atkins and Mrs. Philips!" he gasped. "Oh, this is a dark day for Lucas Lodge. A dark day indeed!" He grabbed their hands and shook them. Never had they seen Sir William ever look so terrified.

"Sir William," Mr. Atkins said, "I am so very sorry for what has happened."

"We must pray," Mrs. Philips said, "and maybe the lord will exercise mercy. Maria will return to us."

"I pray she will," Sir William said, utterly lost. "I pray that she will!"

"Forgive me," Mary persisted, eager to carry her intention forth, "but, if the matter were to become bleak, I would like to see her. Can I please see Maria?"

Sir William was so stricken from the incident that he had a hard time speaking. Seeing that his father was practically speechless, Liam Lucas took over.

"Of course," he assured her, "our mother is upstairs with her now. If the matter should become... never mind, let us not speak of that. Come."

Since it was a lady's bedroom, Mr. Atkins could not join his wife and her aunt as Liam Lucas led them upstairs.

"When our mother saw her, unconscious," Liam said, the color in his appearance quite faded, "I never saw such a change. She screamed, horrified. Never had I seen my mother move quicker than a sloth, and now this. It was..."

To offer him comfort, Mary placed her hand on his arm. When seeing her attempted solace, Liam Lucas's grief softened.

"Quite right," he uttered, "quite right."

~

When reaching Maria's bedroom door, Mary prepared herself.

What if the door opened and she faced Lady Lucas, weeping over Maria's passing?

What if Maria had just breathed her last breath?

Or what if Maria died just as Mary and her aunt reached her?

Such a sudden thing to occur!

It was almost impossible to know what to feel.

Liam Lucas opened the door, and Mary and Aunt Philips entered the room quickly.

There Maria Lucas was. Laying in her bed, her eyes closed, and with her mother crouched down at the side of the bed, like a penitent woman.

She had Maria's right hand covered by her own as she wept into them.

When seeing Mary and Aunt Philips in the doorway, her teary eyes were even more overwhelmed.

"No," Mary said, terror gripping her heart, "please don't tell me that she is—"

"She lives," Lady Lucas wept. "But I don't know for how long. My girl won't wake. My baby is not waking!"

Rushing forward, she fell into Mary and Mrs. Philips arms.

Both women held her as Mary looked over her shoulder. Eventually, Mrs. Philips helped Lady Lucas over to a chair as Mary moved to the side of the bed, leaning over Maria Lucas.

"I don't understand it," Mary declared. "Maria, you are usually so careful. You must wake! If Kitty were here, she would shout at you for not opening your eyes. No, dearest," Mary began to weep. "You must wake. You—OH!"

Feeling the pain and sudden burst, Mary grabbed her stomach and collapsed on the floor.

"Mary!" Aunt Philips cried, holding her.

"Mrs. Atkins?" Lady Lucas asked. "What is the matter?"

Mary remained clutching her stomach as she felt the great and tragic release that she knew of, even without experiencing it before.

With her face being near to Aunt Philips, her aunt could see the horror. The overpowering horror and knew as much as Mary did.

"Mary..." Aunt Philips deduced, her voice low as she knew what was occurring.

In Mary's eyes was the gravest of reactions, as she lamented what she did not want to confront. How could this happen? The agonies that stir the reality of life, but that a person never expects to encounter! Mary knew, even though she never suspected, and she knew why! It was her own sorrow, her own emotional outburst, that led to this.

Mr. Atkins would be equally as horrified as herself, and even more disturbed—because it had been her fault. Having no choice but to be filled with resentment toward herself for letting her sensibilities drive them both to this outcome.

And just as Aunt Philips saw it in her niece's eye, so did Lady Lucas as the bottom of Mary's gown showed the evidence.

Between her daughter's accident and now knowing the horror that the predicament brought on to Mrs. Atkins, Lady Lucas moved back.

"Oh, god," she uttered.

"The baby," Mary sighed, on the burst of tears. "I've lost my baby!"

The tragedy of the moment had affected her. Mary had miscarried.

Chapter Ten

AGONIES OF THE HEART

"If our sisters were here," I said merrily, "as well as Maria Lucas and Diana Long, they would think nothing could be superior to this!"

We had arrived at Faro, Portugal, had made berth and were able to move along the port city. Since England was not currently recovering from war with Portugal, as we had recently been with France, letters could be sent. Those that needed letters sent handed them to Miyoshi, who, along with Trip and Reedus, would deliver our missives to a carrier vessel named the Trepassey.

"Happy to go on shore?" I said to Reedus.

"British in arms!" he cried to me, out of camaraderie.

"British in arms!" I called back, waving to him as they walked in another direction. As he did so, Trip playfully smacked him over the head.

"What did that mean, I wonder?" Arthur Philips asked me as we all walked along the docks and into Faro.

"Reedus is British, like we are," I said. "He could not walk around Cherbourg freely, for fear of being hackled or potentially attacked. Anti-English sentiments run strong there. As passengers, we were given liberties, but not him. Now he gets to do a walkabout."

I looked around me.

"Hello, Faro!" I uttered, cheerfully.

Portuguese architecture was not too dissimilar to England's, but it was enough so that we still felt like we were walking into a novelty.

The men tipped their hats to us ladies as we passed them.

"You must try some Pastel de feijão while we are here," Mr. Blake said. "It is a popular Portuguese pastry that is quite traditional. All we must do is find the correct bakery."

Mr. Blake and Arthur looked at the Faro citizens but didn't pluck up the courage to ask them.

"Men and their fear of asking for directions," Enara pointed out.

"It's not that," Mr. Blake said. "I assure you, but I have had the misfortune to have gone to other regions of the world and assumed someone knew English or French there, and no one did. One becomes humble after that, foolishly assuming that everyone knows their language."

"It's moments like that where you wonder if our education of learning Greek and Latin was a waste," Arthur commented. "Spanish and maybe some Chinese might have been more sufficient."

"Probably so but try telling that to anyone at Cambridge or Oxford," Mr. Blake said. "We'd be laughed out of the classroom and then exit with a heal-mark on our backsides."

"Then I will play the savage foreigner," I said, without any fear of appearances, "and ask someone. I accepted looking foolish about things a long time ago."

"That will not be necessary," a familiar voice said behind us. I turned and Miyoshi was walking with Reedus and Trip. All three were carrying food to bring back to the ship.

Turning to the nearest Faro native resident, Miyoshi began to speak fluent Portuguese. My eyes widened at how she transitioned from our language to one that was also wholly foreign to her. When she finished speaking with the woman, Miyoshi turned to us.

"When you reach the corner, make a left, and you will find a baker's shop. She said that you cannot miss it. Just follow the smells. She says that the baker and his wife make excellent custard tart."

"You speak Portuguese?" Enara asked, amazed.

"She speaks eight languages," Trip explained. "And luckily, none of them is Latin."

"Learning modern Italian made more sense," Miyoshi informed us.

"What languages do you know?" Georgiana asked.

"Japanese, English, Chinese, French, Spanish, Portuguese, Italian and Greek. Right now, I am trying to learn some African languages, but it varies per region. The closest that I could discover being the most common was Swahili, but I am worried that might not even be so."

Since the rest of my party was ignorant of this until now, they looked at her, surprised. She smiled at that reaction.

"In life, you learn that if many odds are against you, learn to be useful."

They left us, continuing to carry the produce to The Lilia.

"Well, does that not beat all?" Arthur observed as we walked to the bakery. "True words though. If the world is going to not hold you of any value, make yourself indispensable."

"She is lovely," I remarked.

"Yes, but she is not of the common way," Emma Watson commented, "it will not be so convenient for her."

As we walked to the bakery, I thought of what Miyoshi and Arthur mentioned. *If you are not of value in the world, then make yourself useful.*

Useful?

Before I left England, I was learning how to tend to horses, cook, clean, and how to be practical. However, I was not an expert in any of those things. I was never given a governess, was never given a well-rounded education, and I never cared to learn music. It was a bitter pill to take...to know that there were experts around you, and you were not among them.

To have no actual skill at anything, except for dancing, well that was a shocking blow. It makes one feel... worthless.

The woman that Miyoshi had spoken to was true to her report. As soon as we turned the corner, we smelled the bakery and followed the pleasant odor to the spot.

Georgiana, Enara, and I rushed to the window, peeked through and the baker waved for us to come in.

From behind us, Emma Watson still walked with Mr. Blake, remaining at his side. He had a trusty companion in her, always.

We all entered, and were a little anxious, because we were without our one-time translator.

"Ah," the baker said, "never fear, I know English."

We all breathed a sigh of relief, and it was very visible, because it made the baker laugh. We asked him for some recommendations of what the best thing to purchase was, and he suggested what would suit our palate.

When we left, we had a couple queques, travesseiros, bolo de arroz, a Pao de Deus, and I bought a set of croissant brioches, for the Lilia crew that I had met. These were all pastries, each delicious, of thick crust of different textures. Mr. Blake, being the gentleman, carried the croissants for me.

Since our time was short, we returned to the ship in proper time. As we carried our new treasures on board, Captain Archer saw us from the larboard, talking with Tepree.

Smiling, he leaned against the wheel, looking as if he had stormed Normandy.

"Did you bring us a gift?" he called out to me.

"Did you ask for one?" I called in return.

He chuckled.

"But as it so happens, we brought you all some croissants."

His expression lifted, surprised at this.

"A gift? Truly?"

"Yes. And with the tone of surprise."

"Can you blame me?"

Suddenly, Gloriana rushed from the other side of the deck, like a rhinoceros.

"But are the pastries edible? I think I ought to be the judge of that."

With one fell swoop, she snatched the box from Mr. Blake and opened it. Her rash behavior alarmed poor Mr. Blake, who was amazed at her presumption, and perhaps was about to say something, when I thought to save us all from their lack of understanding.

"Take no offense," I assured Mr. Blake, "that is just her way."

"Her way?" Mr. Blake asked.

"Yes," I insisted, "her way. In fact, over time you might even take this all as a sort of compliment."

"Precisely," Jesus said as his wife opened the box. "My Gloriana wouldn't snatch a box from anyone unless she cared."

I could see that this sort of logic was wholly foreign to Mr. Blake, but I didn't care to explain it to him. Like Emma Watson, they belonged to that part of England that didn't know a joke if it walked up to them and smacked them on the head. Fortunately, there would always be us other side of England that were born to laughter and understanding that the word 'jest' had its proper place in society. While they did not. No wonder we had our share of civil wars.

Gloriana took a croissant from the box, bit into it, and the satisfaction was written all over her face. But since she was an expert, she suffered from the habit of not wishing to compliment another expert.

"Edible," she grumbled. "Captain! The croissants are edible!"

"Of course, they are," he yelled back. "The Portuguese know how to cook."

"We French can cook a lovely croissant," the passenger, Mrs. Lefevre, said as she stood on the deck, "you all were not on shore long enough."

"A great sin on our part," Georgiana responded.

"Well, as long as you admit it."

As I watched Gloriana take the croissants into the kitchen to keep them warm, I saw Archer watch us as Tepree and Trip made preparations for us to prepare our voyage.

Reedus moved along the deck, ordering the anchor to be raised.

When I saw Archer looking at me, I returned his gaze. Our eyes locked and he smiled at me as the ramp was raised and we were off to Spain.

"What is going on?" Georgiana asked me.

"What do you refer to?" I asked.

"Kitty, he is too old."

My eyes widened.

"That's what you think?"

Georgiana read my expression and saw that, perhaps, she had gotten it wrong all this time.

"Oh."

I sighed.

"I suppose that I have much to explain."

"You think so? Good. Because you do."

~

Later that night, while Georgiana and I were in our beds, trying to let the rocking of the ship lull us into a deep sleep, Georgiana and I had the time to talk.

In the dark, I heard Georgiana's blankets roll around in the bed as she moved over to look at me.

"You are not in love with Captain Archer?" She asked me.

"No," I confirmed, "I am not."

"You are certain?"

"Yes, I am. Indeed, Georgie, you ought to believe that I am in earnest. This is not infatuation. As you said, though he be handsome, he is a great deal too old for me. No doubt there are some ladies who can attach themselves to a man of his years, and more for them, I say. I can understand their inclinations. Admittedly, there was a time where I harbored a great prejudice against the idea."

"Of a young woman marrying a much older man?"

"Yes. I thought her as vulgar for considering him, as he was for asking."

"I feel that way now. I do not understand young women marrying significantly older men. It doesn't seem natural, but merely desperate on her side, and detestable on his."

"Yes. That is precisely how I felt. But now I see why, and maybe I was once too harsh in my assessment. Sometimes, some men have a habit of being more alluring with age and are more approachable to the female sex."

"Archer is that sort of man, isn't he?"

"Yes, he is. One conversation with him, and you will understand. But you need not fear of me being so changeable, Georgie. I am still in love with Colonel Fitzwilliam and Finlay. I wonder that I might always be so, and that maybe, no other love will touch me."

"I do not know if I should applaud you for your constancy or worry that you cling too hard. It's a difficult business."

"Yes, it is. It always is. Georgiana, I want you to understand something."

"What?"

"Being in love is a delight. For a while. But when things become complicated, it is more of a weight than a source of levity. I do not want to add more to that weight. I am not in love with the master of The Lilia. His company does remind me of Fitzwilliam and Finlay, but that's where the attachment lays. He reminds me of comforts from the sort of confidence that I admire. All three men possess the same air, and so I will always seek Archer out, but not to fall in love."

"That is good. Falling in love again is not what you need right now, I daresay."

"No, it is not. There really ought to be a balance between a casual acquaintance and falling in love. We ladies really ought to be allowed to be friends with a man, and that be the end of it. We humans *really ought* to stop swinging between the pendulum of extremes. There is no extreme indifference or extreme affection in this case. I admire him and will always seek him out, but that is all. I just need tenderness. I need a kindred spirit. Just as you do."

"Yes. Though I have not found it, as you have."

"But I thought that you actively did not cling to the concept, especially since you have been spending so much time with Miss Watson."

"Oh, you sound so angry with me."

"I am not."

"You don't say so, but I can recognize subtle rage when I hear it."

"Georgie!" I laughed. "You really are mistaking everything about me, at present. I really am not upset that you are spending time with her. Yes, as I said before, at first, I was upset. Very upset. But I understand why. There is a part of your history with her that I will never be able to touch. Once I resigned myself to that fact, I knew to be happy for you. And I am. But if you are going to dwell on hearts being intertwined, then *that* is where you need to focus."

"Oh! You refer to Emma's feelings for Mr. Blake?"

"It's as plain as the nose on our faces. She adores him."

"Yes, she does."

Now alive with curiosity, I rolled over on my stomach, rested my chin on my fists, and looked in Georgiana's direction. Despite that it was dark, I could still see her outline, in the black.

"She has confirmed this with you? I understand that she will never take me into her confidence, but you know that I can keep a secret."

"Well..."

"Oh, come now," I insisted. "Georgie, you cannot leave me in suspense! That would be most unkind. I am awake, and I will not be able to fall asleep until I am satisfied."

"That is the very problem. I have nothing to tell because she never tells me anything."

"Ah, her reserve."

"Yes, her reserve. I admire that about her, to an extent, but I still like a good open temper. I am too used to you telling me everything, and I like that. But whenever I speak with Emma, and bring up Mr. Blake, all that I get from her is 'he is very amiable and worthy, and that she admires his studious nature and genteel ways'. But that is all. She never reveals more than that, or less."

"She conceals her affections, without even knowing that they are very present in her actions."

"She could be like you and merely admires Mr. Blake in the same way that you admire Master Archer."

"No," I said, shaking my head. "When it comes to reserved ladies, they do not expose themselves in any sort of manner with a man that they only look on casually. They speak to one in the same way that they would speak to anyone else. But when they are feeling a particular regard for a man, they show a greater inclination to be in their company. If Emma Watson did not feel any romantic tenderness toward him, she would treat him in the same manner that she treated us. Difference of gender would mean nothing to her. But it does. She is growing to slowly fall in love with him."

"Yes. It must be that. But here's where I worry."

"What?"

"Mr. Blake is better at being more subtle in his reactions. He speaks to her in a way that indicates that he takes great pleasure with her. But it's complacent—it's too general. His remarks to her are no different than his remarks to me. It could easily be cleverly disguised, and he does feel for her. But in truth..."

"You think that she loves him," I determined, "but he might not return her affections? And that he indulges her attentions toward him, because he is a gentleman, and that is all."

"Precisely. But how do I know? How do any of us know what is in our friends' hearts?"

"We can't. All we can do is predict. Which is a sort of amusement in itself."

"If you find it amusing," Georgiana said, "then tell me. What do you believe?"

"If I knew the sort of man that Mr. Blake truly was, perhaps I could be more deductive. But for now, I can only be inductive."

I rolled over on my back and looked up, into the darkness.

"From what I have seen, he admires her at the same level that she admires him. But if he loved her, there ought to be something more. An accidental touching her back, placing her shawl around her, or a twinkle in his eye. When you are falling in love, your instinct is to touch the other person. She has that instinct, but I don't think that he does. I don't think he is in love with her, at present."

"You believe so?"

"Yes. But then again, maybe my vision is cloudy. After all, Emma and I do not get along. I am prejudiced towards her."

"You would not let that affect your judgment, surely?"

"Georgie, you know that my chief virtue is that I know what I am. There is a pettiness to me, that I might never get the better of."

"Well, she has not been particularly kind towards you. You have a right to be a little cold, in response to her chilly manner."

"Thank you. That's why I am not the best judge. But you asked what my observations are, and I can only tell you from the best of my ability. I do not think that Mr. Blake loves her."

"I fear that you might be right."

"And if I am, what then?"

"Emma would be brokenhearted."

"I do not think so," I responded. "Whatever my relationship is to her, she does possess a tough nature. She would recover. She is young and handsome."

"Not all of us recover from our first big loves."

"Still somewhat attached to Mr. Wickham?"

Georgiana did not immediately respond to me. I heard her shift around in her bed, and then there was a brief silence.

"Yes," she answered.

"Georgie, he is not worth it. He never was worth your consideration and never will be."

"Tell that to my mind. Every time I think I have fully recovered, my mind regresses."

"Quite right. Nothing I say can fully banish him from there. Isn't it so very annoying how some souls haunt us forever?"

"Yes. Emma is no different than the rest of us. If she falls in love with Mr. Blake, and he does not return her affections, it will strike her, in a passing way, or a constant way."

"We'll see in time."

"Yes, we will."

Finally, I fell asleep, happy that it wasn't us who were seized by agonies of the heart.

Chapter Eleven

THE WAIF

Agonies of the heart.

And Jane Bingley's situation had thrown her quite into the epitome of despair.

Often Elizabeth had appealed to her sister, in hopes of wishing to be a proper companion. However, each time that she went to Jane's favorite parlor, or bedroom, she was often shooed off by Lucy and Sarah, who had been given strict orders that their mistress wanted time alone.

Each report was handled differently by Elizabeth.

The first time that she was told that Jane sought solitude, Elizabeth understood.

The second time, she still understood.

The third time, she was becoming worried.

The fourth time, she could not help but grow a little aggravated.

The fifth time, she was beginning to wonder if she didn't do better than to contradict Jane's wish, feeling that her grieving was the worst thing for Jane to do, in solitude.

If the sixth time would occur, then Elizabeth knew what she

had no choice but to do. After all, when a woman is a creature that is as much of action as she is of word, then inaction is her great antagonist. Elizabeth had been denied five times; she could not abide a sixth one.

Although it could prove to be a most unproductive afternoon, Elizabeth sought out Sarah, who was tending to Mrs. Bingley particularly that day. When she found her, she inquired after Jane.

"Mrs. Bingley is not in her room or her favorite parlor," Sarah said, a sort of wild anxiety in her eye.

"Then where is she, Sarah?" Elizabeth asked.

Sarah rolled her tongue behind her teeth, both worried as well as apprehensive.

"What is that look for?" Elizabeth asked. "You only appear that way when you want to say something, but you are afraid to say it."

Sarah's cheeks flushed as she scratched the side of her neck.

"She is in the nursery—where the baby's crib had been placed."

When hearing that, Elizabeth felt as if a gust of icy wind had sliced across her face. Jane was in the nursery that her son was supposed to be placed in, being tended to by one of the most promising mothers in England. But there was no child, save for the child that rested in the earth.

Her sister was lingering in the place meant for the child that was. Without even theorizing, Elizabeth prognosticated what she would see when she arrived there: something frightening.

"And she does not want to be disturbed," Sarah furthered.

Elizabeth was adamant and was possessed with the very fire in her eye that Sarah had been accustomed to seeing when she was living at Longbourn.

"And at some point," Elizabeth declared, "that will not deter me. Sarah," Elizabeth said, taking Sarah's hands. "Be very honest with me. How did Jane look?"

Sarah bit her lip and turned wistful.

"Like not even half the woman that she once was. She's sinking away, and it is terrible to see."

"Then I don't care what she wants. I need to see her. In times like these, the worst thing a lady can do is be obedient. Then again, what has blind obedience ever given me?"

Elizabeth walked past Sarah and headed straight to the nursery.

"That's right," Elizabeth answered her own question, under her breath, "it's never brought me anything of consequence."

~

When Elizabeth arrived at the nursery—the very nursery that Jane had proudly showed her when they both were still with child—Elizabeth stood at the door. She raised her hand to knock against it, to announce her presence first, but she halted.

Once more the feeling of unease washed over her. She recalled what she had foretold herself that she might see on the other end of it.

Jane was human!

And her sister at that.

Whatever frightening image of despondency and depression that her mind had conjured, Elizabeth knew that she was overreacting.

Preparing herself, Elizabeth knocked on the door.

"I do not wish to be disturbed," Jane called from the other side.

Ignoring that request, Elizabeth opened the door anyway and entered to find that there was very little light in the room. The curtains had been drawn over the windows, and they were of a heavy cloth that diminished the light. Elizabeth recalled why that was so. Jane had picked the dense cloth, to shield the infant from unwanted sunlight if it fell asleep during the day.

The crib was no longer on the other side of the room but was in the center of it. While it lacked an inhabitant, it was useful in that it supported the weight of a hand.

Next to the crib, Jane sat there, in a low seat, with her hand rocking it, back and forth. Rocking an empty crib.

Her figure was limp, her shoulders slightly hunched over, and her hair was not held up, but hung loosely around her neck and the top of her back. Since her hair was curly, it fell along her face in a lovely way, but that was where the congenial aspect ended.

The prospect of the room was eerie, the atmosphere daunting, and Jane looked—frightening. With the shadows of the room leaning in one direction, it placed Jane partly in darkness.

It was as if her soul and figure had been reaching to the light, but the darkness was eating away at her person, pulling her into the vastness of desolation.

But it was more than just her body.

It felt as if her soul, the waif inside of her, was also falling into misery, and was being devoured by the anguish that hung about the room.

For a moment, Elizabeth worried that Jane's spirit had been already consumed and that her sister was gone.

Then her courage rose, and she would not be intimidated out of her mission.

"Jane," Elizabeth voiced, her tone gentle and calm. "Dearest..."

"Lizzy," Jane said, not listening to her, "you did not listen. I want to be alone."

"You really do not want my company?" Elizabeth asked, closing the door behind her. "You will not take me into your confidence? Are we not sisters?"

"I love you, Lizzy. You know that."

"And you love Bingley. I have heard that you even turn him away."

"Yes, Mr. Bingley. My poor Mr. Bingley."

Elizabeth moved around the room to get a better look at her sister's face. When she did, it was obvious that Jane had spent a great portion of the day crying. There was the familiar redness that hung about the eyes, and the black bags under the bottom to also indicate that she had not gotten a great deal of sleep.

She was a mother without a child. Hopelessness hung about her, and it really did feel as if she was giving into becoming more wraithlike as opposed to being corporeal.

"How I have let him down so," she continued.

"Nonsense!" Elizabeth declared, pulling up a chair and sitting down opposite her. "Jane, Bingley would never think so."

"He never would, for he is too good a man." Whenever Jane spoke, her words were slow, spoken quietly, and gave even greater indication that she was falling away from them. "But I feel it. Deep within my bones, I feel guilty, as if something is wrong with me. What did I do, Lizzy? What did I do that I poisoned my child, and you did not?"

"Jane," Elizabeth pressed, "you know as well as I do that, often, there is nothing that we mothers can do. It is the product of the situation that some children are not given the chance to live, despite that they deserve to. Too much of life is not fair."

"Even when they have just entered it?" Jane asked.

"Yes," Elizabeth continued, "even so."

"I call that very meanly done, and most unfair."

She closed her eyes and began to breathe more heavily. As she did so, she continued to rock that cradle. The very cradle which there was no child within.

Elizabeth eyed this action with dread as well as quiet alarm. Of course, Jane knew that no baby son was in it, but the action alone indicated that her mind was very afflicted. And, when not accustomed to seeing a sane mind act insanely, she worried that this was not a phase that resulted from losing her son and hinted at a more permanent mental illness.

"Jane," Elizabeth uttered, still watching her sister rock the cradle, "you have done no wrong. You will have your chance again and be the mother that you always wanted to be."

"And what if I lose another one?"

Jane began to weep.

"I could not bear it again. The look of agony in Mr. Bingley's eyes."

Elizabeth was silent. She knew that no matter what she said, Jane was not listening to her. She was so overcome by her grief that she wondered if Jane truly could tend to anything that she said.

"Do you know," Jane said, "the joys of considering names were such a delight for us both. Charles considered the name Osmund, but I wanted him to be named after his father. Naturally, he agreed, to make me happy and please me so. And I clung to the idea with such fervor, of having two Charles Bingleys in my life. And if it was to be a girl, then I would name her after you."

Elizabeth blinked, aghast.

"Me?"

"Yes. So much of my life has been dictated by your considering my happiness. You wanted me to have my happy ending with Mr. Bingley, and you quite convinced Mr. Darcy that my feelings were genuine. It all led to my husband and I finding each other."

"You flatter me."

"I speak as I find."

"And so do I," Elizabeth said, leaning forward. "You may have lost a son, but he is in heaven and will grow up there."

"Oh," Jane gasped, "do not talk to me of heaven. How do we know if it even exists? Do we know anything of the beyond!"

"Jane," Elizabeth gasped, "do not doubt our faith."

"Faith is lovely, but how can any of us dictate what is in the beyond? We merely do it because it helps us feel as if we are in control. But what do any of us truly control? We're always being puffed about through whims of chance, and we grab ahold of what we can, assuming that we have power over our own worlds. But what power do we really have?"

Suddenly, she burst into tears, raced to the fireplace, and flung herself on the floor, pained in the heart.

Rushing after her, Elizabeth leaned down and tried to hold her, but Jane would not be cuddled.

"Please, Eliza," Jane cried, "leave me. I do not want to be seen now, and you tear me to shreds when you see me this way."

"Must I leave you?"

"Please do. I must feel this way now, and I want to feel it alone. Please, leave me."

"Yes, dearest. But I beg of you, when you are ready, I am here for you to confide in."

Elizabeth stood up, turned around and left the room, Jane's sobs tearing at her heart.

As she walked back to the nursery where Hero was, Elizabeth's mind was preoccupied.

Jane was falling away from them all. And worse, Elizabeth had no notion of how to help her. After all, they both had just had children, and Elizabeth could not begin to wonder what trauma she would suffer if she had lost Hero. As such, she *could not begin* to understand what Jane was feeling, while also completely understanding the source of it.

Yet the other half of her was wondering how this all could be resolved. She knew, ultimately, that the best recovery was for Jane to become with child again. But since her soul was so overcome, there was no chance of Jane wishing to attempt it again with Mr. Bingley.

And that was the main impediment: Elizabeth wanted to help Jane but had no notion of what to do.

While she walked, she heard voices.

Familiar voices.

Going to the door that led to the billiards room, she heard Mr. Darcy and Mr. Bingley.

Despite the impropriety of the act, Elizabeth leaned her ear against the door and listened.

"She won't let me near her," Bingley acknowledged, in anguish. "Every time that I approach her, she is cold to me."

"Bingley..."

"No, Darcy, you don't understand. She is changed."

"From all that I remember of when my mother lost my first sister—"

"First sister?"

"Georgiana was not my first sister," Darcy said. "My mother's first daughter was a stillborn as well, and I was five years old at the time. But I remember it. She was in Jane's similar state, somewhat. When a pregnant woman gives birth, their emotions are overwhelming them, and so very out of their control sometimes. Therefore, when a woman loses a child, for the first time, it overpowers her. I have seen this behavior before."

"But she recovered. What if Jane is not like that? What if this takes her over completely?"

"Elizabeth is talking with her now. If there is anyone who can help Mrs. Bingley rally, it is her. Believe me, she will know what to do."

"I hope so," Mr. Bingley said, "I cannot lose my wife, Darcy. I cannot lose Jane. I won't survive!"

As Mr. Darcy began to coax Bingley, Elizabeth had heard enough.

With all speed, she rushed away, went back to the nursery, found Betsy there, with Lucy. She dismissed them, telling them that she would ring the bell, as she pondered what to do.

When alone, she paced quietly around the crib, for Hero was asleep.

Mr. Darcy told Mr. Bingley that she was the source to helping Jane recover and return to the woman that she once was.

The responsibility had been placed on her shoulders, and Elizabeth felt the burden of that.

She did not resent it but only resented that she was entirely at a loss of what to do.

She went to the window barely seeing the lush grounds, then turned back to gaze at her sleeping daughter.

She did not have a plan.

But she would think of one.

Jane's soul would not be lost.

Elizabeth would not lose her sister. She would not!

Chapter Twelve

A BALL IN THE COLD

"Barcelona ahead!" Tepree called from the upper mast.

On the ship, we all raced to the railing and stared. There, ahead of us was Barcelona, Spain, as we would make berth there, for a brief while to purchase more produce and supplies.

There was a problem with the ship, and Merriweather was the chief engineer, so he also needed more tools.

"How long does it take a person to learn how to fix a ship?" I asked him. "Yes, I know, it's a foolish question. But it's not my fault that I don't know any interesting ones."

Merriweather chuckled.

"It takes a lifetime. I've been doing it for twenty years, and I'm still quite the novice." He handed his list of supplies to Trip and Reedus for them to collect the items.

"Why don't you go with them?" I asked, securing my bonnet.

"I cannot, sadly. I have my freedom papers, but I can always get captured, my papers ripped up and be illegally sold."

I felt humbled immediately.

"Oh. Forgive me, I did not even suspect that."

"It's not your fault. It's better not to take the risk. That's also why I couldn't walk around Portugal."

"If that's a possibility though," I asked, curious, "then why did you join a ship where this could often happen to you? Why not stay in a place where everyone would know who you were, so that you would not have to encounter this all the time?"

"Home presents the same dangers. If I stray too far from my home city, I still run the risk of being illegally sold."

"Where is home for you?"

"Trenton, New Jersey. If I were to leave my city, I run a risk. Some of us have roaming feet. We're wanderers and despise being caught in one place. I'm a wanderer. I need a ship to be on. And if I were to be on another vessel than this one, I could still be illegally taken by a British ship, under the Impressment. Reedus and Trip have the same problem as myself, so at least I am not alone in that way. Reedus especially, since he's Welsh. We're all in danger. But Archer is different."

"Well, I learned that much about him, but how can he protect you if a British captain would want you?"

"He promised me that he would tell anyone that I was his son."

My eyes widened.

"Really?"

"Yes. He would say that I am his son."

Looking back on the starboard, I saw Master Archer speaking, with Doctor Phineas.

"He would do that for you?"

"Yes, he would. It's not as scandalous as you might think. Many of you all beget us."

"We do?"

Merriweather smirked.

"Oh, you have no idea. Even in your society. You all are raised to be protected and shielded from the bitter realities of the world. I admit to being surprised at how well you take it. Usually, I shock ladies such as yourself when I speak this way."

That was the wonder of it. Everything about my time on this ship ought to have made me rattled. Discomforted. Alarmed, and I should have been gasping left and right. But the reverse was occurring. I just wanted to know more. When did I develop an intrigue with the horrors of the world?

"I know that I ought to be flummoxed," I said, "and swooning left and right. But I'm not."

"I like it. It makes conversation easier. But as for why I am on this ship. The answer is simple. I am safe here. This is the only home that I could have that would make me happy."

We reached Barcelona's port. The ramp was lowered, and we had three hours to spend ashore.

~

Of all the places that we visited, so far, Barcelona would prove to be my favorite.

The main reason was because it was entirely different than Britain. The architecture was colorful, the tone of the city was vibrant, and many buildings indicated that it was a city that was seldom overrun by any foreign invasion, unlike what I heard of Rome and other famous cities from antiquity.

Despite the brisk weather, the euphoria of the city and the people was enough to bring us animation. Like Portugal, we could speak with the residents with ease since we had no rivalry with them.

While one can never fully make any generalizations of a people based on the few that one meets, it still could safely be said that the people were very pleasant and amiable.

Because our time there was limited, we could only see certain sights from a distance, and some were merely all from our imagination as Mr. Blake described what they would look like.

From the distance, we were able to see the tips of the Catedral de Barcelona, which was in the city's center. We walked down a small portion of The Rambles, which was one of the most famous boulevards in Spain, but not enough to see *nearly enough* of it, and we only were able to do that by hiring a cab that took us there and back as soon as we were able.

It was an exciting city, to be sure, and I knew that, if my family were to ever give us the chance to return, I would certainly wish to return here, more than anywhere else.

When we returned to The Lilia, we found that some of the other passengers on the ship had left us, for Barcelona was where they intended to spend the chief part of their holiday. But with their departure, another set of Spanish passengers replaced them, and we had new arrivals.

From the original set from when we began our journey, we only still had the Lefevres from France.

Therefore, it was a matter of attempting to get to know another set of strangers.

We had a few days before we made Berth at Italy, where many of them would leave The Lilia again, and there would be more farewells, with another set of arrivals.

It is a unique situation, to transition from being in an English provincial town where everyone saw the same people day in and day out, to being on a ship where you met someone, found them agreeable, and then you were to never see them again. A strange arrangement of greetings and farewells.

In my room on the ship, I took pen to paper and began to write about my time in Barcelona, and my wishes for the upcoming festivities.

... more and more, I do so envy the wealthy, but not in the manner

that one thinks. With wealth comes power over one's fate, and control over one's destiny. If I had the wealth that I could possess, I could find the proper arrangement that Georgiana, and my family, could have of traveling around the world.

For inside of me, is a thirst. New scenes and new situations to be thrown into. Even when I go out into the world, and see things that make me dissatisfied with it, I still wonder why I do not fear it. On the contrary, I wish to see more. I want to know the whole world. I want to know everything. Everything that makes the wheel of life turn. Of what makes every society run, or who that society has run over, has hurt, and had to cease hurting. For I do believe, deep down, that we all will recover. Each day, I feel that there must be a sense of progress somewhere, somehow working its way into the thoughts and subconscious of the human character, willing it to a more intelligent way of being.

We just need more time, I feel.

I don't know why I suspect that tomorrow will be better than all the yesterdays before it, as if there will be a better light than all the other days of different shades of darkness.

Or maybe I ramble.

Let me now focus on better things that are definite and that I know to be true.

And that truth is the ball this evening.

As we set out once more, the new Spanish arrivals had found that they arrived at the perfect time for gaiety. I met two brothers, who booked passage, with the interest of taking their holiday at Greece and Turkey, when we arrive there.

Their names are Manuel and Miguel Hernandez, and they look like men who are eager to take the world on, as if they were unafraid of presenting themselves in every situation.

Well, today is the ball. Since it is already somewhat cold on the seas, we must have the ball during the day and end during dusk. As such, the magic that occurs between a man and a woman at night, while dancing a reel, must be put off.

Despite that we must wear our coats and pelisses as we dance, I still plan to wear my best ballgown, and arrange my hair just so, despite that I might have to wear my bonnet the entire time.

Merriweather and White Wolf are bringing the pianoforte up to the deck, as we speak. They are good sort of men, and I hope that I will be able to dance every dance—if any of them will ask me.

But since I have the good fortune to dance with the colorful and charismatic Master, Captain Archer, it might influence the rest of our company to believe that I will dance with any man, as long as he can dance well and smiles at me...

Just as Finlay and Colonel Fitzwilliam always were.

Why can I still not shake them from my mind?

We are parted from each other by land and water, and I still feel the link.

I wonder if they do as well...

Perhaps not. Their duties take them to the world, and it is only a matter of time before they rally and fall in love elsewhere.

Here is the strangest element of all:

If that would be so, I would be devastated.

But I would also be happy if they had moved on. This way, I could say that I hurt neither one of them. For hurt one of them, I must do so eventually. And it would have all been a matter of which one. I could never make that choice; therefore, time must make that choice for me.

Now, I must go, for it is time to prepare.

Closing my journal, I prepared for the ball.

~

"I was a fool!" I laughed, as Captain Archer led me along the set.

"How so?" Archer asked, amused. "Of course, we are all fools from time to time, but I am curious about why you call yourself such."

The ball had begun, and I was able to lead the dance, since I was on the captain's arm. The joy of it! I had never been asked to lead anything before in the whole of my life.

"I forgot about the way one's body heats when we dance."

"You are regretting wearing your coat and bonnet now, aren't you?"

"Precisely! Now I am overheated."

"Well, when we dance the second set, you may disrobe to your delight."

I scoffed.

"For shame, sir, you are being vulgar."

"I used the wrong choice of wording."

"Yes, you did. And I forgive you."

"Very good. Enjoying your first-time dancing on a ship?"

I laughed.

"You find the question funny?"

"No, not the question, but the fact that it is the third time that you asked me that is what is comical."

He shrugged, embarrassed.

"And now you will think that I have no conversation."

"Who am I going to tell and ruin your reputation that way? After all, I am on *your* ship."

"Quite true."

I continued. "Besides, I am not the sort to lay a man's character down by one moment where he was at a loss of what to say. I am not educated enough, when it comes to the ways of the world, to be too judgmental."

"What do you mean by that? Not being educated enough to be too judgmental?"

"It is a theory of mine. The most experienced people in life, who have been given the widest acquaintance with the popular standards, can often be the gloomiest. The effects of their education can either make them properly enlightened, or properly horrid. Mind you, I do not scoff at education, for education helps protect us from being manipulated by those who claim to be superior, but in fact are deceivers and swindlers. But when someone is naïve about life, everything has a cheery aspect. For when you are inexperienced, everything feels like a novelty, and life appears more beautiful. Well, I was never given a full education, and therefore I never learned to hate the history of the world. And since this is the first time that I have left Britain, I haven't had time to develop prejudices. You see? Something must be said of innocence."

He nodded. "No doubt, there is always something lovely about the ignorance of a young mind. Of course, it can always lead you all into danger. But that is what experience is for. Unfortunately, when we elderly must watch younger folk see you all be exposed to the harsh side of the world, we feel sorry for you."

I glanced at him. "You do?"

"Yes. It is like watching someone as they experience the pain of innocence dying. When you are young, you do not see the shift so easily, but we do."

"You have a bird's eyes view? After all, you were once us."

He nodded. "Yes, we were. And sometimes we must tell ourselves that we are not as young as we once were. You don't fully know how to experience the true spectrum of your youth, and all that you could have done, until you get older."

"I have seen that, and that's what I refuse to do," I stated, with a firmness that led to his expression becoming more interested, keener.

"Refuse?"

"Yes. I have spent a great portion of my life knowing that I am not going to live forever, so I was adamant not to walk into my grave at a young age. And I had an uncle to help encourage me in that direction."

"You are very different than..."

"Then what?"

"Than the average respectable lady that I have ever met."

I had to smile at that. “I imagine that you have met a great many of us.”

“I have. Of course, one must not generalize, and I do not aim to. Generalization of manners has more to do with station of life than with nationality. When it comes to British ladies of the lower class, they are more like you. Of course, I do not intend to offend you. You are from an elite circle—”

“Not as elite as you might imagine. I am raised to be a lady, of course, but I never had a governess and was not left to be a woman of information.”

“Ah. I see. Well, I like you the better for it. I like a woman of a good open temper.”

“And I have learned that, even if I have not mastered learning different languages, covering screens, and being accomplished.”

He chuckled. “A good disposition can get you further in life than you might expect. After all, it has gotten you this far, hasn’t it?”

As he turned me, I looked up into his face, the face that felt as if it had been thinned out from the wind blowing it so very long.

“Perhaps it has. After all, it is part of the reason that I am here.”

“What are the other reasons?”

When we separated from each other, since the dance had instructed us to be such, I was given the time to think about what I should say. After all, it was not wise to give myself away or expose my private matters to the master of a ship.

But what important secrets might I have? He was a captain, so surely my affections ought not to be of any importance to him.

When I returned to him, I did not see the harm in being the same open lady that he had admired within me.

“There are several,” I furthered, “but among them, there were some people that I needed to get away from. As well as they needed to be free of me.”

“Am I allowed to know why? Also, I hope that I am, because it would be very horrifying of you to tease me with such a confession, and then do not tell me the whole story?"

I smiled.

"You like gossip."

"I like knowing everything. But gossip implies that I might spread anything that I hear. Although that is not so. I like to know people, but not as a means to ruin them."

"You're implying that I can trust you."

"You can."

"And how do I know that you would not say anything?"

He looked more intently at me, his blue eyes even more direct, as if he was willing me to have faith.

"Trust me."

I rolled my lip.

"Oh, very well. I wanted to leave Britain for four reasons: first, I wanted to go to the world. I wanted to know it, both the good and the bad. Perhaps, I might have done it to show that I was not afraid, and that comes to the second reason. I wanted to prove myself. I wanted the world to see that I could shift for myself, and that I could survive anything. That I was my own woman, as it were. Does that make sense?"

"Of course, it does. My mother was similar. When my father died, when I was young, she did not remarry but looked after me herself."

"Your mother sounds like a lovely woman."

"The loveliest."

"I am certain that she was. I am happy that you understand me. And the third reason is that I wanted to become acquainted with another side of my new family. My cousin, Mr. Philips, is married to Enara, and her family is from Australia. Well, if she came to England to meet us, then some of us had better return the compliment. And since I knew the right thing to do was to leave England, I could make my exit from my homeland also to be an act of familial honor. I was not merely running from something, but I could also run toward something better."

"And what were you running from?" he asked, but there was no worry in his voice. I appreciated that, for it showed that he did not suspect me of any evil, as *honorable* men are often willing to regard spirited young ladies as being such.

"From two men."

"Two men?"

"Yes."

"What did these men do that encouraged you to travel to the other side of the world?"

"They made the grave misfortune to have fallen in love with me."

"And that scared you? You do not strike me as the sort to flee across an ocean over that sensation called Love."

"It's because I am not. If one loved me, and I loved him in return, then that would hardly be a threat to my happiness. If they loved me and I did not love them in return, that would not frighten me either. I would be flattered by it and enjoy that someone thought that I was worthy of being loved. I don't fear romantics just because I do not return their affections."

"Then what was the problem? Did their love grow vicious?"

"Vicious?"

"Sometimes, when we love, we do it so passionately, that we can hurt the one that we love."

"They never hurt me. Well—not physically, but they have hurt my chances of happiness. I fell in love with one of them, he could not afford to marry me, and he left me. I did the wise thing of moving past that prospect and accidentally fell in love with another man. He could not afford to marry me, and he left me."

"Oh, you are looking for a change. A chance to recover?"

"Partly, but I am saving their lives. Captain Archer, have you ever fallen in love so much that it made you forget yourself? That it also drove you to distraction, made you jealous of anyone else who takes your love away from you, even if it is just them talking with her. That love drove you to a bit of madness?"

"Yes. That was what it meant to be so passionately in love that it affects every aspect of yourself. It takes over you so completely, and you wonder how you can survive without that person in your life."

"Yes."

"The terrible time of being in your teens and early twenties. Passions burn hot during that time. Like a blaze that can cause a forest fire. When you age, passion becomes more like a smoldering fire. It warms you, but it does not break you. But I do remember that sort of love that you speak of."

"What was her name?"

"Names. I was nineteen, and I met two of them in one year."

I sighed, so very warmed at knowing that I danced with a kindred spirit. My explanation would not be scandalous to him, because he knew what I felt. While also understanding that falling in love twice in one year is not something that ought to be wholly in the province of men's hearts but had a right to also belong to us ladies.

"The first one's name was Georgette, and the other one's name was Cressida."

"Cressida?" I repeated, amazed, "Now that is a name for the ages."

"Yes, it is."

"And were you her Troilus? Or Troilus to them both?"

"To an extent. Unlike Troilus, I did live."

"And you never married them?"

"I was penniless and had no money to marry and have a family. By the time that I gained some income, they could not wait any longer, and they had married."

"I'm sorry. I know that must have hurt you terribly."

"It did. However, I did not blame them. I took too long. And despite knowing them in the same year, I did love them both."

"As I love both men. If I were to pine over the first one, then the world would call me foolish for dwelling on the past. When I moved on, the world would have it that I am fickle."

"The world will always declare one situation to be too much, and the other half of the world will say it is too little. It will never fully make up its mind of what it ought to do. But what happened that made you truly wish to leave?"

I pondered this. "It was because both men returned to my life at the same time. And I did not have the strength to choose one's attentions over the other. Nor could I turn them away, even when I was a very unsuitable match for them. In truth, I ran because I was weak, but I knew that I was. And I was not going to have them suffer for it."

"Whenever someone admits that they are not prepared to be in someone's life, it is not weakness. It takes great strength to admit that."

"Thank you," I said, relieved. Feeling the comfort of speaking and listening, of understanding and being understood. "You know me."

"If the men move on, will you hate them?"

"Naturally, the agonies of seeing a person you love with a new fiancée or wife is always quite disconcerting. But would I be upset? No, I don't think I will. I would feel Hell in my veins, but I would not let it burn anyone else other than myself."

"What are these men like?"

"They are very similar to you, actually."

"Ah!" He laughed.

His reaction led to me being entirely aggravated at his pride.

"Stop guffawing at me, sir," I said, "and do not become filled with false pride."

"I won't, I won't, I won't," he assured me, "but it is flattering."

"I want to assure you that I don't take interest in you because you remind me of someone else. I just prefer to talk with men and ladies of a certain disposition."

"If I were a young man, you would have fallen in love with me," Archer declared, "admit it."

"What sort of question is that?" I scoffed, my cheeks burning.

"You didn't answer it."

"Because the answer is simple."

"Simple?"

"Yes. Because I have no way of knowing. I can't say that I would have fallen in love with you, when I didn't know the sort of man you were when you were younger, but I also would have a difficulty feeling for any other man than the two men that I am already in love with. But I could have considered you. I do not know. And don't get inebriated off your own greatness, captain! You will get a swelled head."

"Very well. For you, Miss Bennet, I will be a gentleman."

"How delightful. Now, you can tell me about Georgette and Cressida. I have no scruples on a man telling me about other women he was in love with when we were dancing."

"Other ladies would hate me for doing so."

"I am not those ladies, as you very well know. I am Kitty Bennet, of Longbourn, England. And there will never be another."

He smiled and his blue eyes and figure were complemented by the sky as the sun behind him was beginning to set. And that was when I realized something else.

"You would have liked me?" I deduced. "If you were younger."

Archer turned me, raising an eyebrow.

"Now who is asking the vulgar question?"

"One vulgar question might be allowed to be asked if it followed after another one. I have no way of knowing if I would have ever preferred you, when you were young, because I did not know you then. But you see me now, and if I did meet you, before Georgette and Cressida, would you have preferred me?"

"You want the truth."

"I am prepared."

"No, I would not have."

Did I have no pride? Because I honestly did not feel any embarrassment over knowing that he did not find me beautiful in the slightest.

"There," I said, not phased in any manner. "Was that so difficult?"

When seeing that I was unaffected, that I took no offense at all, his shoulders relaxed, and the tension released between us even more.

"No, it was not. Have I hurt you?"

"You told me the truth. I am not afraid of it and understand it. After all, most of us are not meant for everyone. Now that you know that I am courageous in that way, you can tell me all about your two great loves, and know that I truly can hear them, with intrigue and not wounded pride."

"Miss Bennet?"

"Yes?"

"You are the best dance partner that I have ever had."

"I will wear that compliment proudly."

"You should."

~

During our second dance together, Archer told me about his two great loves.

While doing so, Georgiana was dancing with Mr. Blake, who had asked her. Naturally Enara and Arthur refused to dance with anyone else other than themselves.

My third dance partner was Miguel Hernandez, then Jacques Lefevre was the fourth—his wife seemed completely unaffected that he danced with every woman other than herself... then again, they seemed to have an arrangement where she danced with every man other than him—and before my fifth, I approached White Wolf.

"Why do you stand there?" I asked him, for he had remained

there the entire time, spoke little, and was more like a sentinel than an attendee.

"I thought the answer to that question would be simple," White Wolf commented.

"I have an untrained eye on these matters. You must help me."

"It is because no woman here would think to stand up with me."

My smile faded. Once more, I had not thought of the habits of the outside world that existed beyond my own sphere of existence. Finlay had chided me for that, and I was upset. I had a right to be, but now I understood his frustration.

"I didn't know," I responded, quite humiliated.

"It's not your fault. We are from different worlds."

"But then..."

"Yes?"

"Well, you never wholly can know unless you ask a woman."

"What woman would wish of me to ask her?"

"Me. If you will ask me."

White Wolf's expression shifted from strong and silent defensiveness, to emotional. But of course, he did it in a quiet sort of manner.

"You would dance with me?" he asked.

"Yes, I would. But you must ask me."

With his posture more erect, he faced me and offered me his hand.

"Miss Bennet, would you do me the honor of dancing this set with me?"

"I accept, good sir."

Taking his hand, we went to the dance floor and joined the others.

"You dance well." I said to him.

"Thank you. I... I spent a great deal of time practicing on my own."

"That is a difficult way to learn, so well done." As we moved along the set, I had a thought, and I knew that he would not be angry at me for asking. "When you feel unwanted, as if you cannot even ask a woman to dance, because you will not even get an answer, how does that make you feel?"

"Invisible."

"Yes, I imagined so. It hurts when you feel that, I know."

"You do?"

"White Wolf, I'm going to tell you a timeless truth."

"What?"

"Everyone feels invisible from time to time, and it always hurts. And anyone who tells you different is lying. I know how it feels. Loneliest state of being in the world."

"Yes. It is. And it never stops hurting."

"No, it does not."

We continued to dance on, with him telling me about his tribe and the battles that he survived from his time fighting other tribal factions.

It was the last thing that a man should talk about when dancing with a lady.

So naturally, I loved it.

What sort of imp am I?

"I must say," Jacques Lefevre said as we finished the final set of the dance—where Mrs. Lefevre was finished dancing with Manuel Hernandez, "you English ladies in the set are actually respectable enough for me to say that you are almost as good as our French ones."

"Almost?" I said, smiling as we clapped for Merriweather and Gloriana's playing.

"Oh, forgive me, but despite that I found you and Mademoiselles Darcy and Watson to be agreeable enough to look past you being our enemy, nothing will ever surpass our French ladies."

"Well, I can never deny a man who has a proper element of patriotism," I said, "so I will accept being inferior, out of respect for national pride on your part."

"That's the spirit, belle rosa."

While I spoke with Mr. Lefevre, I saw Georgiana and Mr. Blake talking with each other, a little distance away from the rest of our company. Looking over Mr. Lefevre's shoulder, I noticed that they were further along the deck, speaking near the railing, with the sun setting behind them. As they stood there, with the sun's reflection against the water, the reds, oranges, and yellows, augmented the horizon, and framed the two of them in its orb. Like me, Georgiana had removed her coat and bonnet throughout the dance, and like me, she was wearing one of her best long-sleeved ballgowns, the white one that possessed many volumes and augmented her figure. The yellowish tints and shades that fell on them both gave them a fairytale appearance.

I wonder if they were talking of Emma Watson because they were speaking so very animatedly. However, I could not remain inattentive to my present company while watching them both and returned to speaking to Mr. Lefevre.

"And next time there is a ball on a ship," I suggested to him, "you will dance with your wife."

"Oh, there is no need for that. My wife and I have an arrangement."

I squinted, curious.

"Arrangement?"

"Yes, we do," Mrs. Lefevre said, approaching us. "We thought it the best thing for our marriage to always dance with other people at balls."

Now this was an interesting arrangement that I never would have thought made any sense, but different couples guaranteed different marriage arrangements.

"And why is that, pray?" I asked them, not censorious, but eagerly interested. "I judge no one, but it appears that you both look happy, so I wonder about the correlation between domestic felicity and dancing with other people at a ball and not one's spouse."

"We have decided to achieve the wonderful balance of spending time together, versus needing to sometimes spend time apart," Mrs. Lefevre said. "And just because one is married does not mean that they do not often need their own lives."

"We have decided to embark on the ultimate form of a happy union," Mr. Lefevre added, "and achieve the delicate balance of being united in marriage but also maintaining our individuality."

"Basically, what we speak of," Mrs. Lefevre elaborated, "is that the best source to wedded life is for you both to be united, but also to have another part of your life that belongs to you and you alone. Part of our arrangement is that we shall always dance with other people. This way, we can be romantic with others, while still being loyal to ourselves."

"And this arrangement works?" I asked.

"Very much so. You British could learn a thing or two from us."

"I knew that you would say such a thing eventually!" I remarked, boldly. "I admire your tenacity, and you might be right, but forgive me if I make up my own mind on such matters."

"Wait till you get married," Mrs. Lefevre commented, "and you will find yourself thanking us Lefevres, in your prayers."

"Blasphemy, you two," I cooed, still smiling, "blasphemy."

I didn't argue with them, despite that I had no regrets on where I was from and would still choose it over anything. I just thought it was best not to argue, because sometimes the best way to make friends is to let them see that you respect their habits, so long as you don't forsake where you came from. I don't prefer to be at odds with anyone, so sometimes, I don't think my pride is worth the argument, when it leads to nothing.

Pick and choose one's battles wisely and carefully, is what I am beginning to determine. Or else, one would be fighting all the time, for petty reasons. In that regard, my pride was still intact.

Besides, after what I learned of how Henry V really treated France when he was invading, will always make me pardon them. Particularly after how he was during the Battle of Rouen, where Henry V was so horrible, it was pretty much unforgivable. Divine Right of Kings—my foot!

"Miss Bennet," Miguel said, bowing to me, "might I say that you danced remarkably well this evening?"

"Thank you, Mr. Hernandez," I replied, "and one cannot dance so well without a partner who is equally as adept at the activity."

"Oh," he said, sensuously, "so, you are in a right way to be charmed?"

"You are being impertinent." Then I realized what I said made little sense. "But what is a ball, but another pursuit of conquests, I suppose."

"Wisely put," he commented, and he was joined by his brother, Manuel, who bumped shoulders with him.

"Forgive my brother," Manuel said, "this is his way of saying that he prefers your company."

Miguel smiled and was about to say something else, when Georgiana came rushing up to me, and grabbed my arm.

"Kitty, I am quite fatigued," she stressed, "come, let us retire."

"Oh," I blurted out, surprised because she was more so pulling me along as opposed to letting me walk of my own accord.

This rash and insistent action caught my attention, but I didn't argue or press the matter. For there was something in her eye that displayed a panic, a subtle dread. Something had happened to make her resort to dragging me down below deck.

"After all, I am quite tired myself," I said, allowing her to lead us to our room. Turning to everyone, I laughed nervously and said farewell as we went down below.

Once we got to our room, we went inside, and I turned to her directly.

"Georgie?"

I was correct. She was rattled by something.

"I am sorry."

"Sorry?" I repeated. "For what? Last time that I checked, I didn't tell you anything that would incriminate me on any level."

"It's not that. I just realized what it must have looked like to have dragged you down here, in so rash a manner."

"Did something happen?"

Georgiana's eyes became even more filled with astonishment and alarm.

"I am right, aren't I?"

"I can hardly believe it," she gasped.

"I want to understand," I said, grabbing her hands, "but you are not helping me on. Please, steady yourself and tell me what happened?"

"I..."

Visibly shaken, Georgiana moved away from me, went to her bed, and sat down on it.

I didn't know what to do. So much was I at a loss because it was difficult to understand if one wanted comforting, or if they wanted to sit there, alone.

Quietly, I went to my bed, sat down on it, and faced opposite her.

"Dearest," I began, "you are frightening me."

"I don't understand," she uttered.

"Whatever it is, I will help you," I said, "if you will confide in me."

"Kitty..."

"Does it have something to do with Mr. Blake and Emma Watson?"

"Yes."

"Well then it—" I cut off when I looked at Georgiana's face. I made a quick deduction.

No, it could not be.

But I knew that look. I had seen it before.

“Mr. Blake does not love Emma, does he?” I declared. “Georgie?”

“No, he does not love her. He loves me.”

Even though I suspected it, I was still shocked to hear it out loud.

“All this time,” Georgiana said, “Mr. Blake has been in love with me.”

Oh dear.

Chapter Thirteen

ILL MET BY MOONLIGHT

In the pleasure district in London, where all polite society does not speak of, but is as frequently visited by the persistent man who can afford such company, Colonel Fitzwilliam was riding his horse along the street.

While he was unashamed to admit that he had visited houses of such repute before, in the heated hours of night, when his passions got the better of him, that was not what he sought after.

Rather, his errand was of the filial kind. While he was in London, resting at the military headquarters, a messenger had come, giving a grievous report that his brother, Frederick, was passed out, at The Prancing Prince House, quite in the cups.

Feeling the familiar hole that one experiences when they are separate from the woman that they love, as well as from being exhausted from the day's work, Colonel Fitzwilliam was already in a sullen mood. Therefore, when one of his soldiers had come from the Prancing Prince, telling him that he saw his brother inebriated at the house and making a spectacle of himself, the Colonel was even more aggravated.

Leaving the security and comfort from the solitude in his

room, he had his horse called and rode through the London streets, till he reached the front doors of the Prancing Prince.

Soon after he entered, he inquired after his brother, and the head matriarch of the house met him eagerly.

"Colonel Fitzwilliam?" she declared, moving about with such importance, "thank goodness that you are here. Your brother is even more drunk than we have ever seen him."

"I'm sorry that he is like this, Madame Rollins," Colonel Fitzwilliam said.

"My girls are accustomed to his moods," she said, leading him past all the other gentlemen and officers who were making merry with the other ladies who were entertaining them, for the sake of bringing in more clients. Mrs. Rollins escorted Colonel Fitzwilliam up the stairs. "But this time, it's worse."

"Worse?"

"You know he often calls my girls by another lady's name."

"Yes, I know," Colonel Fitzwilliam replied, sighing. This was not the first time that he had to come and collect his brother from making a mockery of himself at this house, nor would it be the last, sadly. And the situation was almost always the same. In a drunken stupor, Frederick would pay all manner of money for pleasant company, where he would use the woman he paid as a substitute for Rosalie, the woman he once loved.

"But this time," Madame Rollins said, "it's nastier. He started screaming at one of my girls, angry that she didn't look like Rosalie. He called her an imposter and then he passed out in the room."

"I'm sorry, Madame."

"Whoever that woman is, he needs to marry her," Madame Rollins persisted. "Or he will always be a drunk."

"That's the problem. He cannot marry her."

"He can't?"

"No. She's a servant."

Madame Rollins sighed, understanding.

"You rich and fancy folk," she commented. "You always make life so very complicated for yourselves, if you ask me. You are all so determined to make yourselves miserable."

Colonel Fitzwilliam gave her a look.

"I meant no offense, sir," Madame Rollins responded, hastily.

"No, you misinterpret my look," Colonel Fitzwilliam assured her. "I just—well, it is a bitter thing to admit that there is some veracity to your declaration."

"Thank you, sir."

They reached the door and Madame Rollins opened it as Colonel Fitzwilliam breathed in heavily, preparing himself.

When they entered, there was a handsome fancy lady standing against the wall, with her face wearing too much rouge, a small star drawn on her cheek to hide a blemish, and she was wrapped in a shawl.

"Madame," Colonel Fitzwilliam said, bowing to her. "I've come to retrieve my brother."

"Good," the young woman replied, "his rantings made him tired, and he's lying there."

Moving to where she pointed, Colonel Fitzwilliam moved around the bed and found his older brother, Frederick Fitzwilliam, lying on the floor, sleeping loudly.

At first, Colonel Fitzwilliam stood there and did nothing. He merely looked down at his brother with disgust and disappointment.

He could forgive a few drunken episodes, but this had become such a habit on Frederick's part, that now the Colonel had lost all patience.

Turning to the young woman, he looked on her kindly.

"He did not do any harm to you, did he?"

"No," she answered, trying to make herself look more presentable in the Colonel's presence. "He shouted a great deal but did not lay a hand upon me."

"Did he pay you anything for any services that he came for?"

"No, not yet."

Colonel Fitzwilliam grabbed his brother's purse, removed two pounds, and handed it to Madame Rollins and gave five shillings to the woman.

"For the inconvenience," he said, "and if you would be so kind as to remain silent on this matter."

"You know my establishment, sir," Madame Rollins confirmed. "Discretion is our motto of the day and the evening."

"Thank you for your kindness and your service. You don't have to remain here for this. I will have him out of the room in a quarter of an hour."

"Very good, sir."

Both women left them alone.

He removed his cloak, picked up a wastebin, carried it over to his brother and prepared for any sort of purging that might occur.

Walking up to his brother, he sat down on the floor, opposite him.

"Frederick!" he cried. "It's time to wake up, brother."

Colonel Fitzwilliam raised his brother up, rested Frederick's back against the wall, and patting his cheek to wake him up.

"Fred...wake up."

Tapping his brother's cheek harder, slowly, Frederick opened his eyes. His stomach began to convulse, and Colonel Fitzwilliam anticipated this as he placed the wastebin in front of Frederick's face as his brother lurched forward and hurled up the food in his stomach.

When he was done, Colonel Fitzwilliam covered the bin, moved it away from them, and began to wipe down his brother's mouth.

"Frederick," Colonel Fitzwilliam said, holding his brother's face, "you must keep your eyes open. I can't have you fall asleep again."

Frederick made a sound as Colonel Fitzwilliam poured some water from a pitcher and forced his brother to drink it.

"We must get you home. I'll return you to your house and you can sleep on your floor to your heart's delight."

"Impostor," Frederick spat.

"What?"

"You did not see her. She was an imposter. She looked nothing like Rosalie."

Colonel Fitzwilliam sighed. "It's not her fault that you tried to put Rosalie's image in her place. It was not fair to her, or to yourself. You must cease doing that."

"I will have Rosalie, or I will have nothing."

Colonel Fitzwilliam didn't bother to respond, for he knew that there was no point.

"Well, if you will have nothing, then there is no more reason for you to be here. Now is there? Come, you must help me."

Gathering his brother's items, and placing Frederick's arm over his shoulder, Colonel Fitzwilliam hoisted his brother up and helped him as Frederick half-walked, half-limped down the steps.

Madame Rollins had Frederick's carriage drawn, and Colonel Fitzwilliam just managed to get Frederick out of the establishment. Just as they had come down the last step, Colonel Fitzwilliam froze.

For just as he was exiting, he came face to face with Lieutenant Finlay, who had been standing in front of the Prancing Prince.

Both men looked on each other with alarm.

With them both, there was a slight humiliation of seeing them in such a situation.

Especially on the Colonel's side, because with his brother being so inebriated, they must have presented a vulgar picture.

No doubt that Finlay must feel undoubtedly superior, in that moment. His brother may have been rich, but Finlay looked more presentable in this situation.

As for Finlay, he could see that the Colonel was merely tending to a wayward gentleman, and that he had come to this establishment for release.

But they had to speak.

There was nothing for it.

"Colonel Fitzwilliam," Finlay said, standing at attention, despite that he was not in the Colonel's regiment.

"Lieutenant Finlay," Colonel Fitzwilliam said. "We seem to be ill met by moonlight, don't we?"

"I fear that we do. I know what image that I must present."

"And I feel the same."

Finlay looked at Frederick. "A friend who was making too much merry?"

"A brother who was making too much merry."

"Oh."

Finlay looked behind him and saw the carriage.

"Can I be of assistance?" Finlay asked.

"Thank you."

Finlay helped the Colonel get his brother into the carriage. After he closed the door, the Colonel ordered his horse to be brought around, so that he could escort his brother back to his townhouse.

Rather than make a hasty retreat, Finlay remained near the Colonel.

"Is there something that you wished to ask me?" Fitzwilliam asked him.

"Yes...have you heard any word from Miss Bennet?"

"*Our* Kitty, you mean."

Finlay smiled sadly.

"Thank you for believing that I have as much a right to her heart as you do."

"You are her first love, and I am her second. We both belong to her, and I am not overpowered by that reality."

"I was, for a time. I was undergoing my selfish phase."

"I am older than you. I have had more time to overcome that side of myself. And no, I have no word from her. But so has none of the family. They could not send a letter when at France, because they feared how they would be received there. They will not send a letter to us until they reach Portugal or Spain. But, unless Kitty decides to breach protocol, as we have wickedly pushed her into that sort of manner before, we cannot receive word from her ourselves."

"Is it evil of me that I wish she does write me?"

"Yes. I feel the same."

"I came here to meet friends. In fact, these establishments are losing their appeal to me."

"And me as well. Finlay?"

"Yes?"

"What if Kitty does return and she is married to a wealthy man?"

This was a thought that raced across Finlay's mind, from time to time, but he always settled on the same conclusion. Perhaps he did it for his own peace of mind rather than out of being objective.

"She won't," Finlay determined.

Colonel Fitzwilliam gave him a side glance.

"You don't think so?"

"I could be wrong, but Kitty fell in love with both of us, despite herself. I don't think she wants to fall in love anymore, in another direction. She does not seem like the sort who can fall in love for a third time so soon."

"You are telling yourself that to make it easier on your own heart, aren't you?"

"I might be. But I hope that I am correct."

Colonel Fitzwilliam's horse came. He mounted it and looked down at Finlay.

"We must try to move on," Fitzwilliam said.

"But we won't," Finlay declared, knowing the Colonel's heart as much as he knew his own.

"No," Colonel Fitzwilliam said, "we probably won't. I do so hate being confused."

"Me as well."

"Farewell."

"Farewell."

Colonel Fitzwilliam rode off, escorting his brother home, while Finlay stood outside of the House, still thinking away of the love that would be across an ocean.

~

When reaching his brother's townhouse, the servants assisted in taking Frederick Fitzwilliam upstairs and washing him up.

While sitting downstairs, Colonel Fitzwilliam prepared to leave, but the housekeeper, Mrs. Doran, was adamant on keeping him to stay.

"Colonel, please," Mrs. Doran said, "of course, Master Frederick naturally is a little spirited, and we have come to understand that."

"Thank you for being euphemistic, Mrs. Doran," Colonel Fitzwilliam said, "but what you call spirited, I call a refusal to finally grow up and feel one's age. Being inebriated is all well and good when one is at university or when a loved one has passed on, but he takes to the drink too keenly and too often."

Colonel Fitzwilliam realized that he was speaking too much on the matter.

"Forgive me. I am not in the best of moods."

"Nonsense, Colonel. I can never begrudge brothers from

knowing what their siblings are about. If anyone can properly label them, it ought to be each other. But are you really going?"

"I must," the Colonel said, putting his hat back on.

"But at so late an hour? The servants can quickly make up your guestroom, and you can have a bath and receive your brother when he becomes more aware of himself. He always is so after he bathes."

Taking one look at her, Colonel Fitzwilliam sighed. He knew what she was about, for Mrs. Doran was wholly aware that Frederick would be easier to handle with his brother around. After suffering the effects of being too far in the cups, Frederick Fitzwilliam was always a little difficult to manage. Therefore, with the way that she looked at him, Colonel Fitzwilliam relented, giving way to all the powers of chivalry that his spirit contained.

"Very well, but Mrs. Doran, please make sure that one of the servants wakes me at sunrise. I need to return to St. John's headquarters by then. I must be awake before all my soldiers."

When hearing that Colonel Fitzwilliam would stay, Mrs. Doran's shoulder relaxed, and her anxiety lessened.

"Very good, sir. Do you need any soup and bread prepared?"

"As much as it would pain me to wake the cook," Colonel Fitzwilliam said, removing his cloak, hat, gloves and handing everything to the doorman, "if it would not be too much trouble."

"It shall be done. And what of the master?"

"The usual proscription: some clean water, a little bit of bread to sop up the good wine that's filled him and then after the water, bring some green tea in."

"Very good, sir."

The Colonel remained in the billiards room, playing a game with himself when he was informed that his room was prepared.

"Doran," Colonel Fitzwilliam said, "my brother and I are the same size. If you could procure some of his nightclothes, he will not argue on seeing me in them."

Doran chuckled.

"Never fear, Colonel, I already had that thought. Your night-clothes, or should I say, 'your brother's', are already in your room."

"Mrs. Doran, you are invaluable."

Colonel Fitzwilliam went upstairs to the room that he usually inhabited whenever he visited his brother.

~

Wearied, the Colonel enjoyed the comfort of seeing his old room and fell into the comforts of all the memories that were there. After the servants had finished stoking the fire, he was left alone to disrobe.

Removing his redcoat and placing it in the closet, he then removed his necktie and undid the button at the top of his shirt. As he unbuttoned his waistcoat, he looked at the blaze in the fireplace. Walking up to it, he leaned over it and let the heat wash over him.

Despite his best inclination, his mind could not help but wander over to all the women that he loved in his life, and how he could never lay with them as man and wife. As woman and husband.

From his first great love, then to others such as Fiona Prescott, Phyllis Hayter, Claire Godwin...and Kitty.

All of them rested deeply in his mind and how he had to release them from his company, one by one.

One by one.

Each of their images dashed against the logs, his imagination turning the firelight into their figures. And no wonder because each of them had the same fire in their eyes.

"That is why you cannot forget them," Colonel Fitzwilliam said to himself, seeing their beauty in the light, "and you never will."

The painful agony of being a man, secretly driven by sensibility, already affected him greatly. However, as time wore on and he aged, he thought that experiencing such losses would not affect him so. After all, such passions usually occurred when one was young and felt everything so keenly.

He laughed, sardonically, at his own folly. He was not the sort to release his affections from his heart. And his memory.

But Kitty Bennet!

This had been the most violent of his adoration. Despite the first three women being from when he was younger, and his romantic inclinations were more tense, Kitty rested stronger in his heart.

Her image affected him, still.

It did not help that their attachment had grown to a level of physical stimuli. With Fiona and Phyllis, he never touched them further than their hands holding when they danced.

With Claire, he had kissed her a couple of times, but they both did it so very ill that it killed the very affection that they possessed. As such, the Colonel and Claire only had a dream between them, but never could it be a reality, because longing looks at each other do not hold much validity when there is no physical connection.

But with Kitty, the physical blended with the emotional to such an intense level, that it reached the full apex of reality and dreams in his eyes and mind.

Their skin had melted into each other, and he knew that he had found a lady who when they laid together, their bodies and spirit would satisfy each other, and he could pursue the precise same affection that Beatrice and Benedick shared in Shakespeare's great work, while also sharing the passions that a man can usually only experience with a fancy lady or courtesan.

It was so unfair that only those sorts of women knew how to please the thirst of a man's more wanton side, but the wives that his kind were expected to procure were so obsessed with purity that a true bond could never be reached.

Until Kitty came into his life. She was not obsessed with purity to the point where it got in the way of a man and a woman achieving a true bond. She knew the sort of marriage that he would want. She was the perfect blend of goodness and wickedness. After all, love is a magical emotion. Wickedness is a part of it.

And so...he would always love her.

He was interrupted when Mrs. Doran knocked and entered.

"Ah, Doran, is the soup ready?" he asked.

Mrs. Doran grimaced, but not at him.

"It is, Colonel, however, the servants have placed Master Frederick in his room, after his bath. He's awake and he wants to speak with you."

Not surprising at all, the Colonel did not even take the time to button his waistcoat or put his jacket on. Rather, rolling up his shirtsleeves, he told Doran to keep his soup warm, that he would see to his brother, take a bath afterwards and then eat.

"Well," he whispered to himself, "best to get on with it. After all, what is the worst that could happen?"

When he went into his brother's room, Frederick was sitting in his favorite armchair, by the fire. He was in his robe, nightclothes, and had a blanket wrapped around him while some water and bread were on a tea-table next to him.

With there being only a lamplight on the other side of the room, Frederick Fitzwilliam's figure was illuminated by the flames, and Colonel Fitzwilliam felt as if it cast a demonic hue on him.

Contributing it all to his imagination, Colonel Fitzwilliam closed the door behind him and noticed that the bread was untouched.

"You should eat some bread," he advised.

"Ah," Frederick said, still a little intoxicated. While the wine and brandy were subsiding in his system, the aftereffects were still prevalent. "Willing to administer your proscriptions on my life?"

"Just say that you are happy to see me and be done with it."

Colonel Fitzwilliam sat down opposite him, tore the bread in half and handed it to Frederick. His brother took it and began to eat it in small bites.

"You know, very well, that I will never admit to that," Frederick said.

"No, you will not."

"Brother?"

"What?"

"If you'd like to gloat about coming to my rescue, you may."

Rather than be baited into an argument with a slightly drunken man, Colonel Fitzwilliam decided to shift the turn of the conversation.

"You got angry with the woman that you hired at the House," he noted. "You shouted at her for not being Rosalie."

A quick flash of regret and remorse filled Frederick's eyes as he bit into the last bit of his bread.

"Do you remember that?" The Colonel pursued.

"Yes," Frederick whispered. "I do."

"Oh, Fred..."

"Are you about to lecture me again?"

"Yes! Are you surprised?"

"Not in the slightest. In fact, if you did not, I would declare that you were not my brother, but rather were a strange entity who had killed him and taken over his body."

"Well, that was a strange theory."

"I'm drunk. What do you expect?"

"Very true. What should I have expected? Far be it from me to lay down your cruelty to that woman to you merely being too far in the cups, but I know you better. When you drink, you speak about things that are still haunting you."

"You do not need to be a philosopher to know that, surely."

"Frederick, what are you thinking?" Colonel Fitzwilliam blurted out. "Or have you relinquished any attempts at restraint? Your tiresome displays of pining over Rosalie have reached such a point where you are letting the whole world see it."

"Richard, are you so different?"

"No," Colonel Fitzwilliam said, shaking his head as he stood up, "do not place your behavior on me. Why do you do that?"

"Do what, pray?"

"Shift every situation into a way where you make yourself into being the victim."

"And force you to see a bit of yourself in me? What can I say, but that I cherish it. I tire of being lectured on what I am, when every aspect of myself is in a little bit of everyone?"

"This is where you label your actions down to the pursuit of truth, is it? Where you tell yourself that, since what you feel is real, it does not matter how you impose yourself on the world? You could have hurt that woman."

"Did I?"

"You were prevented."

"I would have prevented myself. You know that."

Richard said, "I know now, but what about tomorrow, or the day after that? I cannot predict what you will do anymore, in this tiresome display of your broken heart."

"Tomorrow evening, I will return and make my apologies," Frederick said, "unless I forget. Oh, the delights of forgetting."

"There is no delight, in times such as this."

"But there is. Nothing tears more on the soul than guilt, and you know me. I prefer to be light as a feather."

"Guilt also helps us not to repeat the same mistakes, and you love to sing the same song and dance often."

"I prefer the same melody."

"Then it's time that you learned a whole new one. If you are going to go to a House, then you had best act like a gentleman when you do so."

"Dear Richard, acting like a gentleman is the last thing that they want there." Frederick chuckled.

"Not true. Even those ladies prefer a man who respects them, so do not delude yourself."

"You are just as romantic as I am. Do not deny it."

"I have no wish to deny it. Love all you want. Remember past affections all that you want. But do not let it affect your day to day life. Rosalie was a good woman."

"And now you speak evil and act it," Frederick hissed.

"Do I? Pray tell me, how does that make sense?"

"Rosalie was not a good woman. She is a *great woman.*"

Colonel Fitzwilliam sighed, accepting that he ought to indulge his brother on this score.

"Yes, I suppose that she is," he agreed.

"And always will be." Frederick looked ahead at the fire. "A man never forgets his first time, now does he?"

Richard's eyes widened when hearing this. Was this the truth?

"She was?" he asked.

"Yes, she was."

Richard rubbed his eyes. Now it accounted for so much. Rosalie was the first woman that Frederick loved, as well as being the first woman that he was intimate with. She had his first time, and therefore, she also had his virtue in her hand.

"Why did you never tell me this before?" he asked Frederick.

"I don't know. Perhaps I thought it would be a delight to keep the secret to myself. Remember, brother, any other man would have boasted of becoming a man, in full, but not myself. In that, you can praise me, to balance all the times that you must find fault in me."

"I do not want to find fault in you, but at least I would like to have known that. In one moment, you want me to know you, and then you do not want me to know you."

"You know that I take delight in being a card of the wild," Frederick uttered.

"I would allow you to be so, if it did no harm."

"Perhaps a little harm is what this family needs."

Richard snorted. "Oh, so you are that sort? You must invent a little hardship for us all, to feel more like a man."

"A true man braves the evil sides of himself."

"A true man also overcomes them, and you do not. I am sorry for Rosalie, but at this point, you don't know yourself."

Frederick flashed him a look.

"Do I not?"

"No, you don't. At this point in your life, you would have turned your burning passion for Rosalie into a firelight that would have warmed you in cold nights, and in solitude, and helped you rally into a better way. However, that is not so now. You use her memory as an excuse to burn everyone around you. It has reached a point where I think you like the idea of clinging to the idea of her, because it gives you the excuse to be miserable. And misery gives you purpose."

Again, Frederick scoffed. "Ah, you think that I am in love with the notion of lost love, rather than loving her. That idea has danced across your mind, I see. Of me being in love with the idea of love, and not the true lady."

"Am I wrong? When is the last time that you saw her?"

Frederick did not answer. The silence made the Colonel more curious.

"Frederick, when is the last time that you even saw her?"

Frederick closed his eyes.

"Two months ago."

His brother was utterly surprised to hear this.

"Two months ago?" Colonel Fitzwilliam repeated, sitting back down.

"Yes," Frederick answered slowly, "I managed to contrive a meeting with her. Despite learning of a new development."

"What new development?"

"Nothing so small. Only that she is engaged to be married to another man."

Now it all was coming together. Frederick Fitzwilliam's extreme behavior could all be attributed to his recently seeing the woman that he loved now being attached to another. He felt sorry for his brother, however, it did not signify any fault on Rosalie's part.

"Frederick," Richard coaxed, "while I am sorry for your situation, it's been years. Rosalie had to move on."

"She hasn't though. She still loves me."

"I am certain that she does."

"No," Frederick said, leaning forward, "you are saying that to be kind to me and put me in a calmer state. I am saying it because she told me so herself. You are right. She marries him because she must. It is the only path for a woman to take sometimes." His eyes were on fire with insistence. "But she still loves me. She told me so."

"Did she?"

"Yes. And if we had the time, I could have pressed my advantage, making the man a cuckhold without even knowing so. She would have been willing."

"Frederick, don't lie to me."

"Am I lying?"

Colonel Fitzwilliam gave him a stern look.

"Ah," Frederick smiled, "is this where I admit to not being a gallant man? That I took advantage of her love for me, that I contrived any means to find time alone with her, that I fell into her, enjoying the pleasures of years past—or do I deny it all? Do I say no, that I overcame my passions and exercised prudence, that I gave way to a better habit? That I wished her well, and respected the unworthy sot who proposed to her?"

Frederick chuckled.

"No," he finalized, "I do not think I shall tell you, Richard, but leave you thinking better or worse of me."

"Because it amuses you?"

"Yes, it just might."

"And then you will tell me, years from now. As is your habit," Richard said.

"Yes. I think that I might do that."

"Frederick, enough!"

This was the desired effect. This was what Frederick wanted all along since his brother had come to his rescue. After all, in his eyes, his brother's superior habit was repulsive, because it always placed Richard as the hero. It made Frederick feel worse, and so, like the impish creature that he was, he would not be satisfied—no, he could not be—until he had reduced Richard down to his level.

"I cannot stop you from always doing as you do," Colonel Fitzwilliam stated, "but your behavior puts a great deal of strain on our parents. You must learn not to let your heart run away from your head."

"As you have done with Kitty?"

Despite that he knew that Frederick would bring up his last romance, Colonel Fitzwilliam still ground his teeth.

"Leave Kitty out of your lectures."

"Why, when she has everything to do with it? Especially since, when you look at me, you are looking into your future."

Richard finally felt his temper flare—in just the same manner that Frederick had wanted.

"Am I? Fred, do not slander me so."

"Slander you?" Frederick laughed. "Now that is a true insult toward me. I thank you for that bit of hurt."

"You hurt me first."

"By making you see the true reality. Miss Bennet and Rosalie are the same sort of woman. We both are drawn to the same qualities in the opposite sex. You cannot deny that I am right."

"Yes, you are. But it does not mean that I am the same sort of man. I refuse to let my agonies affect my daily life."

"Kitty is still unattached, and you still have the dream."

"What dream?"

"The dream that you both might marry. It is still possible. But wait until the dream no longer becomes a possibility, and then you will know what I feel."

"I will rally. I promised Kitty and myself that I would, and that is the end of it. I will move on when the time comes."

"Strong words for a strong man. But I am as strong as you and look at myself. With us strong men, we tell ourselves that nothing will break us, but our hearts are as fragile as any lady's heart is. You will learn that in time. And besides, stop acting like you are so much mightier than I am, though you be the better man. You have given way to liberties with Kitty. Do not think that those circumstances have not reached my ears, even though I did not witness them with my eyes."

"Anything that I have done was done in secret. If you refer to the one kiss that we shared in public, it was when she left England and no one of note was about to spy on us. What you have heard is the gossip of servants, who need to embellish news for the sake of telling a good story."

"Tell yourself what you wish," he continued, laughing bitterly, "but I am certain that when Lady Catherine heard of it, your Kitty had to own to it."

"She did not deserve..." Richard trailed off when he thought of Frederick's words. He might have been tired, but he was able to deduce something that Frederick accidentally revealed.

"How did you know that?" Richard asked.

"Know what?"

"That Lady Catherine had known about my feelings for Kitty, and that she had chastised her for it? How did you know that?"

"Our mother and father do occasionally write to me, you know? Considering that I am their eldest son and heir."

This was the last burden placed on the camel's back. Richard now began to let his anger rise, for he had caught his brother out in a lie. Usually, he was never able to catch him, but this time, fortune was entirely on his side.

"They might have," he stated, his eyes like ice, "if they had known about it. But since Lady Catherine owes Kitty, due to Kitty saving Anne's life, Lady Catherine never wrote anything to Matlock. The only reason that I am aware of it myself is because Kitty told me, and I wrote to Lady Catherine afterwards about it all. But our parents never learned this, just as I know that they never told our aunt anything about my affection for Kitty."

Richard's eyes flared as he bore down on his brother, who saw that he had taken a step too far.

"It was you," Richard hissed. "You wrote to Lady Catherine about my love for Kitty, so that she could cause trouble between us. Didn't you?"

Frederick did not respond.

"Didn't you!" Richard yelled.

"Shouting? That's not particularly gentlemanly of you, Richard."

At his wit's end, Richard slapped Frederick.

The sudden violent act was not the end of the disagreement, but the beginning. Richard grabbed his brother, raised him up and spun him around.

"Don't lie to me!" he spat. "You are the one who told Lady Catherine about Kitty and me."

"She ought to have known it."

"No, she should not have. It caused Kitty to feel even more dejected, and now she is traveling to the other side of the world, to overcome that sensation. That same sensation that has taken her from me. You helped cause this. You are a villain, Frederick."

"Perhaps I am. Or perhaps I am helping you."

Richard shoved his brother back into his seat, and Frederick did nothing to fight against him. After all, what could be said of Frederick, always, was that he knew when he ought to be punished. Although, this tendency of self-torture was not a balm for Richard's seeking of retribution. It only made him angrier.

"No more of that. I've heard your tedious excuses for your ill behavior all being attributed to me being the one of us to have an heir to Matlock. And I don't believe that you wrote to Lady Catherine on that incentive. No. It is more selfish, isn't it? Tell me, Fred."

Frederick didn't respond but sat there.

"Tell me!" Richard cried.

Despite that he always preferred to have an ace up his sleeve, the good wine did unhinge Frederick's tongue enough that he confessed the truth. Or part of it. When it came to truth, Frederick didn't always know if he was speaking it or not, sometimes. So much was his mind a combination of twisted knots and turns. For a man to know himself and not know himself seems illogical. Perhaps it is. But that does not make it any less of a truth.

"You know, surely," Frederick admitted, "that I could not stand to see you have something that I could not have."

The confession duly came.

When hearing it, Richard was satisfied, but not less happy. Rather, it only transformed his anger to a quiet resentment. He scarce could speak, though he felt so much.

"I hate you," Richard whispered.

When hearing that declaration, Frederick relented. Abandoning his ambiguous tone, his inconsistent behavior, and shifty meanings, he was humbled. Only then did he realize that he had taken a step too far.

"Richard," he said, his eyes filled with contrition, "I..."

"I hate you," Richard repeated, before he rushed out of the room, dashing past Mrs. Doran.

He went into his room and slammed the door, rattling the windows.

'I will never forgive him,' he said. 'Never again'.

The next day he left before Frederick woke—but Frederick knew. Frederick knew.

Chapter Fourteen

RIDDLES OF THE HEART

Oh spite! Oh hell!

Sitting on my bed in our cabin, I was still frozen at the spot. And so was Georgiana, with her back pressed against the door, as if she was warding off any sort of intruder, be the intruder physical or mental.

"You?" I barely spoke louder than a whisper. "Mr. Blake is in love with you?"

"Yes," Georgiana said, her face still horrorstricken.

"Oh, my lord!" I professed. "All this time that he was paying attention to Emma Watson, and..."

I stood up and began to pace back and forth.

"But then you are her friend," I noted. "And sometimes people find it easier to talk to a friend than the object of their affections."

"Yes," Georgiana said, "*now* I know that. Kitty, when they spoke together, he often would speak to her about me. He told me that when I confronted him on how he could profess any affection for me, while paying attention to Emma."

I stopped pacing when I realized that I had been unkind toward Georgiana by not acknowledging the sense Mr. Blake took in preferring her.

"Georgiana," I insisted, "do not think that my reaction is meanly inconsiderate of you. I can very well understand why Mr. Blake fell in love with you. In fact, despite Emma's manifold attractions, I find you to possess more virtues than her, and a more agreeable air and countenance. I just am surprised because I did not see any indications toward this."

"I did not either."

"If he was contriving to be a lover, Mr. Blake did a very poor business of it and of making his sentiments known," I commented. "He has done you both ill. Of course, maybe I am being too hard on him, for he might have been unaware of that."

"Perhaps he did not."

Once more, I was not touching on the more important matters. Yet, in discussions such as this, where people were so much star-crossed, it takes time to know what one is about. And since I was never very accomplished on perfect conversation, things often had to come on me gradually.

"And what of your heart? What did you do? What did you say?"

"Kitty, I was horrified, and I still am."

"Of course, I am to understand that you rejected his advances."

"Yes, I did."

"Did he take the rejection like a gentleman would?"

"He had no choice. We were in public."

"Yes. The ball."

"Also, I told him the truth of us thinking that he preferred Emma's company. I chastised him for proposing to me when it was Emma that he had always shown a preference for. It was an accident."

"It would do better that you did say that. By expressing that you never held any special regard for him, because you thought that he preferred your friend, was the easiest way to refuse him."

Georgie sighed. "But I have potentially exposed Emma."

"Forgive me, but I care more for you than I do for her."

It was coldhearted to say such, but it was true.

"I cannot help it," I explained.

"And I won't ask you to explain. We are friends. I am not upset with you. Especially since I am the one who is thrown into a friendship with a woman who does not favor my current friend, while she prefers a man who prefers me instead. This is an egregious sort of business."

"Oh!" I groaned. "Why must life be so complicated? Nothing ever goes smoothly where it ought to. The next thing that would occur would be if Captain Archer dies from heart failure. With our luck, that is just the sort of thing to happen! Oh Georgie! I am so sorry about this."

"Now I sound ungenerous!" Georgiana cried. "Now I cannot stand the sight of him. And he won't stand the sight of me. Tomorrow is going to be so awkward."

"True. When it comes to situations such as this, distance helps a person, but you both are thrown together on a ship where your circle of friends is limited. He was a fool to propose in this manner."

"Yes, he was. I know that he didn't intend to ruin anything, but he has."

Leaning forward, I took her hand.

"Georgie, do you want me to talk to him?"

"No," she replied, automatically, "you must not."

"Why not? When a man receives a rejection, and still must face the lady, there will always be discomfort. Sometimes, another person needs to enter and smooth the way. Or I can speak to Arthur about it, but I am sure that you do not want more people to know than those who already do."

"Yes. Of course, with Arthur, it might be a great deal better because he is a man."

"La! We women can speak as strongly and as adept as a man can. In fact, in circumstances like these, sometimes, we women can be a little more intimidating."

"You plan to scare Mr. Blake?"

"If I must. But I do not believe that it will come to that. It is just that I mean to utilize the plan that we had before. We made a plan when we set out, to inform everyone that your fortune was very little, contrary to reports. When I speak, I am not setting Mr. Blake's feelings for you on your fortune, but very rarely do tutors and clergymen not consider a woman's purse while they consider her hand. You have charms that any man should consider, and ought to. But if we were to tell Mr. Blake that your future was lost, or never what it was considered to be, then perhaps he would—what I mean is..."

Georgiana took my hands.

"I know what you are trying to say. You are trying to tell me that you think I am worthy of an excellent match, but that if Mr. Blake believed that I had no fortune, he would revoke his affections for me. And that part of his preference for me is that I am an heiress, whereas Emma Watson is not, and her aunt left her scarcely anything at all."

I winced, afraid that she would not understand that I had meant well, and to protect her.

"Yes," I answered, "Georgie, I don't mean it as any slight to your excellent person."

"No, you are right to worry about me. And, if this were the case, then it would make it easier on me. I would have preferred it if he chose me for my money. In that way, I could refuse him with no pain on my part, as well as inform Emma that he is not worth her consideration. But that is not so."

"How not so?"

"After Mr. Blake proposed to me, I told him that I felt it incumbent upon me to explain that he heard false reports of my inheritance. I told him that I had only been given two hundred pounds a year, and that was all."

"This did not deter him?"

"No. He said, that since he was to live in Australia, life would be decidedly easier for us here, and that his income could sustain us both."

"He was willing to marry you, despite your lack of wealth?"

"Yes."

I sighed, immediately feeling remorse for how cross I was with Mr. Blake. He proved his choice to be disinterested, at least. And his choosing Georgiana over Emma showed that he had exquisite taste.

"Then perhaps I may have wronged him," I said. "He loves you for the sake of loving a superior woman. Now I regret what I said."

"Kitty, regret none of it. In cases such as these, one ought to gratify and censure such a man as Mr. Blake."

"If you wish to talk more of this, I am very much willing. But there is the other matter."

"What other matter?"

"Georgie, what will you say to Emma about this?"

Georgiana's eyes widened.

"Oh, good god."

She had no notion of what to do.

And truly, what could Georgiana do? Tell Emma, and risk her friend feeling such a painful sensation of knowing that she was not the preferred lady?

That was the spell that caused all kinds of mischief.

Georgiana laid down on her bed, frustrated.

"Kitty, would it be so horrible for me to acknowledge that I do not intend to tell Emma at all?"

"That's what I would do."

Happy to have a supporter in this, she turned to me, her eyes wistful.

"It is?"

"Of course. Whatever Emma and I feel for each other, I know

that she is not the kind of woman who would let this sort of thing put a strain on your relationship. But I have been wrong about people before. Even if she were to rally, these entanglements are very difficult to forget. She might say nothing, but it can put an invisible break on such bonds. It makes a person feel inferior to their friends, and friendship depends on both sides being on equal footing. Also, just because Mr. Blake feels toward you now, his heart can always shift to the friend."

"You propose that after he feels for me, he could learn to feel for Emma."

"It is possible. For some, a bruised heart heals when it finds affection elsewhere."

"But would I want Emma to attach herself to a man who is using her as a means to recover from myself?"

"Perhaps not. However, everyone has the right to move on eventually. When I return to England, to find Finlay or Fitzwilliam married, I would not label them as fickle, but adaptive. If Mr. Blake were to swing away from you, and then swing towards Emma, that would be cruel. But if he were to take time to reflect, and then eventually fall in love with her after discovering that his heart was open to the prospect, then why not?"

"Or he could fall in love with someone else entirely."

"And that as well. And she would have to recover from that in her own way. Again, she and I may not be particular friends, but I can sympathize and not want to see her undergo unnecessary pain. There is no point in telling her this now when it does not help her in any sort of outcome. If he never falls in love with her, you will not be the means through which that occurs."

"Then it will be between us."

"Yes, it will," I assured her.

Georgiana kissed my cheek.

"Thank goodness that I have you for a friend," she said, to which I felt at ease, and I smiled genuinely. While Emma may have known Georgiana longer, Georgie and I were bound by secrets and experiences on both our parts that Emma could not touch.

I could not help but find joy in this.

"But are you certain?" I asked. "About me not talking to Mr. Blake. Maybe he does need someone to speak to about the matter."

"But what would you say?"

I thought for a second, and then I listed everything that I would suggest to help smooth the way between them. When I finished, Georgiana relaxed.

"That is what you would say to him?"

"Yes."

"Then I would be most appreciative if you did. Thank you."

"Well, if you think that I am a worthy friend, I had better earn that title, mustn't I?"

We both sighed, relieved. I was happier to see her in a better way. Depend upon it, I would do everything in my power to make sure that Georgiana did not experience any more unpleasant scenes from that direction.

She came with me on this journey, and it was only right that I protected her from any awkwardness. If I were to ever be a poor protector, it would not be now.

We prepared for bed, and as we laid down in the dark, I could not sleep.

Mr. Blake had proposed to Georgie?

She refused him, naturally.

He would marry her; despite being told that she had no substantial dowry.

Emma Watson favored the man who favored her friend.

We were on a ship where Enara and Arthur were meeting Enara's family, while undergoing all this.

And I was caught in the middle of this all.

I left my heart behind in England, and only for other hearts to be exposed on the open seas.

No matter where one goes, there will always be something to get in the way.

"Georgie?" I whispered in the dark. "Are you still awake?"

"Yes. After a ball like this, I have no choice but to be."

"Well, your situation has just made me realize something."

"What?"

I said, "One of the largest problems in the world is not just violence, oppression, prejudice and poverty, but something else."

"What?"

"One of the biggest problems is that people always have a habit of falling in love with people who don't love them. Or people falling in love with the wrong people."

Georgie gasped. "By Jove! I think you are right. Truly, there must be some kind of way out of here."

"Yes. It causes so much confusion; we can't get any relief."

"No, we cannot."

"But you and I, we've been through that, and this is not our fate."

"So let us stop talking falsely now. The hour is growing late."

"All along the watchtower of life."

"Yes, all along it, we keep our view. Too much of life feels like but a joke."

Chapter Fifteen

FATHERLY AFFECTION

Rushing back to Longbourn in the carriage, Mrs. Bennet's nerves were all afire, with her heart being so thunderstruck at Mary's misfortune. When she reached home, she called for the Hills, and Mrs. Hill immediately rushed forward to help her remove her pelisse and bonnet.

"How does Mrs. Atkins do, Madam?" Hill asked, urgently.

"She has taken to her bed, and it is best that she remains there. The sad girl should not have been walking about. I blame the Lucases for this all."

"There, there," Mr. Hill said, coaxingly, "surely we cannot blame Miss Lucas for this occurrence."

"Precisely," Mrs. Hill said, "these things are natural."

"Well, it does not matter, then!" Mrs. Bennet bellowed. "But what does matter is that my poor girl has lost her child, and she did not deserve it."

Mrs. Bennet turned to them both.

"And through all of this, what has Mr. Bennet been doing?"

The Hills looked in between each other.

"Sitting in his library, reading a book, I daresay?" Mrs. Bennet observed.

"We are sure," Mrs. Hill declared, "that he must be expressing his grief, in his own manner."

Mrs. Bennet, as could be expected, did not let this remark placate her. On the contrary, it only made her more determined and fortified her behavior. To sit there, while Mary had miscarried, and never gone to see her, was a horrid action on Mr. Bennet's part, and she would not let him ignore her, nor shoo her away in the manner that she was suffered to endure.

"Enough of that, I declare," Mrs. Bennet hissed, going to the library, and entering before knocking.

There, she found Mr. Bennet, sitting down, and reading a novel that he had read twice already.

Mr. Bennet looked up at her, coolly.

"Do you come to me because you are unwell?"

"Sick of the heart, yes."

"I can imagine so."

"But not sick of good judgment, which you lack in this circumstance."

Mrs. Bennet slammed the door behind her.

"Mr. Bennet, that is quite enough, sir!"

With his wife having raised her voice, this left Mr. Bennet no choice but to close his book and focus on her.

"I am glad to at least see that you showed some respect and lowered your book," Mrs. Bennet said, her tone no less ferocious. "Mr. Bennet, what is wrong with you?"

Mr. Bennet did not reply but only looked at her over his spectacles.

"No, truly," Mrs. Bennet continued, "I am not candid, but I will be as honest with you, as you always deem it correct to be. And I say this now, with great feeling. Our daughter is in Meryton, having recently lost her child, and you have not even visited her, to inquire after her. At a time like this, a person's parent is precisely what is needed during such an instant, to offer comfort."

"You are a mother who underwent the precise sort of thing. If anyone can offer solace to our grieving child, you are the sort who is up for the task."

Just as he was about to raise his book up, to continue reading, Mrs. Bennet's temper was fully flared. He was to return to his novel, abandoning all parental responsibilities and leaving it to herself.

A sudden burst of maternal altruism fueled her, and affection for their child rested in its proper place as Mrs. Bennet grabbed the book and threw it into the fire.

Mr. Bennet, very hard to rally to any sort of voluble behavior, stood still as he looked on her with a fury. However, his expression was no match for his wife's resolution.

"If you pick up another book in your deceased book's place," Mrs. Bennet declared, "then that book too shall meet an unfortunate end."

Mr. Bennet leaned back in his chair, folding his hands over his chest, and looking squarely at her.

"You have my attention, Mrs. Bennet, for however long I choose to give it."

"You will give me your attention," Mrs. Bennet overrode, "for however long I choose it to be given unto me. What are you doing?"

"What am I doing?" he repeated, raising an eyebrow.

"Yes, sir, what are you doing? You sit here, while your daughter just lost her first child. She is heartbroken and after seeing her, it would help if her father were to exert himself to leave his library and inquire after her."

"Her Uncle Philips is there and would do the duty admirably."

"Her uncle is not her father. He should not have to make up for your inattentiveness to your own child."

"When you miscarried, you rallied, and I did not sit at your bed and nurse you into a better way. You understood, like myself, that losing a child was a natural side effect to maternity. You rallied quickly, despite all your sensibilities. Does it not occur to you that Mary, with all her sense and education, would rally even faster? She does not need me in the same manner that you did not."

"First, Mary is not me. She is her own person, and secondly, you are wrong. When I miscarried, I did need you beside me. I cried often, I felt my spirits low, and I spent so many years lamenting that the child I lost might have been a son, and that I had poisoned him."

Mr. Bennet blinked.

"You did?"

"Yes. When alone, I often gave way to my despair and cried." Mrs. Bennet quieted down. "And I do it still, from time to time, when not in your presence."

Mr. Bennet leaned back in his chair, utterly speechless. For, in such circumstances, what could be done? What cynical words, what wit, could be a proper reply to such a naked truth?

"Often," Mrs. Bennet continued, her tone heavy and her words slow, "I wonder about that time. Of what I could have done to have lost my child. And of if it was a boy, and how I could have saved the family, and Longbourn, if I had been less active, had took my daily walk less, and had been more stationary."

"Am I to understand...is that why you no longer took daily walks?"

"Yes. I feared losing a child again. And I was tired of being to blame to possibly losing our home ever since."

"You were not to blame. This is merely how motherhood is."

"Yes, that is so. But don't you understand? For god sakes, man, don't you ever know, that in times like these, logic does not win, because the mother is too devastated. We don't want you to move away from us and ignore us until the problem is over. We want you beside us, holding us, and making us wholly aware that we have your support. And from a daughter, who is probably brokenhearted, how about you get off your bum, and you show it!"

When hearing his wife reach such a level of profanity, Mr. Bennet flinched, his eyebrows raised in slight alarm. But in times like those, a person grows defensive, rather than humbled. Feeling ill-used and judged by a person as inferior as they are, they must seek to bring them down to their level of mistakes. And for Mr. Bennet to feel despised, suffering under the weight of his wife's censure, when knowing that she was no better than himself, was enough to push him in a proud direction, and not in a reflective one.

"Your verbosity is astounding, my dear, and you have embraced a colloquial coquettish sort of manner. How theatrical."

Mrs. Bennet glared at him.

"And yet," Mr. Bennet uttered, "I cannot help but wonder if this new parental virtue stems from its proper place, or from either an angle of losing one's memory, or from guilt."

"Losing one's memory or from guilt?"

"Yes, Mrs. Bennet. You are having an exquisite time at dissembling my defects. I wonder if you do it to shield yourself from yours. Or do you forget so easily how you refused Mary's marriage, at first?"

Mrs. Bennet looked away from him, and so Mr. Bennet leaned forward, pressing his advantage.

"Or out of guilt," he continued, "of the fact that Kitty has run to the other side of the world to get away from you, because of your failings to be a proper parent for her. That you have always been wrong about Elizabeth. So now, you must replenish that deficit in any way that you can. Do you do this now to replace the feelings of inadequacy of letting our middle children down, in such a manner? You say that I don't know myself, Mrs. Bennet. But do you know yourself?"

Mrs. Bennet turned to him.

"First, I do not see how my failures as a mother have anything to do with this moment."

"It has everything to do with it. And you know that it does. You just don't have the ability to blame yourself for anything."

"I ask you to care for our child, and you sit here, complaining about your wife. Do you see how vicious that makes you? That the man I have been married to, all these years, is as coldhearted as I always suspected him to be."

Once more, Mr. Bennet was silent.

"But you forget, Mr. Bennet, I may have been wrong about Elizabeth, but we both were wrong about Mary, as well as Kitty. And Kitty did not leave England to be rid of *me*. She did it to be rid of *us*. Now, stop listing my failures as a parent to shield your own, and take this moment for what it is: you sitting in your library, not inquiring after our daughter who just lost what could have been the light of our lives. Or do you forget what it was like when you saw Jane and Elizabeth as infants, and held them for the first time?"

Jane and Elizabeth.

For a moment, time undid itself and Mr. Bennet recalled when he was a young man, and the midwife emerged from the room, with little Lizzy in her arms. Still idealistic and not imagining that he would never father a son, Mr. Bennet immediately held Elizabeth in his arms, cherishing the notion of being a father once more. She was so small, and though she was weeping, as all babies do when they leave the womb, soon her cries quieted down, and she tried to open her eyelids to look at the man who was her father.

Cooing down at her, Mr. Bennet recalled placing his finger in Elizabeth's little hand and watching her try to close her fingers around it.

In that moment, he found her to be the bravest thing in the

world, and time made him happy, because it proved that he was correct.

How different it all was when Mary, Kitty, and Lydia were born.

But that one moment, that one incredible moment when he held Elizabeth for the first time, then went into their bedroom and saw the midwife wiping down Mrs. Bennet's face. Her blonde hair was still wet from the sweat that drenched it from her exertion, and she was as beautiful as ever.

That was the time when he still was madly in love with her, ignoring all the folly that she often displayed, and he believed that they had the whole world ahead of them.

And that was when he knew how Mary must have been feeling now.

It only took a memory.

His silence both startled and aggravated Mrs. Bennet. She wanted him to agree with her quicker and with more eagerness. Seeing that it would be best to swell his pride, Mrs. Bennet decided to give a little on her own behalf.

"What you say of me is true," she admitted. "Perhaps, at some point, I failed as a mother toward our younger daughters. I did love them, but I made egregious errors on their part. But are we not the same in that manner? Have we not faltered somewhere, on the same level? Very well, if you cannot find yourself to agree to that, then can you withhold your criticizing my character and focus more on our daughter, who is hurting? Let us save this argument for later. She is more important now."

Mr. Bennet removed his spectacles.

"Well then," he said at last, "what are we waiting for?"

They arranged for the carriage to be brought round, and soon they were headed into Meryton, to the Philips' residence.

When they got there, Aunt Philips received them eagerly, happy to see her sister bring Mr. Bennet to move to being a more active parent.

While her reception was kinder, Uncle Philips was the reverse. After Dennison informed him that Mr. Bennet was sitting in his parlor, Uncle Philips left Mr. Atkins to look at the business as he received his brother-in-law. When seeing Mr. Bennet, he accosted him and decided to have a private word.

"You come to see Mary," Uncle Philips said, sardonically, as he led Mr. Bennet upstairs, to Mary's bedroom. "How fatherly of you."

"You sound vindictive, Thomas," Mr. Bennet said.

"I am happy that you are as perceptive, as always. Except for matters such as these. It took you long enough to come and see her."

Uncle Philips never concealed his views on Mr. Bennet's skills as a father, even to Mr. Bennet himself. Both men, who had once been friends in their youth, had long since abandoned their friendship, because they disagreed on how to be a proper parent. Simply put, Uncle Philips despised Mr. Bennet's angle of parenthood, and had a history of telling Mr. Bennet that, to his face.

"I am well aware of your perspective on my sense of fatherhood," Mr. Bennet said.

"Yes, you do. But I am not in the mood to argue about this, at present. Go to her, man. And be kind about it."

"When have you ever known me to raise my voice? You do me a dishonor."

"A person can be unkind and not speak loudly. Mary is hurting. Speak *kindly* to her. And again, let's not argue about this now."

They reached Mary's door.

"Do well," Uncle Philips said, and then he left Mr. Bennet alone.

~

Mr. Bennet raised his arm to knock on the door, but then he froze.

A new sensation overcame him. It was an emotion and state of mind that he had not experienced in so long; he was nervous.

So terribly nervous.

He was not accustomed to being so overpowered by the emotion. Yet he had to sojourn forth. There was no running away from this encounter.

At last, he knocked on the door.

"Mr. Atkins, is that you?" Mary asked, from the other side of the door. "Never fear, you don't need to worry over me. I don't want to take you from your work any longer."

"It's not Mr. Atkins, Mary," Mr. Bennet said, "it's your father. Can I come in?"

"Father?"

"Yes."

There was a moment of pause.

"Very well, come in."

Mr. Bennet opened the door, and he saw Mary sitting in bed, with the sheets over her as she sat up against the headboard. Her eyes were a little red, and it was obvious that she was crying.

When seeing her like that, Mr. Bennet acknowledged how much he was clearly not made of stone.

Mary was heartbroken, and his initial reaction was to do nothing.

"Mary..." he uttered, quietly.

"I never thought you would come to see me," she said, gasping and in despair.

"Oh, my girl!" he professed, going to the bed, sitting down on it, and holding her in his arms. Resting her head on his shoulder, Mary was limp, her energy spent.

"Oh, Papa!" Mary cried. "I cannot stop crying. I killed my baby. I killed it."

"No, you did not, Mary," he assured her. "You did not. This is a part of motherhood. I cannot begin to understand the pain you are feeling, but I promise, you will recover. This was not your fault. You must know this."

"I know. Aunt and Uncle Philips told me so. Mama told me such. And my husband has been so kind. But I cannot stop crying, Papa. Why can't I stop crying?"

"The answer is simple, Mary. It's because your love was real. That's why you feel so hard. Your love for your child was real. Please, my girl, do not feel ashamed of what has happened. These pains are agonizing because they ought to be. But every day that rises and falls, you will feel the pain less, and you will turn this tragedy into an incentive to be a mother again. Then you will become so, and you will go forth, and be the best that you have ever been. It will be the making of you later, even if it is the breaking of you now."

"I feel as if I hurt Mr. Atkins when I am this way."

"He understands, just as I understood when your mother underwent this same situation once. And when you are ready, he will be as open and in love with you as ever. I am proud of you."

Mary looked at him, amazed.

"You are?"

"Have I never said that before?"

"No, you have not."

"Oh," he replied, humbled. In times such as those, Mr. Bennet could not help but reflect on his life. His mind raced across all the history of when he was Master of Longbourn, and now he knew. He never did tell Mary, Kitty, or Lydia that he was proud of them. He did it, under the impression that he did not want to spoil them, as their mother did. Yet perhaps he spoiled them in another way. Perhaps, he spoiled them by *not* saying it.

"I am proud of you. I always have been."

"Thank you, Papa."

"No thanks must be rendered unto me. I ought to have said it long ago. I am proud of you all. So terribly so."

He kissed her on her forehead and held her a little longer.

~

When he left Mary alone, he went down the stairs, only to come upon Mr. Atkins, who had eagerly come to meet him.

"You saw Mary?" Mr. Atkins asked.

"Yes, I have. She will recover, I promise."

"I know that she will. She is a match for anything."

Mr. Bennet chuckled. Mr. Atkins really did love his daughter.

"Yes, she is." Mr. Bennet placed his hand on Mr. Atkins's shoulder. "Give her time, Atkins. She may be sad, sometimes, but do not turn away from her. She needs your strength, and your company, in this trying time."

"I will. Depend upon it. I know that she and I are in this together."

After sitting with the family for a brief while, Mrs. and Mr. Bennet left for home. While they did so, they were silent on the way back, and even when they entered Longbourn, they were quiet.

When Mr. Bennet removed his coat, he began to walk back to his library.

Braving speech, Mrs. Bennet called to him.

"Mr. Bennet."

He stopped.

"What did you say to her?" she asked.

"What ought to have been said." Looking at her over his shoulder, his face displayed humility. "You were right. You were right."

Feeling embarrassed about having to admit that, Mr. Bennet retreated to his library, leaving his wife to stand there, transfixed to the spot.

Clutching her sides, Mrs. Bennet felt every nerve in her wake up.

He told her that she was right.

Never, in their marriage, had he ever said that before.

For one moment, she was right.

Chapter Sixteen

A STRESSFUL SET OF SITUATIONS WITH A BEAUTIFUL VIEW

Rome!

Once we arrived on the shore, there was a sense of liberty for everyone. A couple of the sailors on the Lilia were Italian, so we were given a five-hour time on shore, so that they could return to their families and there would be a rotation of new sailors coming in.

"Well," Marie Lefevre said, as she and her husband had their belongings taken on shore. "This is where we leave you all."

"You are breaking your journey here?" I asked, a little apprehensively. Despite the differences between us, I had come to like the Lefevres. They were animated and distracted me from the tension that was within my party.

"Alas, dear ladies," Jacques said, "yes, now we come to the end of our acquaintance."

"I'm sorry that we didn't get the chance the know you better," Arthur Philips said. "I suppose we took your acquaintance for granted."

"Indeed, we did," I concurred. "It did not occur to us that we would separate so soon."

"That is the way of ships; lots of comings and goings and then never meeting again."

"Miss Bennet, Miss Darcy, Mrs. Philips and Miss Watson," Jacques said, each kissing our hands, "it was a true delight to have danced with you all."

"You danced very well," Enara said, "and you are a partner that I did not regret having."

"I better not have been."

Monsieur Lefevre leaned in close to Georgiana and me.

"I will never have a love for the English and always will wish your country bad weather and that your battleships always sink to the bottom of the sea before they ever make any progress. But allow me to make an exception for yourself. Miss Bennet and Miss Darcy, you are the precise sort of ladies that I prefer. If all of England were like you both, I would think Britain and France would get along tolerably well."

We kissed him and his wife on the cheek, feeling such a loss.

As we went on shore, there were cabs aplenty. Since we had the time, we planned to ride into the heart of the city, and we knew that we could visit the Circus Maximus site and even visit the Coliseum. As we hailed a few cabs for ourselves, I watched the Lefevres load their luggage into two cabs and get into them.

I caught their eye and waved farewell to them. Smiling, they waved as well and rode off into the distance.

I would never see them again.

I suppose that was the way of traveling; you came, you met many strangers, they no longer were strange, and then they exited your life just as quickly. And that you didn't take the time to get to know them as well as you ought to have.

As we arranged for the cabs, I decided that this was as good a time as any.

"Mr. Blake," I said, as we all assembled, "being a tutor who has also mastered Latin and Italian, I trust that you have much history as we ride along."

"Very much so," Mr. Blake said, surprised that I had sought him out so directly. After all, I had never been very determined in ever seeking him out. I was not, nor ever would be, inclined to see the charms in him in the manner that Emma Watson did. He was not a disagreeable man, to say the least. And he was comely, and gentlemanlike, in his own manner. However, I didn't really care. After all, I had seen superior men in my time. Mr. Blake would never fall into that category.

"Well," I said, giving him no chance to argue about my company, "since you must be more enlightened than I on this legendary city, we shall ride together, so that you may point out the highlights of the city to me."

Out of the side of his eye, I saw him glimpse Georgiana and Emma Watson.

Out of the side of *my* eye, I saw Emma Watson eye me, suspiciously.

Also, Enara and Arthur exchanged a look, where afterwards Arthur gave me a 'what are you doing?' expression. I had to remind myself to explain it all to him later, without informing Arthur about Mr. Blake's failed proposal.

Since Mr. Blake had been silent for most of the morning, clearly affected by Georgiana's rejecting him, this situation was entirely in his favor, so that he could be far away from her. Also, since I was Georgiana's particular friend, he had no choice but to be curious about why I sought out his company.

Emma Watson would not thank me for this. But I dare say that she was not the sort to seek revenge in any sort of way. After all, she was too refined for such a thing. I trusted that I was right, in this regard.

Although he might not have preferred me as a companion, Mr.

Blake could not refuse me, or he could not call himself a gentleman.

"I should be very happy to be your guide," Mr. Blake said, helping me into the cab.

Enara and Arthur got into another.

Georgiana and Emma got into the third.

Looking over my shoulder at Georgiana, she gave me an appreciative glance, and my heart was warmed. After all, I was not going to emerge from this interview with many friends on my side, excepting herself. Emma, perhaps, might like me even less than she did before. And while Mr. Blake did not despise me before, he might do so now.

As we left the harbor, I saw Trip, Reedus, Merriweather, and Miyoshi rush down the ramp and run along the port, with a great deal of mirth and delight.

"What makes them so happy?" Mr. Blake wondered, also watching them as we got further away.

"Italy is a safe haven for them," I explained. "There is no threat to any of them here. And since they are with Miyoshi, they will look after her. Italy is the only safe place that they can all relax and enjoy themselves."

"We are living in strange times, are we not?"

"Yes, we are."

"On the one hand, sophistication, and on the other hand, barbarity."

"I heartily agree," I said, "but I am of the suspicion that your maxim can be attributed to any period of human history. After all, since every human is such an odd mixture of virtue and vice, I daresay that we can never fully escape such a paradox to our existence. I have had to reconcile myself to that reality."

"You suggest that, since vice and wantonness is inevitable, that we ought to succumb to our passions?"

I scoffed inwardly. It was as if he was deliberately attempting to misunderstand me.

"I deserve no such translation to my findings. I was merely stating a reality. We all can believe in a better way and a brighter tomorrow, while still confronting the way the world is around us. Are you asking me to be blind, sir?"

Mr. Blake's face was a little blanched as he rubbed his chin, evidently mortified.

"I have both offended you and now I feel like quite the dunce. And I call myself the tutor. Forgive me, Miss Bennet. It is merely that...well, today, you might not find me at my best. Forgive me for embracing common phrases, but it could be said that 'I woke up on the wrong side of the bed'."

"You apologize well. I forgive you."

Mr. Blake's face lit up.

"Then I propose that we talk about happier things. You were friendly with the Lefevres."

"Yes, I was. I wish that I could say that I had gotten to know them very well, but that is not true. I enjoyed their company every time that I spoke to them, but I took my time with them for granted. We always tend to put off conversations for the next day. I know their personalities, but I never took the time to learn what part of France they were from, what their family was like, and what were their dreams, passions and aims in life. And now, all I can do is regret those missed opportunities."

"You confess to that freely. Admirable. Many of us in life, who do not wish to waste it, are not repaid with getting what we wish."

This was the precise statement that I needed. It helped me transition into the heart of the matter, in a way that suited me most.

"And by that, you are speaking of what you experienced after the ball," I informed him.

My declaration was followed by all pretense dropping within him, and shock overcame him. But it was only for a few seconds before a calm expression of defensiveness replaced it. He was a man of the world; he had no choice but to look confident all the time.

"I cannot understand what you refer to, in a cab, in a city where such discussions are meant to be concealed," he uttered. Quite frankly, I was no longer in the habit of being patient with such propriety when it did no good.

"And we are in this city for five hours," I said, "in a cab where if we speak low and do not use specific words, no one will hear it. And since we are *in a cab where if we speak low and do not use specific words, where no one will hear it,* and in a city that we might never have the chance to visit again, how is this not safer than other places? After all, we shall be on a ship for days upon end, where you might have no one to take into your confidence."

"Miss Bennet, I do not think it wise to speak of the matter to the friend of the woman whom I—"

"Who you had such an unpleasant scene with," I finished for him, to speak in ambiguous terms.

When seeing what I was about, he sighed, relieved.

"Yes," he said, "that is the best term for it."

"Also, are you troubled by the fact that I am a lady addressing you thus?"

"Precisely. Such behavior is something that must be objected to. We ladies and gentlemen ought not to speak of such ordeals together."

"No, none of that," I refuted. "I neither have the time nor the patience for such outdated thinking. What does a man speak of that he could not do it with a lady? Truly, let us move past this."

"Really, Miss Bennet, I know that you have been attributed to having a reputation—"

He stopped talking when I gave him a side glance, and I am certain that it scared him to his very core. Such a reaction ought to make sense, for I did not withhold any sort or resentment on my behalf.

"A reputation? A reputation of what, pray?"

"I spoke hastily."

"No, you started something. Therefore, you might as well finish what you have begun."

"Miss Bennet, I do think well of you..."

"But you have given rise to accepting other's labels on my person. As I said before, finish what you started. What do I have a reputation of being like?"

"Of being too liberal in your manner, and wild in others."

In another life, I would have let these defamations of my character affect my confidence. But now, I was only slightly affected.

"I am free, whereas others are constantly chaining themselves down," I said. "Perhaps the rumors of me are correct. But you can either sit there and set my person down by cruel comments that you are encouraging by censoring me, or you can allow me to help you."

"I just do not wish for you to do anything further that can give rise to more gossip on your behalf."

"I thank you for your concern, but I do not need it. I can fend and shift for myself. Now, can we continue?"

Mr. Blake was silent, until he looked out of the window, a happy smile on his face.

"There it is! The Circus Maximus."

I leaned my head out of the cab window and sure enough, there it was. The Circus Maximus.

When it came to the Circus, the most impressive thing about it was knowing its history and that the location was there. Unfortunately, there was not much there at all, and mostly an empty lot.

"Has it been overrun by conquerors who tried to take Rome?" I asked.

"Well, since it was a racetrack, there was never very much architecture to begin with," Mr. Blake said, "but yes, many of the historic sites in Rome are no longer present, since raiders felt as if they must have their way. The truth is, Miss Bennet, civilizations rise to epic proportions and prominence, and so, there must always naturally be an equal and opposite force that seeks to tear them down. It's the way of history."

"Yes," I said, sad as we rode past the Circus, "it is the way of history. But, of course, one must take into account the manner in which a society became great. If it was a society founded on the oppression of lesser nations around it, then the empire that established itself might eventually crumble, due to imperfect foundations. For a nation to last, fate must be on its side. And fate is rarely permanently on the side of the one whose house was built on fragile bricks and stone."

"That is very wise, I grant you."

"The product of a wild mind, I suppose," I replied, assertively "It winds its way down pathways that others prefer not to tread."

Mr. Blake looked at me curiously.

"What sort of lady are you?"

"I am Georgiana's friend. That's the sort of woman that I am."

When hearing Georgiana's name, the storm cloud of gloom returned to his face. I did not fear it. In truth, I was happy that we had arrived at the chief point, for I feared that I would not get the chance before we reached the Coliseum.

"And we return back to the beginning, I see," I pointed out the obvious.

"Yes, I must say that we have."

"I am not here to repeat every word you said to Georgiana. My reason for my impertinence is not gossip, but as an intermediary only. The fact is that you are two people who have undergone a disagreement, and you both are confined to the same ship until we reach our destination. That will not be for weeks. Therefore, I am here to assist you both through this ordeal."

"You are?" he asked, softer.

"Yes. I can imagine that it will be difficult for you both, and you do not have the wonderful gift of there being any distance between you, to allow any chance of recovery. No. You both are plagued with the task of having to see each other repeatedly. Do you find that to be a daunting prospect?"

He sighed, but he did not reply.

"Come, man," I insisted. "We do not have all the time in the world."

"Yes, you are quite right. We do not. Yes. I do find it to be a daunting prospect. But also, it is a contradiction of a prospect as well."

I adjusted the shawl around my shoulders, confused by this statement.

"I do not follow."

"What I mean is that, yes, the cure for my passions would be to place as much distance between myself and your friend. Seeing her hurts me, but it is also a pleasant sort of pain. Am I to presume that you don't know how it feels to suffer under a rejection?"

"I do have some experience on the matter. I once preferred a man who preferred a relative over me."

When hearing this, he turned to me, all tension in him relaxing. From his eyes down to his feet, I saw that knowing that we both shared similar experiences put him at ease and established a link between us. That was very good, because that was precisely what he needed.

"Truly?"

"Yes," I answered.

"And, if you do not mind me asking..."

"You may ask. After all, I was the one who began this discussion."

"Well, how did it make you feel?"

"Embarrassed," I answered. "And mortified. As well as heartbroken."

"Yes, quite right."

"Is that what you felt when Georgiana gave her answer?"

"Well, yes. I am not afraid of her knowing this."

"I can understand how hard this is for you. However, it would help to write about it. In a journal, so that you cannot force your feelings to remain inside. It helped me, for what it is worth."

"Thank you."

"When it comes to pains of the heart, it does not do to suppress the pain, no matter what anyone says to the contrary."

"Do you still love the man that did not prefer you?"

I grimaced, disgusted at the very notion of once feeling anything for Mr. Bingley.

"Oh, dear lord, no! In fact, I regret ever having such an inclination. Truly, I wonder what I could have been thinking. Then again, I was younger back then."

Mr. Blake laughed at my reaction.

"See?" I said, giving him hope. "It gets easier. That is what I wish to tell you. And it was not as if I was no longer in the man's company. I saw him often after that."

"And writing about it helped?"

"Yes, it did. And also, as time wore on, I opened my heart to other possibilities, and I fell in love again. I suppose that finding new affections did help. I am not advising that you shift your adoration to another woman quickly. That is not fair to the next lady, because she will suffer for your hasty transition. What I conclude is that, when you are ready, open your heart again. And you will see that there are many worthy women in the world. This is not the end for you."

"But in the meantime, what ought I to do? What do you advise?"

I groaned, distinctly wishing that I could say 'I told you so'.

"Oh, is this where you ask the advice of the *wild* woman?"

He blushed.

"I spoke cruelly there, didn't I?"

"Yes, you did. Oh well, I still might as well tell you what I came to say, regardless. I know that it will be difficult, but when you see

Georgiana, always try and be agreeable to her. Maybe even acknowledge the awkwardness of the situation to her."

"I cannot do that."

"Yes, you can. It will help you both, a great deal. For sometimes, our history can be the barrier that we placed between ourselves and others, and it won't go away until we have confronted it. It might even help you and her learn to become friends over time."

"Miss Bennet, forgive me, but I must ask. Last night, she said that she was unable to love me. Is that true? Have I no chance of succeeding with her?"

"She has no choice," I said. "She knows someone who prefers your company, and she will not betray the lady from back home."

While that was a lie—after all, Emma Watson was right there in the cab behind us—hopefully this acknowledgement would do the trick. Instead, it fueled his hopes.

"Her refusing me was based on the affections of another lady back in England?"

"Yes."

"Then there is hope. For that means that her lack of affection for me is done out of loyalty to another lady, and not cold indifference."

"But it is," I stressed. "Mr. Blake, this will be hard for you to hear, but Georgiana holds fast to friendships. As you saw, it is one of her charms. She will never consider a man that one of her friends prefers. She cannot even find him alluring or attractive. The only way that she would do that is if her friend's heart was seized elsewhere. And it's not." Looking at him, I sighed. "You will still hope anyway, won't you?"

"I cannot help it."

"Even if I advise you to move on, I know that your heart will not listen. Instead, it will do as the heart always does; find its own reason and take you along for a ride."

Mr. Blake nodded. "Yes, I suppose that it would."

"It's natural. But still, when the time comes, see if you can find affection elsewhere. There are many ladies who would feel their fortune in having a husband such as yourself."

"You flatter me."

"No, I do not. In fact, I prefer not to flatter you at all. I say it because it is true. You have many fine qualities, and other ladies will consider them, for even Georgiana was aware of them. As does her friend, Miss Watson. In fact, I would encourage you to continue speaking mostly to Miss Watson, for her company always seems to put you at ease, and it might prove very diverting."

He sighed.

"Quite right. Quite right. And here we are."

I looked out of the window and there was the Coliseum!

Speechless, we all exited our cabs and stood before the legendary monument.

Despite that time had worn it down, and perhaps there might have even been thieves who stole parts of the architecture, it still was there, as strong, and prominent as ever.

When standing before something so incredible, all you can do is sit there, gazing at such a remarkable feat. The design still represented the incredible magnitude of the human capacity. Of all that we are capable of, of all that we could create. Such a piece of work was man!

As we walked around the exterior, we discovered that we had time to visit the interior. We paid our tickets, and the tour began as we were led around the inside of the structure where the Roman games took place.

Not only were we amazed by all that we saw, but also there was an element of amusement. For, not frequently, but occasionally, there was a cat or kitten who wandered about the ruins.

The guide told us that the Italian people let the cats remain there, because cats were both a symbol of good luck, while also keeping the vermin out of the ruins, protecting it from mice and rats.

Arthur, Enara, and I even got one of the cats to let us pet them.

While the tour guide threw one of the cats some dried meat that he had in his pocket, Georgiana quietly came up to me and addressed me from over my shoulder.

"Well?" she asked.

"Mr. Blake will not ever force you into a scene that will arise that will cause discomfort between you both. The only thing that I must prepare you for is that he might wish to talk to you about the matter, from time to time. Not so that he can convince you to love him, but to ease his curiosity. That is all."

"I can weather that."

"And if he ever were to say anything provocative, then come to me again. I will protect you."

Georgiana pressed her forehead against mine.

"Thank you, Kitty."

"Always, Georgie. Always."

I might never be a popular sort of person, but I would always be a true friend to Georgiana Darcy. Hopefully, that must count for something.

Sadly, we had to leave the beauties of Rome's greatest ruin and return to The Lilia.

With all the affairs settled between Mr. Blake and Georgiana, I felt as if my work was done. Therefore, I thought it would naturally follow that he would choose Emma Watson to join him in his cab.

Ergo, imagine my surprise when he approached me and asked me to join him.

Once more, I spied Emma by way of a side glance, and I saw her look at the ground, discomforted.

But since I knew that there was no reason for her to feel any sort of envy, I accepted, and Mr. Blake helped me back into the cab.

As we rode away, I looked at the Coliseum one last time.

"Miss it already?" Mr. Blake asked.

"Of course, I do," I replied. "Mr. Blake, the wonders of the human skill and achievement! What mankind can set itself to do when it puts one's mind to it."

"Yes. It is all those things. It's also enough to make one feel like they have been born again."

"Precisely. Even though I know the history of what occurred in the gladiator games there, we must not blame the building. Rather, going there does give me the feeling of rebirth." I turned to him. "Now tell me why you wanted me to ride with you? For I did not foresee that."

Mr. Blake's eyes lost their luster and they looked more resigned.

"You were right."

"Right?" I echoed.

"I did need to talk about it. And I felt that, since you seem to be an amiable sort, maybe it would help to voice my feelings. Do you mind if I talk about what occurred the night before? And how it makes me feel?"

"Go on," I said, "speak now or forever hold your peace."

He chuckled, and so did I.

"And once more, the *wild woman* wins the day."

"You are never going to let me forget that, will you?"

"No, I will not. I can forgive, but I am dreadful at forgetting. That is just what my character is. You will grow accustomed to it. Or you might not. The choice is yours and is quite out of my hands."

"Yes, I suppose that it is. Well, since you are showing a unique display of letting me speak as I wish, I shall choose to grow accustomed to you. Miss Bennet, I wish that your friend had said yes to me."

I smiled. "I can understand why. My friend is the greatest woman in the world."

"Precisely."

"Now, I acknowledge that I know the events of last evening from Georgiana's perspective. You may tell me yours."

He sighed.

"Thank you. First, I confess that I was so nervous that I could barely speak, and then when she looked at me, with the moonlight in her eyes, I was dazed. Never did I see anything more beautiful. And then I began to speak, and I said..."

He spoke the entire way back to the harbor. And I let him, overjoyed that I was amidst a romance that I was not a part of. Ah, freedom!

When we all boarded The Lilia again, we were met by new sailors who had joined the crew. Interestingly, one of the sailors was German, and his name was Elias Durchdenwald.

As we climbed aboard, I looked to the captain's wheel where I saw Archer talking with a strange woman.

Seeing me looking at him, he turned, smiled, and waved for me to come over and see him. Always eager to obey him, I excused myself from my party and walked across the deck.

As I passed Merriweather, Miyoshi, and Durchdenwald, they gave me a look.

"You both look like you know something," I said.

"We do," Durchdenwald said, with his thick German accent, "this ought to be interesting."

Walking up the steps, to the captain's deck, I approached

Captain Archer and now I was able to see the foreign woman on closer inspection.

She was wearing the traditional habit, but there was something about her that spoke of superior strength. She was taller and appeared to be more muscular than the average woman.

"Well, Master of the Lilia," I said, in a coquettish manner, "what tidings do you bring me?"

Archer chuckled.

"I bring you a new subject to fascinate over."

"Oh," the lady said, in an Italian accent, "I am a subject now?"

"Who isn't?" I retorted. This made her raise an eyebrow, but not from feeling offended. Unless I was mistaken, she looked amused.

"Oh," she said to Archer, "she is different. Very good. I was worried that she would be too refined."

"I cannot claim that accomplishment," I said.

"And that's why I thought you would be excited by our new arrival," Archer instructed. "Miss Bennet, this is Senorita Rafaela Benelli, from Firenze."

"You are from Florence?" I asked her.

"Yes, I am," Senorita Benelli confirmed.

"And Senorita Benelli," Archer introduced, "this is Miss Catherine Bennet, from Hertfordshire, England."

"You may call me Kitty," I said, "for I answer to that."

Rafaela looked at me, curiously.

"You seem different than the English ladies that I have ever met."

"Yes, I am. English ladies of my stock are a rare breed, but we do exist. There are at least five of me in every English city. Or maybe just three."

Rafaela smiled while Archer chuckled.

"I told you that Miss Bennet would be worth your notice," Archer said to her. "Miss Bennet, I think that my old friend here is notable enough to go into your journal. Rafaela, Miss Bennet loves to write our adventures and exploits in her diary. But I think she prefers to only write about interesting people."

"And people that I do not like," I admitted. "That is the best place to say all that you wish to say to them."

"You are witty," Senorita Benelli said. "I prefer that. After all, our journey to Australia will be a long one. As such, I will need an interesting person."

"I will try, but sadly I fail under performance."

"If you do," Archer said, "then Rafaela will help you. She is a hunter."

At first, my response was casual, because I did not fully gather his meaning. Then, after four seconds, I began to. My jaw dropped open as I was agog.

"Hunter?" I turned to Senorita Benelli. "Did he say hunter?"

"Yes," she responded, "he did. I am on a mission to New South Wales to gather more knowledge of the wildlife and report back to the Italian Philosophic Society. Since they heard of the interesting animals there, they knew that they might require my services. After all, a preservationist would not have the skills to survive the place."

"You really are a hunter?"

"And yet I am a woman."

"Yes." I grinned like a madwoman. "You must tell me everything. I will plague you with every question in the world."

"You will hear it all when you and your company join me for a special dinner in my cabin," Archer invited me. "I issue an invitation for you and your company to dine with me this evening. Rafaela shall be there."

"I prefer to save my story for when the audience is the largest," Senorita Benelli said. "For I do not have to suffer repeating myself whenever a new person approaches me."

"Well, Miss Bennet," Archer said, "what do you say? Will your company enjoy a dinner in the master's quarters?"

I smiled.

"Captain, did you even have to ask?"

Chapter Seventeen

WELL, THAT WENT TERRIBLY

Once I removed myself from the Master and Senorita Benelli, I rushed down below deck and arranged for our entire company to meet in Arthur and Enara's cabin.

When we were assembled, I told them the news and they were all excited.

"A huntress?" Arthur said. "Senorita Benelli?"

"Yes, she is," I confirmed. "And when looking at her, I believe it. Imagine all the stories that she will have to tell us."

I danced around Georgiana and Enara.

"I shall write it all down and be amazed in knowing that she will not depart when we reach Greece, but rather, she will go with us for the entire rest of the way."

"You take such an eager interest in these sorts of ladies?" Emma Watson asked me.

"Of course, I do." I looked at her, alarmed at her calmness. "First, we have Tepree, then Miyoshi, and Gloriana. And now we have this woman. They have lived more than I ever will, to the point where they are the peak of womanhood."

"And that is where your wildness presents itself, Miss Bennet,"

Emma Watson said. "It is not just your behavior now, but also your perspective. How can you admire these ladies when their behavior is too masculine, and not like that of a proper lady at all?"

Once more, there was that word: wild. Yes, perhaps I was, but that label was not the point. Emma never took the chance to know these women, and what they signified. She committed the most egregious offense—and common one—of believing that she was enhancing the female position in society by limiting it.

"Too masculine?" I repeated. "Just because you are jealous of them, or ignorant that they are superior to you, does not give you the right to label their actions as improper for a female. What is wrong with you!"

My last sentence was not spoken quietly, but I spoke it with such a fury, that everyone in the room flinched. Especially Emma Watson.

Seeing that my outburst only confirmed the rumors about me, I groaned inwardly and rushed out of the room. Closing the door behind me, I came face to face with Elias Durchdenwald.

"Miss Bennet?" he said, gently, clearly overhearing everything that I just said.

"Please," I whispered, "do not look at me just now."

"I do look at you though," he remarked, "and I do not do so in disgrace. Not at all."

I squeezed his arm, affectionately.

"Thank you."

I rushed past him, went to my room, collapsed on the bed, and buried my face in my pillow.

Well, that went terribly.

And there was no going back. Emma Watson and I were probably enemies now.

Oh, what was I saying?

We were already enemies before. Now, we had just cemented what had been subtle.

Chapter Eighteen

EPIPHANY

At Godfrey Park, Darcy and Elizabeth emerged from under the bedsheets, having just finished making love. Their bodies were still perspiring as they collapsed against each other, with Darcy resting his head on Elizabeth's breasts as he kissed them slowly, still amazed at her.

"Do you enjoy that motherhood has made them larger?" Elizabeth asked, amused.

"Oh, with great enthusiasm," Darcy responded, in between kisses.

Elizabeth laughed as she placed her hands over his head and began to rub his scalp and hair. This massage always calmed him and was precisely as he liked it.

"My beautiful Fitzwilliam Darcy," she cooed, her breath ruffling his hair that was next to her lips.

"You call me beautiful?" he responded, running his hand down her stomach, and rubbing her thighs, then at last driving his fingers deep within her. Elizabeth moaned.

"Please do not stop, dearest," she said, gasping heavily. "I know that you may be tired, but..."

"Never fear. Time has taught me that when we men are spent,

women sometimes still have more energy to them. We finish sooner than you do."

"You are very astute." She moaned again, squirming with pleasure. "Then again, I suppose that I am the only novice in this situation."

Raising himself up, Darcy looked down on Elizabeth's nude form and marveled at her. As she writhed underneath him, with his stroking her harder and harder, the waves of sensations that rushed through her added even more beauty to her face and figure. Her eyes were alight, with pleasure, bringing even more sparkle to her fine eyes, then he kissed her breasts once more, until her body spasmed, her hands clutched the sheets, and she lay limp.

"Now," Darcy declared, resting against her, "I daresay that you are happy."

"Happy? Me?" Elizabeth decided to tease him, as was often her way. "No, not at all."

"You wicked creature," he said, pinching her nipples in his fingers.

"You would not have me any other way, and you know it."

"True, I would not."

"How did I manage to find someone as handsome as you?" Elizabeth questioned. "I cannot account for it."

"You think me the lovely one."

"Hero has your eyes."

"She does?"

"That's what Lucy says. She has seen quite a few childbirths in her time, and she says that Hero has your visage."

"I will never forgive myself," he uttered.

"Why?"

"A girl should look wholly like their mother. Especially if the mother is you."

"I am certain that she will be beautiful, and knowing you, you will dote on her."

"Yes, I probably will. But we must take care not to spoil her. Though I am tempted."

"Every father is."

~

As they lay together, Elizabeth sighed.

"You sigh? What is that about?"

"This is the worst time to be thinking of just now. Why do we humans, when in a happy time, always think of things that make us miserable?"

"You are thinking of Jane and Bingley," Darcy surmised.

"I cannot help it. Does my husband dare judge me?"

"He does not," Darcy answered as Elizabeth massaged the back of his neck. "It is natural to worry. Especially with how things are going. Lizzy, Bingley is very frightened."

"He has reason to be. Usually, when Jane rebukes my company, I sometimes see her anyway, and she looks like she is fading into the shadows around her. It's as if her despair is bringing her down. I've never seen Jane like that in the whole of my life. Even her serenity had sparkle to it. When seeing his wife like this, I can see why Bingley is afraid. He is not made of stone and thank the lord for that."

"He does not know how to help her rally, or how to make her happy again."

"I'm afraid for them both, and I am still thinking of how to resolve this. I think..."

"What?"

"As drastic as this sounds, maybe they need to return to Hertfordshire. While our mother is..."

"Your mother," he finished her sentence.

"Yes. Despite that, she is still a comforting presence. Maybe we need to take Jane back to Longbourn, where our mother will be there as a balm."

"You think that would work?"

"Yes, and—" Elizabeth stopped abruptly when she came to a realization.

"Eliza?"

"I just realized that it is a terrible plan. Our mother is horrible at coaxing anyone. In fact, she might spend a great deal of time always bringing up the subject and not offering the maternal needs that might be necessary for Jane to experience."

"That is sadly true," Darcy said. "Elizabeth, that plan would work for a brief while, but Longbourn is not the answer. I am sorry that it is not, but it is no less true. But I do see the need for a change in society, and some diversions that might help her predicament."

"By being here, her emotions probably do prey upon her so very meanly. Oh!"

"What?"

"Why did I not think of it before? The Gardiners! Maybe we should take Jane back to Gracechurch Street. Especially since Aunt Gardiner miscarried twice. She would know precisely what to say."

"Oh! Well, that is a delightful idea. Yes, your aunt and uncle would be beneficial for her safety. We must make certain to have Hero safely looked after as we travel."

"I'll keep her with me the entire way," I said. "We must withstand some crying every now and again, but I do not want to let her out of my sight."

"Nor do I. I will suggest it to Bingley tomorrow."

"Do so. And I will tell Jane."

"Will Jane say no, possibly?"

"If she does, then I will attempt to convince her. Darcy, I do not want my sister and your friend to fall away from each other. I want them to recover from this."

"As do I."

~

Elizabeth rolled over and mounted Mr. Darcy as if he were a horse. When doing so, Darcy placed his hands along her hips and ran his hands up and down her stomach and thighs.

"It is strange," Elizabeth declared, "that of the two of us couples, it is not us that has experienced any marital rift, but them."

"Yes. Then again, we overcame all our disagreements and came to the marriage with our flaws realized. Whereas Bingley and Jane came to the marriage perfect for one another."

"True. I suppose, there is something to be said for getting your mistakes out before wedding vows are exchanged."

Looking down at Darcy, Elizabeth ran her hands along his chest and then covered his hands in hers.

"Darcy, I make a promise to you now."

"What promise is that?"

"I cannot fully declare that I would be any different than Jane if I were in her circumstances. After all, I love our Hero, almost as much as I love you."

Darcy's expression changed from pleasure to subtle amazement.

"You love me more?" he asked.

"Yes, I suppose that I do. I have always been told that no love for your spouse will ever measure up to love for one's child. I must be perverse."

"I am not upset by this," he answered. "I know that you will be a superior mother. It is merely that, you really will always love me best?"

"Yes," Elizabeth confirmed. "I will always love our children, but it took a while for me to wonder if I would regret it no longer being merely you and me. For I had just found my love for you only a year and a half ago. I was selfish, in wanting you all to myself, but we didn't have enough time for it to be solely us, to my liking.

"I love Hero, more than my life. But you, Fitzwilliam, are my soul. I will always cherish this love, for it took so long that it was entirely worth the earning. And maybe that is what would fortify me. No matter what happens, no matter what tragedy would strike us, as long as I have you, I will never despair. I would regret losing a child, but I will never fall away from you. Because you and I are too connected, for me to not recover from any other loss."

Slowly, Mr. Darcy raised himself up, wrapping his arms around her back and holding her closer to himself.

"You mean all this?" he asked, his tone harsh from the rapture.

"Yes," Elizabeth said, looking deeply into his eyes, "I do."

Mr. Darcy let out a sharp breath, amazed by all that he was hearing.

"Two years ago," he said, "I almost gave up all hope of us being united, and now this?" He placed his hands on her cheeks, to ensure that their eyes were locked together, in one gaze. One long and intense gaze that marked the connection between them both. "Now this. Elizabeth, please tell me that it will always be this way. That you will always be so much tied to me, in a binding manner that will not allow any severance?"

"I do."

He kissed her passionately and pressed his forehead against us.

"Always find your way back to me."

"I will. And what of you, Fitzwilliam?"

"What of me?"

"You must promise the same. Will you be bound to me like this always?" Elizabeth insisted.

"You know that I will always desire this. Always."

"And that you will always come to me in this manner. I believe in this passion. This grand achievement of intimacy like this. Always fall into me this way. For this is true love."

"Yes, it is. And I will cling to it, for there is sanctity in it."

"Yes, there is."

"My Elizabeth...always be a part of me."
"On that, I can swear," Elizabeth vowed.
Laying in bed, they fell asleep in each other's arms.

Chapter Nineteen

ANOTHER WILD WOMAN

Fearful of seeing the rest of my company after my outburst, I spent a great deal of my time above deck and watching the water as we sailed along and awaiting any land as we passed it. I enjoyed the wind on my face.

"That strip of land is Messina, Sicily," White Wolf said to me as we passed between two lands. Messina was on our right and there was another land on our left.

"What is on that side?" I asked, pointing.

"That is Reggio di Calabria," White Wolf answered. "It took me a while to learn about all this geography. I was raised in a world where our land was all that we needed to know."

"I can well believe it. North America is a large place. Faith, there are some Colonies there that are larger than Britain. We are big people, with big ideas. No wonder we colonized so much, to the detriment of the natives. I do not think one island is large enough for us."

"You still call the States the Colonies?" White Wolf asked, amused. How interesting that I was to have this same conversation again.

"Oh yes," I said, not ashamed to own to it. "I am of the suspicion that we always will call you lot our Colonies. Perhaps, secretly, we will never fully cut the metaphoric umbilical cord. I think that it's our habit, and affliction, to reject you sometimes, while also clinging to you. It does not make a great deal of sense, but it is true, nevertheless."

"I can well believe it. After all, the States are your offspring, but they are also independent. You take pride in the first and then take prejudice against the second."

I reflected upon this statement.

"Well, yes. I suppose that it is a proper way of putting it. And a very intelligent one." I looked up at him and saw the feather that he had tied to the braid in his hair.

Raising my hand, I ran my fingers along it.

"I'm sorry," I said. "For when we took your land from you."

White Wolf smiled.

"Do you know that you are the first pale face to say that to me?"

"I can imagine so. Do you have any more time to spare with me?"

"Yes."

"Are you in the spirit to tell me your life's story? What is it like to live in a tribe?"

"Oh, it's a whole different world to what you are accustomed. I can do my duties and tell you everything at the same time. Come."

As White Wolf performed his daily chores on the ship, he told me about what life was like in the Dakota tribe, of the duties that women and men did. Of the ritual that he had to undergo when he had to become a Brave. Of when they first met us pale faces. Of the women in his tribe that he had been in love with. It was enough to keep me occupied until we had to dress for the Master's dinner and also gave me many things to write down in my journal.

~

While I was listing all that occurred that day in my diary, Georgiana entered.

It had been the first time that she and I were alone since before my outburst.

When we faced each other, we both blanched and looked down at the floor, avoiding each other's eyes.

Was this how our friendship was to end? In that moment, I realized how fragile camaraderie could be. Sometimes, time and distance ends bonds. Other times, a friendship can be snapped like a twig, forever torn into two separate entities, and to be connected no more.

Placing my pen down, I closed my diary and folded my hands against it.

"Georgie..."

"Kitty..."

"I know that I acted very indelicately," I said. "And that you must be upset with me."

"I'm not."

I turned my head so sharply to her that it hurt a little. All my despair and avoiding her had been for nothing?

"You aren't?"

Georgiana sat down next to me on my bed and took my hand.

"While I advise you to always exercise moderation of speech, Kitty, that was an argument. And I understand why you reacted the way that you did. I suspect that you admire Tepree, Miyoshi, and Gloriana, don't you? And now you are becoming intrigued with this new woman in our midst, Senorita Benelli."

"Well, I confess that I am. I am intrigued by them. How could I not be? They seem filled with new horizons. And they—well, they are stronger than I am. You know that I am not the jealous sort and am never afraid to admire better women than myself."

"I know. And you never feel inadequate in their presence, which makes you worthy of being around them. But Emma is not raised to admire what these women are like, and she was offensive toward them. I think that hurt your feelings and your respect for these women."

"It did."

"And...quite frankly, while I love Emma, maybe she did need to hear someone speak like such to her."

I became more alert when Georgiana supported my actions, immediately feeling more comfortable with her returning to being my ally.

"Thank you, Georgie. But I think it is more than that. I think her perspective on womanhood is so much akin to the maxims of the rest of the world: that there is only one definition of what a woman is. I cannot agree to that."

"It is more than that," Georgiana elaborated. "Kitty, I am about to say something that will be trying to you. Try not to be too angry."

"I will try. But I make no promises."

"The more that I consider the matter, I think that Emma does not treat you correctly and does not do you proper justice."

"She calls me wild, doesn't she?" I inferred.

Georgiana looked surprised, but not at my declaration. She was surprised that I was already aware of it.

"You know?"

"Yes," I assented, "I do know."

"At first, I attributed your differences to the fact that you both are two entirely different ladies, and that Emma was raised to be so refined, and you were raised to fend for yourself, sometimes. But after you returned from helping me by talking with Mr. Blake, she spoke about you in a very jealous manner."

What? Oh, surely, she would not think that... but when a person is in love, they can be so terribly foolish.

"She thinks that I am now setting my cap at Mr. Blake?" I asked, aggravated.

"Yes, and she began to voice her opinion of you in a more vocal way. I corrected her, of course, but I think she deserved what you said to her. And, in part, I think she knows that she deserved it. Emma is not without feeling. She is merely young and has had less dealings with the world than us. She prides herself on her sense but still acts off her sensibilities."

"I am angry with her. I cannot help it."

"I know that you cannot, because maybe you have every right to be angry. Do not exact any revenge on her, because I think that Emma has already received her comeuppance. She let her jealousies get the better of her, and it rendered her looking ugly in her company. You chastised her, the rest of us understood, and now she has to spend her time knowing that we all think a little less of her."

"You all do not despise me at all, then?"

"No, we do not."

Smiling, I grabbed hands with her.

"And I spent the whole day avoiding you all." I laughed. "Now I feel like such a dunce."

"Yes, I had a feeling that is what you were doing. Well, it was all for nothing. We actually thought you gave Emma a dose of reality that she now must administer to her education."

"Well, it was not all for nothing, I think. I learned how moccasins are made."

"You did?"

"Yes, and about how a man can become a Brave. It would frighten you out of your wits. I loved hearing it."

We got dressed for dinner, and I had a spring in my step, comforted at the prospect that I still had my friend. I still was not alone.

The dinner party in Master Archer's cabin proved to be very easy to experience. Since Archer was the sort of man who believed in a host's duty to start a conversation, he began it in the right way.

My entire company was there, along with Tepree on his right side, next to her was Senorita Benelli, then the Hernandez brothers were next to her.

The way that he arranged for us to sit was me on his left side, and Enara next to me, and the rest of my company filed along as they wished. I preferred this because I wanted to be near Archer. His company was warm, and it rubbed off on anyone near him.

As the food was brought out, I voiced how lovely it all looked.

"Well done," I said to Jesus and Gloriana, touching her arm. "The food looks heavenly."

"Thank you, and it is because it is," Jesus responded.

Gloriana tapped my shoulder, consolingly.

"You poor English girls...there is no one to cook anything proper for you. No wonder you are always so thin."

"I thought I was plump."

Jesus and Gloriana took one look at each other, laughed, and then left.

I rubbed my face, hiding the blush in my cheeks.

"Do not be offended," Archer said, chuckling. "When they talk like that, it only means that they are comfortable around you."

"I know. I just always thought I was properly plump."

Everyone at the table laughed, except for Emma Watson, who merely looked a little flushed.

"Do not get too disappointed, Kitty," Enara said, "when it comes to different cultures, 'plump' means different things."

"It does," Manuel Hernandez said. "Beauty is subjective, pending from culture to culture. We Spanish men find your figure to be quite plump enough for our tastes."

"Sir!" Arthur stated, reprimanding him. "That's my cousin you are speaking to."

"Oh," Manuel rushed out, "forgive me. I spoke very wrongly. And I do apologize."

Unable to suppress his laughter anymore, Archer laughed again, and this time, Tepree and Senorita Benelli joined in.

"No matter what," Archer said, "we boys shall always be boys, I daresay."

"True," Mr. Blake said, eyeing Georgiana. "Very true. There will always be a little savage wantonness in us, try as we might to expel it from our characters."

"But we cannot," Arthur said, "which is why marriage is such a wonderful sacrament. It satisfies our warmer sides, and places it properly in the realm of sanctity."

"Pretty words, sir," Archer said, "now I must ask, how did you find your Australian beauty?"

"By being a sailor who had no desire to remain in one village," Arthur said.

"And what of you, Mrs. Philips," Tepree said, "what part of New South Wales are you from, and helped you find Mr. Philips?"

"Ah, I do love retelling this story," Enara said. "I am from Sydney, Britain's initial penal colony. My family are descendants of Matthew Flinders. He was one of the explorers who traveled along the Australian coasts in open whaleboats. In 1802, Flinders charted the entire south coast of the continent from Cape Leeuwin to Bass Strait. The next year, he continued his exploration up the east coast and round the northeast tip of the continent into the Gulf of Carpentaria."

"Oh, really?" Senorita Benelli asked, astounded. "You're descended from one of the cartographers who explored and charted New South Wales?"

"Yes. Flinders was my uncle."

"Well now," Captain Archer remarked, "goodness me!"

"Flinders was really your uncle?" Tepree responded. "This is quite a remarkable thing. To be eating with the niece of the navigator who explored New South Wales alongside the likes of George Bass."

I sat there, amazed that their reaction was similar to ours when Enara first visited Hertfordshire. There will always be something remarkable for when history and experiences repeat themselves.

"It's one of Flinders associates who has arranged for me to come to Australia," Senorita Benelli said.

"Truly?" Enara asked.

"Yes, it is. Arrangements were made with the Italian government that they might consider an expedition to Sydney. This way they could get firsthand accounts of the wildlife and if Italian explorers might take an interest there. I was sent by an agency to learn as much as I could about the terrain and animal life, so that I could send more detailed reports. When down there, I will be met with a set of brothers and father named Llullian. They are locals to the area and are from some of the Aborigine tribes."

"How did you find a way to be given that chance?" I asked. "I never thought that we would even be considered for such a mission. How did you achieve it, despite all obstacles that would have been in your way."

"And you are right," Benelli responded, placing a loose strand of her hair back behind her ear. "My good fortune is connected to my father. Senor Benelli made our family famous through his political connections and trade that he established between Holland and Italy. This proved very good for the Benellis and the Italian infrastructure. The trade provided many opportunities for our country, and it raised my father to a level of distinction. When he became powerful, we were respectable through association. If it were not for him, I never would have been given the power to make my own life. And sadly, that is always what it results in. Having money, power, and a room of one's own. Those are the three main ingredients to being able to order one's life."

"But you are a huntress," Emma Watson said, having spoken for the first time since we all had sat down. Her sudden utterance immediately made me sit up, alert. What was she about to say? Would it be censorious and prejudiced? And Emma was not unobservant herself. As she spoke that last sentence, she saw me look directly at her. In my eye was a quick rush to disagree with her about any negative comment that she would give to Benelli. Therefore, we both were standing at attention.

"Yes, I am," Benelli responded, evenly. "I specialize in smaller and larger game, such as the Eurasian lynx, the Italian wolf, the Marsican brown bear, Pyrenean chamois, Alpine ibex, common genet, the Sardinian long-eared bat, fallow deer, and the crested porcupine."

"You've hunted those?" Georgiana asked.

"Yes, I have. I also am trained as a fisherwoman. I spent some time whaling, until I found it to be a cruel sort of practice."

"Cruel?"

"When you hunt on land, you do it for preservation and so not to overwhelm the terrain with too much wildlife. That is the side effect of not having adequate hunters in an area. You learn of that tendency called overpopulation. Each creature, like us humans, is vital to maintaining balance in the circle of things. But when we hunt whales, it leads to imbalance in the ocean, and also, we kill them for the oil that we gain from them, mostly. There are other means of achieving such oil."

"But the oil helps make the world run," Mr. Blake responded, "and can it be argued that if we do not hunt them, could they overpopulate the ocean?"

"I respect your viewpoint, Mr. Blake," Benelli replied, "but on this point, we will always be in disagreement."

"As long as we peacefully disagree, that is all that matters."

"Yes, it does."

"Now, I confess that I cannot give into any side of this discussion," Arthur said, "for whenever people start discussing oil, people say that I ought to care, but I am ignorant, and they say that I am ignorant, and then there's an end on it!"

We all laughed.

~

After our laughter died down, I saw that Emma was about to open her mouth to speak again.

Apprehensively, I gave her a sharp look. I could not tell if she perceived it, or wholly ignored it, but she continued, nevertheless.

"If I might ask," Emma Watson continued, "how did you become a huntress, Miss Benelli? Usually, we ladies are not so."

"We are not so, due to a combination of our nature and of how we are nurtured," Benelli responded. "We are born naturally physically weaker than men, a fact that I do not fear to admit, as well as being the gender who reproduces. That gives the implication that we naturally are not as adept of mighty deeds, and also that our natural and obvious role is to raise a child. The latter does make a great deal of sense, because being motherly is as natural to many of us ladies as breathing.

"But with my father, it was the reverse. He had fathered a few sons, and none of them survived longer than five years old. Only my sisters and I were the ones who remained. He could have railed against fate and life for not giving him an heir, as many patriarchs have been known to do. But he did not. He accepted that he had three daughters, and so one of us ought to take on the role of the son. Since I showed the most obsessive of being most like him, he chose me. Also, ever since I was a little girl, I gave all the displays of never wishing to be a mother."

"You don't?" Emma asked.

"No, I do not. And that has continued, which is the chief reason why I am able to achieve all that I do. A mother's duty is to raise her children, to the best of her ability. I lack the selflessness to do that, and it was best that I learned that at a young age, rather than becoming a mother and learning too late. So, father saw that I was the best to learn all that he knew.

"He made certain that there was always a lady around us to teach us the refinements of being a proper woman, and I was given a good education, but he taught me everything he knew. He taught me how to shoot, be it from pistol or musket. He also taught me how to hunt and skin one's prey, to prepare pheasant, and how to fish. Also, I spent much of my education learning about every animal, who they are the predator of, and the prey to. It was him who taught me the balance of nature and how it ought to be maintained. And he took me on expeditions. That is why I was able to maintain my position in society; he paved the way for me."

"And, I wonder," I said, "that you never experienced opposition in your pursuits."

Senorita Benelli grinned, but it was a sad sort of smile.

"Oh, I have, I can assure you. When my father was alive, he braved most of the conflicts that I faced and would have no argument against me. But when he died, I lost much support and had to spend years proving myself. I faced many a harsh word, and risked defamation against my character, out of other's attempts to destroy my chances. It becomes a matter of endurance, courage, and braving the odds that are inevitably stacked against you."

"But you continued on," Tepree persisted, "as many of us find ourselves doing. The trick is to have a champion on your side." Tepree looked at Archer, who smiled.

"Yes," Benelli continued, "and when my father died, I lost my chief champion. So, I had to become my own and then find one who would assist me. But my father warned me that such a day would come when I lost him. I was prepared. Besides, sometimes, nothing in life that is worth having, ought to come easily. Or we would all be spoiled. Sometimes, overcoming the obstacle displays a great deal of character. Maybe I needed the struggle because it meant that I had proved myself. It's a difficult path, but that's the road that some of us must walk down."

I looked at Tepree, who did not respond, but I knew what she was thinking. If it were not for Archer believing in her, she would have to be constantly fighting for her place in the world.

Out of the side of my eye, I felt as if I was being observed. Turning, I saw that Emma Watson was looking at me.

For a brief few seconds, our eyes locked gazes. It has been said that the eyes are like windows to the soul. Well, Emma had learned to be a proper lady, in every way. The tendency of the lady was to not give oneself away, or to show any emotion other than pleasantness and informative. Sadly, I did not know what her expression meant.

Although, what I could determine was that her look was not one of resentment or judgment. She was not angry. Faith, I wish I knew what she meant. But I was not prepared to ask her.

~

The dinner came to an end, and in my eyes, it was a great success. Senorita Benelli was a very interesting woman, and Archer told us about his time in Canada, and the women who were similar to Benelli and the ladies who served under him on his ship. Between them both, we were all very entertained.

Sadly, while I was very interested in everything that they had said, I was filled with a sense of inadequacy. It was a common and familiar pastime, so I was not foreign to the sensation. But this time, the inspiration behind it was different.

When we all separated, we thanked Archer for giving us a delightful evening.

As we left, I had a thought.

"Arthur," I whispered to my cousin.

"What is it, Kitty?" Arthur asked, his voice equally as low.

"Have there been any rumors going around that I am wild?"

Arthur may have looked a little uneasy, but there was no lie in his eyes.

"Yes, there has. But don't worry. No one thinks you to be a loose girl, and those who do, are miserable sots and you do not need to care for them, and they are not worth a jot."

"You think so?"

"I know so. Never fear, Kitty. You will not suffer from slander on this ship. Depend upon it."

I went back to our room, and Georgiana was as talkative as I was about the evening as we undressed to get into our nightgowns.

"What did you think of it all?" I asked her.

"I think that I can understand why you admire them so," Georgiana said. "And I think even Emma has been changing her mind about them."

"You think so? Has she said as much to you?"

"No, but she was quiet for most of the dinner. I will talk with her tomorrow when we arrive in Greece. But I truly do believe that she might regret her hasty judgments and that she might be wishing to gain your good opinion."

"I did not think she would care for my good opinion at all. But if she is considering enhancing her perspective of what we ladies are capable of, I encourage it."

As Georgiana helped me out of my stays, I began to undo my hair.

"Georgiana, I felt something."

"What? Did I accidentally stick you, somehow?"

"No, it's not that. I have felt insecure before, under the weight of being inadequate. When growing up, I was always aware that I was insufficient as an accomplished woman, and that I lacked the refinement that was attributed to gentility. But I did not mind it. But now, I feel inadequate all over again. Now I feel insecure of not being like Tepree, Benelli and Miyoshi. In one direction, I was inadequate for not being enough of a lady, and now I feel inadequate for being too much of one, and not revolutionary enough. In other words, in both directions, I do not feel as if I am woman enough."

"I knew it!" Georgiana cried. "I knew that was what you were feeling."

"How did you know of such a thing? I barely realized it myself."

"Believe that I know you as much as yourself, and sometimes more than yourself. Kitty, society has claims on us all. And that society has torn you in every direction that it can. To the point where it has taken you in two directions at once. You will be confused for a time. After all, on the one hand, we have conduct books who are defining a lady's role in society as confining her to the home. And then we hear tales of Joan of Arc, the Amazons, and the likes of Mary Wollstonecraft. I think the world will never know what it wants."

"If that is the case, then the only way that I can discover myself, is to do it of my own accord. And ignore the world altogether."

"That is a frightful possibility," she said as I placed my stays in the chest and then helped her with hers. "And maybe that is the point."

"That we are confused on how to be a lady."

"Maybe. After all, like Benelli said, maybe the struggle is worth it."

"Yes," I said, getting a faraway look in my eye. "Perhaps it is. Poor Emma Watson. Perhaps she is even more confused than I, at this time."

"I think she just might be."

"I am so evil. I like that she is forced to recollect, and maybe even doubt herself."

"I knew that you were going to say that!"

I groaned, in jest.

"Stop knowing me so well!"

Chapter Twenty

HEALING

Returning from Meryton, Mr. Atkins had returned to Mr. Philips with all the paper and ink that was required. Recently, two farmers had a land dispute, and one of them hired Mr. Philips to supply his services. Willing to give Mr. Atkins more experience, Mr. Philips allowed him to lead the investigation and add to his clerk's expertise.

As both men sat in the study, going over the map of the general area and tracing the history of past ownership of the properties, Mr. Philips looked at Atkins.

"How does Mary do?"

"She is a great deal better today than yesterday," Mr. Atkins said. "Whatever her father said, it did help the matter. I confess that I never knew that Mr. Bennet possessed how to be so congenial, as opposed to being more inclined to his caustic wit."

"My brother-in-law has always possessed the ability to be a good father to all his daughters. He merely never wished to exert himself."

Mr. Atkins gave his Master a shrewd look.

"You've always known the man that he is, haven't you, sir?"

"Yes. And I was very forward in my opinions. Perhaps that is what ruined our friendship."

"Your friendship? Were you and Mr. Bennet good friends at one time?"

"Oh, yes. We were, and always in each other's confidence. Time wore our friendship down, and we both didn't agree on many things. First, he did not support my belief that ladies should be given the precise education as ourselves, and that he ought to have hired a governess. He called his daughters silly, but he never gave his daughters a chance to ever learn any serious subject matter. He believed that I was wrong to let Arthur be a sailor, since he was my only son. Also, I had a son, and he did not. That added to the existent strain between us."

"What was Mr. Bennet like when you both were young?"

"As determined to be witty as he is now, but more open to jollity. He wanted to enjoy life. We both did. I do not know what happened there."

"He stopped loving his wife and you didn't."

Mr. Philips looked at Mr. Atkins, pointedly. Mistaking this for censure, Atkins apologized.

"No," Mr. Philips said, "no need to fret. You are right. I think that is the chief difference. He no longer loves his wife, and I still do. That probably made all the difference in the world. I always managed to make time for Mrs. Philips and me to do things that always helped us maintain a level of intimacy."

"That is what I want," Mr. Atkins pressed. "Mr. Bennet helped Mary's spirits rise, but I want to solidify it and know that I helped her."

"You both need more time alone."

"Yes, we do."

Coming to a decision, Mr. Philips sat down at his desk, putting his spectacles on.

"Tonight, we all arranged to dine at the Lucases. You and Mary will not come with us."

"We won't?"

"No. If you go to the dinner party, you will be too exhausted to want to spend time with each other. And you both need more time with the house to yourselves. When we are all out, comfort her. Knowing that you both are still each other's chief entertainment is vital to this part of your marriage."

"You would do that for us?"

"I would do anything for my nieces' happiness."

Mr. Atkins smiled.

"Thank you, Mr. Philips. You are the best employer that a man can have. And uncle."

"I know."

When night fell, Aunt and Uncle Philips left for Lucas Lodge, and Mary and Mr. Atkins watched them depart.

"Why did they want to leave us behind?" Mary asked, now that they were alone.

Mr. Atkins looked at her fondly, and his eyes were soft as he raised his hand. Even without him saying anything, she understood that gesture.

With great affection, she placed her hand in his as he closed his fingers around her palm. Raising her hand to his lips, he kissed it.

In his eyes was everything, as they were overcome with passions and proof of his love.

"You know why," he professed, gently.

"Yes," Mary said, her voice low as she fell under the very spell that he always seemed to cast on her. "Yes, I do, don't I?"

Slowly, he led her up the stairs and they walked to the bedroom.

When they stood at the door, Mr. Atkins turned back to Mary, his expression sensuous as his intention bore into her mind.

"Do you remember the first time that you and I first came into this room, as man and wife?" he asked.

"I do. Do you know what?"

"What, Mrs. Atkins?"

"With that look on your face, and that fire in your eyes, you look the same as the first day that I realized how much I was in love with you."

"Now I am going to remind you."

"Remind me of what?"

"That whenever we go into this room, it should always remind us of the first time that we became one. As I do."

Slowly he opened the door, and they entered the room that had been theirs for months.

And yet, the spell had been cast, and Mary felt as if she had walked into it for the very first time.

Behind her, Atkins closed the door and he faced Mary again.

"Mary?"

"Yes?"

"I am going to kiss you now."

"I know."

Slowly, Mr. Atkins kissed her, as she wrapped her arms around his back, to hold him tighter toward herself.

While doing so, Atkins began to undo the pins in her hair so that her locks would fall free, along her shoulders.

When their lips separated, he went behind her and raised his hands to the lacings and ties on her gown.

"And now I am going to undress you," he uttered, his voice romantic and masculine.

"And I will never forgive you if you do not," Mary said, her tone filled with wantonness.

"Very well. I go to it."

Atkins's hands were nimble as they undid all the fastenings to the back of her gown as it fell to the floor, next he undid her stays, removed all outer garments, and Mary remained there, with nothing but her stockings that were tied at her knees.

"Mary," he said, but he was prevented from speaking any more, for Mary had turned around and kissed him passionately.

"My husband," she uttered in between kisses.

"Yes! That I am."

Pulling him more toward herself, they collapsed on the bed together, while he removed his jacket.

Continuing to undo his waistcoat, Mr. Atkins kissed Mary along her neck. Afterwards he threw it on the floor, he pressed her legs around his waist, grabbing her bottom in his hands and pressing it tightly, while still kissing down her neck and along her chest. Running his lips along her breasts, Mary cried out when he repeated their wedding night.

Every action that he performed, it had been from their first night together as man and wife. Due to her recovery and condition, he was gentler, however. Flattered she was, so very much, by him remembering it all, that Mary moaned out, not caring for how she sounded as she bit his ear affectionately.

Further and further, he lowered his lips along her breasts, down her stomach and then he kissed around her thighs as he ran his fingers in between them.

Rolling her over, Mr. Atkins kissed down the spine of her neck, and then he kissed further along her backside, then he rubbed even further into her as he pushed his mouth further along her bottom.

"Tell me that you love me," Mary cried.

"I love you," he cried. "And now all will know it."

Rolling her back over, he unfastened his breeches, Mary held him against her with her thighs around his waist as he drove himself into her.

While doing so, they looked deeply into each other's eyes, feeling the power of becoming one.

"I love you," Mary said to Mr. Atkins. "I love you."

"And I will always be here," he promised. "I will!"

With one final thrust, his body tensed up, their figures were united at the apex and Mary felt completion as they fell into each other.

At last, exhausted, they held one another, under the bedsheets.

"On our wedding night," Mary said, "we performed this activity three times."

"I know," Mr. Atkins said, his eyes closed. "Give a man time to rest. After all, I am not a machine."

"I know. I just..."

"Yes?"

"I never tired of having you in this way. Dearest, can we do this every night?"

Mr. Atkins opened his eyes and looked at her, wholly interested.

"You want to?"

"Yes."

He laughed.

"Why do you laugh, sir?" she asked, tickling his chest.

"Because I always want to do this with you. But I thought that by doing it nightly, I would exhaust you or be too wanton for your piety."

"No," Mary stressed, "do not ever think that. I love this activity and I always am open to you when you wish it."

Amazed, he kissed her passionately.

"Mary, that is a promise that I willingly make."

Resting his body against hers, Mary closed her arms around him, protectively.

"I am sorry if I frightened you for these last few days. I was like a flake of snow, wasn't I? Fragile."

"I understood. And I want you to know this, Mary, for it is very important. I will always love you and I will always be here for you. As long as you will always find your way back to me."

Mary ran her hands through his hair.

"Of course, I will," she stressed. "My love, there will never be a day that I abandon you from my affection. I just lost my way for a little."

"We will have another child, I am sure of it. I don't want to lose you."

"And you never will again. This first time was the hardest, for it being the first. From now on, I will be stronger. And I will remain fast to you and forever bound. By God, you and I will never be anything else, but one. To this, I vow."

"I know. That is all that I needed to hear."

Raising himself up, he kissed her as he ran his hands deep in between her thighs again, rekindling her desire.

"And I am ready again."

"Thank goodness."

And once more, they molded into one, wholly unaware that, in the North, the eldest Bennet sister was undergoing the same crisis but needed more time to reach the place that they had.

And another sister was across the ocean, about to be tossed into another predicament that she did not foresee.

Chapter Twenty-One

TENSION UNTYING

Rhodes!

The Lilia had made berth in Rhodes, Greece, and one look at it was all the confirmation that I needed to know that I had arrived at one of the most beautiful places in the world.

Rhodes was a Greek Island that, from what I saw was entirely encased by castle fortifications. There were a few entrances, but it was obvious that in the historic times of kings, colonization, and conquest, Rhodes would have proven to be an almost impossible island to conquer. When going ashore, seeing it was more confirmation on me being correct.

Rhodes was an Island that was bustling with life and beautiful people. Despite the weather still being quite cold, it was warmer than being on the open seas, and the people had a congenial air about them.

When we arrived, we literally landed amidst the main road and marketplace.

"Greece," Myoshi said to me as she prepared to disembark with Merriweather, "the safest place in the world for our crew to cross over to."

"You all are safe here?" I asked.

"There is intolerance everywhere, but they are less harsh of that here, than other places. Especially for the men. No one could capture a sailor here without there being many witnesses."

"And then there is the other matter," Trip said as he prepared to go ashore as well, alongside Reedus.

"What other matter?"

Reedus grinned.

"Women, women, women."

"Yes," Trip said, grinning, "and we'll always be novelties."

"Happy hunting," I replied, "but break no hearts!"

"There will not be sufficient enough time for that," Trip said, tipping his hat to me. "Tread lightly. We are not the only novelties here."

As our company went into the main square, we all separated into groups. The chief surprise was how Mr. Blake remained alongside me as we walked and offered me his arm.

This surprised me, and I let him know this as we walked along...

"...especially since my outburst towards Miss Watson must confirm the rumors of my vulgarity," I said, "and that I did not follow your definition of a traditional lady."

"Still will force me to confront that?"

"Like I said," I laughed. "Always. Now, answer my question. Why do you seek me out especially? Is it because I am Georgiana's friend?"

"Partly. I suppose that is a great part of it. I know what I say might be conveyed to her." He looked ahead and watched as Georgiana and Emma were walking ahead of us. Georgiana was wearing a lovely red bonnet that matched her red pelisse, and it was very flattering a look, which set her off from the others around her. "She looks beautiful."

"It's because she is."

"Yes," he sighed. "She is. So much so that it hurts a man."

"I can see what you are feeling."

"I'm certain that you can. After all, you and I are so much alike."

"And that is the other reason for which you chose me as your walking companion?" I guessed.

"Yes, it is. Still dwelling upon misery loving company, I am still there. Also, your outburst to Miss Watson was not the actions of a woman who did not care at all. On the contrary, I think it is because you cared very much about something."

"I did, and I do."

"That alone makes your actions pardonable. And there is something to be said for youthful passion. To care so much about something that you would fight for it. You possess spirit, and I was like you once, when I was your age."

"You are not very much older than me, are you? Or is that a direct question?"

"I am thirty."

"Oh. I never would have guessed it."

Mr. Blake smiled.

"Thank you. But despite how the world would have it, when you reach my age, you discover that thirty is still quite young. You do not feel very different than you did when you were in your early twenties. You are only a little wiser. And in my case, not so much, sadly."

"You cannot help that you fell in love with the woman that you did."

"True. It hit me like a thunderbolt, and age and wisdom could not be my defense. Nothing ever can when we fall in love, can it?"

"No, it cannot. All that we can do is feel as we do."

"And believe that everything shall work out, in the end."

"But there is one matter that I still request satisfaction about."

"I am at your command," he said as we looked ahead and admired everything around us.

"Why did you wish to speak to me when you could talk to Miss Watson? After all, you have more of an equal footing with her, you are better acquainted, further in each other's confidence and her company is more to your liking. After all, she is very refined."

"A good set of questions."

"Are you afraid to give me the answers?"

"Not at all. First, I am widening my ideas of what proper company is. Second, yes, Miss Watson and I are better acquainted, but as you said, she is refined, and there are certain things that a gentleman cannot talk about when it comes to ladies such as Miss Watson. And thirdly, I know..."

"Know what?"

His eyes darkened as he looked at me, and I perceived. Did he really know?

"I know that Miss Watson favors my company, but not in a disinterested fashion," Mr. Blake pointed out. "I have reason to believe that she prefers me... romantically."

I looked ahead and saw Emma and Georgiana talking. At first, for her sake, I was determined to deny it, but when she turned and looked at Mr. Blake and I, her eyes narrowed on my arm linked in his.

Brilliant!

For as she looked at us, her eyes betrayed her again and there was a subtle pain in them. I could deny Mr. Blake's observations all that I wished, but Miss Watson's expression only proved him right.

"Well," I said, "the truth is in the eyes. I wanted to help her on, but I was very unlucky there. I could not deny what you said, because what would be the point?"

"Precisely. There are some things that cannot be unseen."

"How long have you known that she favors you?"

"At first, I merely rendered her preferring my company as it being the fact that we were on a ship and there were few people that one can converse with. But after I began to take more notice of Georgiana, I noticed Miss Watson's changed behavior to me. It was not such as yourself, where your indifference toward me only made you braver in my presence. However, with her, every time that I see her, there is a pain in her expression. She looks at me as if I hurt her."

"And that was when you knew."

"Yes. Our emotions, very often, have no choice but to betray us."

"Something you and I know all too well," I commented.

"Yes."

"So," I said, "that is why you speak to me. Because you cannot talk to Emma. Your company must be irksome to her, and so you are sparing her."

"Yes. After all, I proposed to her friend," he extoled, still watching Georgiana most acutely, "and I still am drawn to that quarter."

"This is a tangle, isn't it?"

"Yes, it is. I've caused all sorts of trouble, and, to my surprise, you are the only peace that I can find through all this."

I looked up at him, amused.

"Never before would I have known that feeling nothing would make someone at ease around me."

"Oh, it's more common a tendency of life than one would know. Those who feel so much lose so much. And those who coast from day to day, wholly indifferent, win much."

"If that is true, Mr. Blake, then that is not fair."

"No, it is not. My feelings led to me losing Miss Darcy's company and then losing Miss Watson's."

"And now you have only me. Indifferent little me."

"Yes. This is a strange sort of friendship, isn't it?"

"Believe me," I said, rolling my eyes, "I've experienced stranger ones."

Mr. Blake smiled.

"I think I am beginning to like your open temper."

"Oh. Well, that is nice."

He raised an eyebrow.

"You are still going to remind me of how I called you wild, won't you?"

"I cannot help it, Mr. Blake. Perhaps I take amusement in making you squirm."

We looked at each other and grinned.

Well, this was a strange turn of events.

We had no choice but to return to the ship. It was hard, because I could have spent a whole week walking the whole of Rhodes, and sad that I could not.

"If you ever get the chance to return to this part of the world," Mr. Blake said, "you must also go to Turkey. It is a worthy place."

"When I earn my wealth, I just might," I said.

"Earn it?"

"Poor choice of words," I said, confused with myself. "I do not know why I said that. Oh well, we all have the right to forget ourselves, from time to time. And there is something that I must ask you."

"Yes?"

"Could you see yourself falling in love with Miss Watson?"

He sighed.

"It would make sense for me to fall in love with her. She is beautiful, is going to live where I am about to, and is agreeable."

"And yet, she means nothing to you."

"And I don't know why."

"Yes," I sighed. "I am so sorry for you."

"Thank you. I will need some sympathy because we still have a voyage ahead."

We returned to the ship.

Over the next part of the voyage, to Egypt, it remained this way. Mr. Blake often sought out my company, and we spent a great amount of time in discussion.

I was afraid that this arrangement would only make Emma Watson return to finding the very sight of me unbearable—again. Although it was not so. True, she did not speak to me at all, for the most part, yet she no longer eyed me with disdain.

Between Rhodes and Alexandria, she and I managed to ignore each other, peacefully, until we found ourselves walking down the hallway below deck, in opposite directions.

Having no choice but to walk past each other, we braved the confrontation.

I nodded to her as I passed her by.

She did the same.

As we crossed paths, with me walking to the deck and her to her room, I heard her stop her footsteps.

"Miss Bennet?" she called me, over my shoulder.

I was a little overwhelmed internally. Breathing in, I gathered my social courage—social courage is truly the most difficult thing to ever muster up—and faced the lady whose company gave me so much pain.

"Yes, Miss Watson?"

"Georgiana and I have been talking."

Pause.

"Yes," I said, "and?"

"And she has done me a great favor, as is always her way. I am aware of her predicament, and she has told me that you speak with Mr. Blake, for the sake of relieving her from his company. And he from hers. That is what you are doing, are you not?"

Finally, she knew! No longer would I have to suffer miscommunication and misunderstandings, as I had done before. I was utterly sick of suffering under those two things, for it happened to me a great deal too much.

"Yes," I said, "that is my intention."

"Ah."

Standing squarely at her, I folded my hands in front of me.

"I made a promise to Mr. Darcy and my sisters. I said that no matter what, I would protect Georgie. No matter what others think of me, I will always do just that, even at the expense of my reputation."

"Well, as you did it, you protected me as well. Even if you did not mean such."

"Is this helping you?"

"Yes, it is. I cannot stand looking at Mr. Blake just now."

"I understand."

"Well, that is all that I wished to say."

"I hope that you can recover from this."

Emma did not respond to that. Perhaps it was because it was too early for her to do so. Instead, she nodded at me, and walked back to her room, shutting the door behind her.

She and I still were not friends. But we despised each other less. That was saying something, at least. Yet one thing was certain. She and I would never press our company on the other. That's all that we could do.

Chapter Twenty-Two

NIGHT TERRORS

A couple days later, we arrived in Alexandra, Egypt, which would be the last place that we would make berth, before we would cross the vast ocean and our final destination would be Sydney, New South Wales.

Of all the places that we went to, Alexandra was my least favorite. The city itself was not at fault for it, but merely the time. Due to arrangements, we only had an hour to walk along the shore and had rarely any time to see anything.

All we had time to do was post some more letters, and see the people, who had a very compelling look to them. The main thing of interest was that White Wolf and Elias Durchdenwald joined our company and White Wolf turned more heads than we did. After all, Egyptians have been seeing Europeans for centuries, but not Indians from our American Colonies. Since White Wolf was tall, impressive, had long black hair that he had two feathers in, and he wore some of his tribal necklaces, he was the ultimate novelty.

Indeed, some Egyptian children even ran up to him and tugged at his hands. Laughing, he had to bend down and give them the feathers from his hair to appease them. I suppose I was not surprised. From what I had seen of Egyptian art, White Wolf would look like a deity.

And, from time to time, we all need to feel beautiful, now, don't we?

Our time came and went without us being able to see anything remarkable at all, which was a pity.

It was not until we returned to the ship and sailed away that we were able to see the vastness of the city and how lovely it looked.

"To be so close to something remarkable," I said to Elias Durchdenwald, "while also being so far away."

"Yes," Elias said, "antagonizing, isn't it?"

"That title feels as if it is the story of my life."

Nearby, Arthur approached me and pinched my cheek.

"Chin up, Kitty. You are a Bennet girl. All you girls do is find your footing."

~

By the end of the evening, we were now in the Indian ocean, and there was no land to be seen.

This was the beginning of us traveling a great distance, and at the beginning of seeing no land for weeks. While in Alexandra, Captain Archer had made certain to purchase enough food for us to continue our journey with ease.

But now that we were on the open water, it felt as if our journey had reached a new level of realness.

And all the excitement that came along with it began to prick away at my nerves.

That night, I did my best to sleep, but I found myself unable to. Everything about the experience seemed to keep my eyes open and my emotions alert.

I felt as if I must get up and move about, or I might burst.

Quietly in the dark, I stood up, found my shoes, slipped into them, reached out and put on my cloak. I tiptoed out of our cabin, making sure that I did not wake Georgiana.

When I entered the hall, I silently moved along until I got to the stairs that would take me above deck. I knew that I did not need to worry about being in danger, because there was the night crew, who had to see to the sailing duties in the darkness. Quietly, I crept up the stairs and watched as the crew was cleaning down the deck and lowering the sails.

As I emerged, some of the sailors looked at me, aware that I was not where I ought to be.

"Miss Bennet?" I turned and Merriweather came up to me, clearly having distributed a shift change.

"Mr. Merriweather," I said, "sorry, I just... well, I could not sleep, and I was curious to see what the sea looked like at night."

"You come at a thoroughly unromantic time. At night, there is maintenance."

"Is that Miss Bennet?" Captain Archer called from his spot.

"Yes, it is, sir."

"Am I in trouble?" I asked Merriweather.

"I do not think so. Go to the captain. Tepree and Trip are sleeping. He might want your company."

Eager to stay atop deck, I crossed along, moving around the sailors, and joined the captain.

"You are awake?" he asked, wearing his overcoat.

"And so are you," I said, "doesn't a ship's Master need rest?"

Archer smiled.

"He does. But for some reason, I found that I could not sleep. Are we similar in that way?"

"Yes, we are. I could not sleep either."

He rested his arm on the railing, looking at me casually.

"Your restlessness is my benefit. I would like some female company."

"Then I shall try and suffice."

"What keeps you awake? Or is it general wakefulness?"

"I should like to think so. I suppose that I am a little excited. We are now at the meat of the journey, and the beginning of where my exploration might be." I breathed out heavily. "I ought to be looking back, worried of home. After all, a great deal of my heart is still there. And yet, I am happy to leave my heart behind."

"Why?"

"Why what?"

"Why would you want to leave your heart behind?"

"Because it belongs there. And it is best that it remains there, safe and sound."

I shivered.

"You are cold." he noted. "Allow me to be a gentleman."

"I do not fear a gentleman being so," I said, as he removed a heavy blanket from a chest and wrapped it around me tightly.

While he did so, he looked firmly at me. In the moonlight, the blue of his eyes was even more augmented, and his gray hair only appeared to be black.

"You are thinking of the two men you loved back in England," he noted.

"Yes."

"And that's why you do not want to bring your heart here with you."

"Precisely. Best to let it remain there. You know that I am still in love?"

"Because of how I just touched you. I placed my hands on your arms, and you did not call me impertinent. That could mean only one thing: you were in love before, and you let the man take certain liberties."

Sighing, I looked down at the wood below us.

"Forgive me, I spoke too much, didn't I?" he realized.

"Perhaps, you did. But to set any rumors of me at rest, I will clarify. Truly, it is best to get on with the truth. I am still a maid. But yes, I have already had my first kiss. And my second, and third.

I shall be even more honest than before. I could not control myself."

"I have been in your same predicament on many an occasion. Come, let me show you some constellations."

He led me to the railing, and he placed his arms around me, to help me get warmer.

"You are being too bold, sir," I said, "but I am not offended by it."

"I am trying to keep you warm."

"I know. And thank you."

Looking up, we saw the stars in the night sky.

"Beautiful!" I remarked.

"Yes. Even though the night is lovely wherever you go, there is nothing more incredible than looking up at it, on a ship, where the dark waters are below. It only augments its beauty more. Here a man or woman can look up, question their place in the cosmos, and feel as if we all matter."

"You are right."

I was amazed, for the inner parts of my secret soul did cry out that observation. Here, under the night sky, with the universe only there as our judge and overseer, I felt an electricity surge through me. In truth, I was more awake than ever, as the stars reflected in our eyes and danced across our subconscious, waking up the part of ourselves that refuses to submit to any particular mode of being. We feel as if our spirits can go up and out, anywhere and everywhere, in touch with every aspect of the heavens above, and the inferno that is below.

To fear neither wrath, nor ruin, no prying eyes of society and its limitations. Raphael's 'The School of Athens' contained its own veracity, for what are geniuses but like Plato as he points to the heavens above, and we flawed mortals are like that of Aristotle, and are always pointing to the world around us, concerned with the petty and the very human. And I was human, but I dared to look up at the stars and find my own genius in them.

"I feel that way now," I submitted. "How provocative you are, for knowing what I would usually conceal."

"I do not believe that you are upset with me. You lie, Miss Bennet."

"Of course, I lie. I like your perceptive nature. However, one deception deserves another."

"How have I deceived you?"

"You lied to me when you told me about your past loves. I understand, because the last woman you loved is closer to your present life, and you did not wish to give yourself away."

"You have been reading my past?"

"Yes. You never told me that you were in love with Tepree."

When I looked at him, he did not look away but instead directed his eyes firmly at my face. I suppose that I should not have been surprised. After all, he was a brave man, so he would be brave enough to face me.

"Or am I wrong?" I asked.

"No," he acknowledged, "you are not wrong. I must ask, how did you know?"

"You protect everyone in your charge. I suppose that it is your habit."

"The product of being a child of Canada and the United States. When being a child of two worlds, you have two identities, and so, it helps you understand many truths and that there is a plurality of life. Many people have a singular sort of mindset. I think I felt that plurality so keenly, that protecting uniqueness is all that I know. And, so, I find the different beautiful."

"And that's what drew you to her, wasn't it? Tepree was different, and the world does not want that. So, you protect that difference. But by the way that you look at each other, I can see that there is more to it than that. Eventually, you fell in love with her."

"I had no choice. You've seen it yourself. She is superior. Like Senorita Benelli and Miyoshi."

"Yes, she is. Is that why you have never told her how you feel? Because she is superior, and it can be intimidating?"

"No, that's not the reason. You know the real truth behind why I never married. Because every great love that I ever had did not work out for me. For one reason or the other. While it is bewitching to have attached yourself to your great love during the most romantic period of your life, not all of us are so fortunate. And I lost the women who chose me and lost another friend during it. With Tepree, I love having her in my life. But I will not whisper sweet nothings into her ear, because I am afraid."

"Afraid? You? I never would have suspected that the Master of the Lilia would fear anything."

"The Master of the Lilia is a man, like any other," he replied, amused, "and we all fear something. The men that you love also have their fears."

"Yes," I said, "I suppose they do. And I do not despise them for it. In fact, I think that their humanness is what renders them even more handsome. And so, I will not despise you. And of Tepree, you chose to never tell her that you love her, for fear of losing her."

"Yes. But I think she prefers it that way. Sometimes, the second that you tell someone that you love them, you lose them. We both do not wish to lose each other, and what we have."

"Do you think that she loves you?"

"Yes. I believe that she does. But due to our lives, we can feel it, but never fully pursue it."

"What's that like? To have a love near you, day in and day out, knowing that you both feel as you do, and yet you are never fully united?"

"Why don't you tell me how you bear it? After all, aren't we the same in that way?"

My mind returned to England, and I thought of Finlay and Fitzwilliam, and our times together as we spoke in drawing rooms. My soul had found its weight again, I felt the pressure of it, and I had to reflect. Were Archer and I the same? And was I looking into my future when I saw him? Was that why I felt a kindred spirit with him, without being wholly aware of it until now? Of course, he had power over his life in the way that I did not, but of our characters—were Archer and I similar all this time?

"Yes," I confessed, "I suppose that we are. Torn between our lives and how they are not in accordance with making a proper match."

"I hope you are more fortunate than I," he said, "and that you are able to not lose much when you choose to care."

I sighed and moved away from him.

"Or am I speaking too much in a way that hurts you?" he asked.

"No," I said, suddenly needing support as I felt feint. I rested my hand on the railing and watched as the water bubbled around the ship. We humans are like an ocean, with so much depth within us, that no one will see. "You speak correctly, and that's what startles me." Turning to the Master, I looked squarely at him. In the dark, his peach skin was illuminated by a lamp that was near him. He stood there, his posture erect, and his figure elegant. "You merely present a frightful reality."

"And what is that?"

"That my fate is already decided, and that I will end in a way that I did not expect. Alone."

"I made you too frightened of what the future has in store for you, didn't I?" he asked. "I suppose that maybe I am just being elliptic because it is nighttime. This is the hour where we men and women can be capable of saying so much nonsense."

"No, it was not nonsense." I moved and stood next to him. "I do believe that you were exchanging stories to find a parallel with another person. A connection if you will. We all do that, so I do not begrudge you. But maybe, I do need to confront that about myself." Then I smiled. "Or maybe I will defeat the odds. After all, if we are alike, then I make my own destiny."

In the moonlight, he smiled and tapped my cheek.

"Once more, you do not fear a man touching you," he observed. "You must have cherished these men very much."

I looked up at the stars again.

"They are a part of me. As Tepree and all the other women you have loved are a part of you."

Archer leaned closer to me.

"Do you regret falling in love with them?" he asked.

I considered this.

"At first, I did," I said, "because I hated favoring two men at one time in my life and being confused over it. But now that I am away, I do not regret it. I suppose that it is because they are so much a part of what has helped me grow."

"Precisely. To the point where it does not matter if you marry them or not. You feel better for knowing them and once having their hearts in your hands."

"Yes."

"Then now you know. That is the way it is with Tepree and all the other women in my life. I am better for knowing them. And with Tepree, I am better when she is here. And so, I hold her, by not having her. You have these men, even though you do not hold them."

"I suppose," I realized, "that I will have to find comfort in that."

"You will. And when you do, life becomes richer."

He took my hand and kissed it.

"Miss Bennet, might I call you beautiful?"

I blushed, looking down in the darkness.

"If you promise to never hurt me, then yes, you can."

Archer smiled.

"You are beautiful."

"Thank you. But why did you tell me that?" This time, I was the one to lean closer to him, pressing my influence on him. "Do not be afraid, sir. After all, you are the master of a ship."

"I just..."

"Yes?"

"I just needed to call a woman beautiful, and for her to thank me."

"Why?"

"Because, even in older age, we still need to feel young every now and again. If I could go back in time and be young again, I would."

"Would you marry one of your great passions?"

"I don't know. But I would have spent more time with them. I suppose I just needed to speak with you like this, because it reminded me of how I used to talk with them."

"You are trying to relive your youth in me, aren't you?"

"Perhaps I am. Or perhaps you have drawn me in, and I do see the women that I love in you."

I was not afraid of this. Nor was I afraid of him. I suppose it was because, like he said, we were similar. We were harmless; just romantic and blindly moving around in the buff, looking for acceptance wherever we could. Therefore, I just stood there, wholly unaffected.

"You would have done things differently," I said, "if you had the chance. I know it."

"Yes," he acknowledged, "perhaps I would have." Slowly, he walked up to me and removed the blanket from my shoulders. As he did so, his eyes remained fixed on mine. "And I think it's time that you went to bed."

"Perhaps it is," I said, staring at him boldly in turn. "But I go on my own terms."

"Your own terms?"

"Yes. Admit that you do prefer my company, and don't be afraid to say it. It will help you."

"How will it help me?"

"You may have not chosen your loves in your youth," I said, "but you still have time. When you are ready, tell Tepree. It's never too late to fall in love again."

I curtsied to him and went to leave.

"Miss Bennet?" he called to me.

"Yes?" I said, in response.

"I lied before. If I was a young man, you might have been one of my great passions."

I gave him a sly smile.

"I had a notion. And the truth shall be your friend, sir. I know that it has helped me on more than one occasion."

"Would you have loved me?"

"I can happily say that there is no way of knowing. Would you have been a rake, or real? But I can also say that you would have been a hero of mine. And I would have placed you as having every chance in the world."

He smiled gently.

"Thank you."

"You're welcome."

I left him and returned to my cabin.

I crept back in and snuck back in my bed. I remained looking upward, and into the darkness.

Reflecting on the conversation with Captain Archer, I wondered why I was not disturbed by it at all. Everything about the conversation was vague and seemed to be aimless. And yet, I felt as if it was a sort of foreshadow and foretelling something that I would have to do eventually. But more importantly, I was not afraid the entire time, nor intimidated by it. I suppose that it was because I knew that I was offering a heartbroken man a moment of peace.

Men such as Archer, Colonel Fitzwilliam and Lieutenant Finlay were meant to be kings in life. But they were not and would never be. However, what they did need was a lady, every now and again, to make them feel as such. Maybe that was the point of me.

Who knows?

~

Boom!

The sudden shouts and commotion roused me from my slumber, and I practically fell out of my bed.

Despite that it was still dark, I saw Georgiana's outline as she also woke up with a start.

There were shouts coming from above, the scurrying of many feet and of people preparing for a battle.

"What is going on?" Georgiana cried.

"I don't know," I said, fretful as I looked above at the ceiling and heard many shouts. Anxious to know what was going on, I jumped up, put a blanket over myself and put my boots back on.

"Stay here!" I ordered her. "I am going to discover what is going on."

"Kitty, no!" Georgiana said, grabbing my hand.

"I must see. I shall return."

Closing the door behind me, I saw many sailors rushing about as us passengers were looking out of their doors, scared.

From the furthest cabin, Senorita Benelli emerged, carrying a musket with her.

"Miss Bennet?" she cried, rushing up the steps. "Stay here!"

Despite her warning, I could not help myself. With all speed, I rushed up the steps and jumped onto the deck. All the sailors were rushing to different spots, with swords and muskets, while Archer was shouting orders about preparing for battle stations.

"Miss Bennet!" White Wolf declared, grabbing my arm. "Get down below, now!"

"What is going on?" I asked, but the answer came to me quickly as I saw another ship on our larboard side, gaining on us. I saw the crew, and they were a ragged and motley sort.

"Pirates," White Wolf said, "they snuck up on us. Get down below, now!"

My spirit froze in me as fear swept over my face.

It was a pirate ship, true enough. The crew looked ragged and utterly like savages. They were going to board us. There was a battle ahead.

"Miss Bennet," White Wolf said, "Kitty, please!"

Hearing him say my first name brought me back to life. Remembering myself, I did as he bade me and rushed down below. Just as I reached my door, to tell Georgiana what was going on, I heard gunshots.

My eyes widened from the shock.

My mind was filled with horror.

We were being attacked.

Danger and evil now was coming into my life.

I had driven Georgiana into horror.

I would never forgive myself.

Afterword

Reader, thank you so much for reading this one. Of all the books that I wrote, this one was the greatest risk, because I had taken Kitty from all that was familiar, and hurled her into the unknown. As such, the reader had no choice but to go with her.

First, this is a novel that began one way and ended entirely differently than what I had intended.

Initially, I had written it to be a story entirely from Kitty's perspective, and no intercutting between her experiences and what was happening in England. It was originally to be a story entirely about her adventures.

Soon into writing that, it felt weird, and I realized that it was a terrible idea. It felt natural that the reader would want to know what was going on back in England. After all, when you throw the reader into an entirely different world, then it seems wise to also give them flashes of the familiar. So, that led to this story being a mixture of the different, but also the familiar, all in one section of the saga.

This sadly led to Kitty's story being more drawn out, because I had intended this story to also incorporate when Kitty and Georgiana had reached Australia, but I hope the reader understands why I had the instinct to put as much focus on life back home, making this chapter of the series more of an ensemble tale, rather than one from a sole narrative. I hope that I was correct and gave the reader what they preferred. But only time will tell.

The only negative aspect of this is that now there is more story after this, but all one can do is allow the story to unfold where it may. Please forgive me for that.

Also, when reverting the narrative back to England, there were several themes that were important to touch on. And that brings us to...

The Loss of Innocence

When in England, there are a great deal of characters experiencing many setbacks to their domestic joy. Particularly losing one's child. This was done for two reasons: first, miscarriages and infant mortality were very common back then, and so it brought an element of reality to the story. Secondly, it presented a loss of innocence in this story. Mary and Jane lose their firstborn, and now they must feel the sad effects of life turning their world upside down. They've suffered, and so the innocence of their lives has quite fallen away, and they are forced to meet the bitter parts of motherhood. Kitty, naturally, undergoes many setbacks in her life because she is the main character. Obstacles and conflicts are a given for her. But with the other sisters, they too, sometimes, must suffer their share of these conflicts as well. These trials will be arduous, but the sisters will persevere, in the end. What I mean is that there had been no books in the series where the lead characters were unsuccessful or lost at the moment. This book was there to present many obstacles that the heroes and heroines cannot fully defeat.

Kitty & Emma Watson

Now this was a deliberate choice that I made for good reason. As the series unfolded, whenever Kitty encountered another character from Miss Austen's other novels, Kitty always got along with them. And if she did not favor them initially, she did respect them when they confront their mistakes. But, overall, Kitty was never against them... until now. Emma Watson is the precise sort of woman who naturally would not get along with Kitty, for they were so very different than what they expected.

Kitty and Emma were so much the reverse of each other, and both were the exact opposite than what either lady would expect or want in a friendship, that it will take them both some time to become friends, if they ever do. This also offered a great deal of reality, because very rarely do friendships like that work: where two people are friends and then another friend enters the group, there is often tension or discomfort. That's how relationships often unfold, and we cannot easily command friendship from each other so easily. Also, it offered a different type of relationship for Kitty because it might have been unexpected. This aspect of the story was actually pinpointing something that many of us go through: having a close friendship, and then another person enters that group, shaking the bond that we have with that person, and a little friction occurs. I took what I have observed that many of us undergo and gave it to the heroine. I hope I wrote it in a way that was relatable.

Kitty, the Friend

Another risk to this tale was that Kitty is not the love interest. Or not the chief love interest. She spends the entire story away from the men that she has fallen in love with, while still holding fast to them. And probably always will. There was a brief second where I even considered that maybe she could fall in love with someone else, but that was a terrible idea! Sometimes, if you readers knew half the bad ideas that we writers have, and reconsidered before we committed ourselves to such lunacy, you would laugh.

Either way, this placed Kitty into a whole new role: as the friend in the story to others who are tossed in love. From her company to the crew, Kitty experiences many people who have been in love, never could commit to it, fell in love with the wrong person, or has undergone marital problems. And with the main character, Georgiana, being proposed to, Emma Watson being not considered, and Mr. Blake being rejected, Kitty is now an observer of all these situations. She gets to be on the outside, looking in. This suits her and gives her time to reset her life. This also shows that Kitty is no longer around people who are accustomed to her verbosity, her rambunctiousness, and her liberal mindset, and so she must deal with that as well and not being shielded any more. This leads to her having to defend herself all over again.

Also, since the first eight books of the series center around her experiences with Colonel Fitzwilliam and Finlay, it gave the series a chance to put Kitty in a new setting, with new people. But in this tale, by Kitty being focused on being a friend and wishing to always look after Georgiana, it presents another part of when someone is in love: of learning how to maintain even when the love interest is not around, and how to establish your identity throughout it all. That is the hardest part of one's life: the moment after. And she pursued something that the others were in pursuit of throughout the tale...

Freedom

All throughout this tale, there was the concept of the pursuit of freedom in some way, which is what the Lilia was symbolic of. Captain Archer associated himself as being both Canadian American and from the USA. This plurality of nature, and him embracing it, was felt keenly by him, and it taught him to accept difference rather than being a biased person. Also, with him being a male, it gave him the power to protect difference. Ergo, the Lilia, represented a place where differences were accepted and could be protected from the outside world, always inviting strife and discord. All the Lilia crew were a collection of people who had no qualms with others who were dissimilar to them and just wanted that one part of the world to call their own. This gave them the chance of liberty that they might not have if they were to leave the Lilia. And Arthur displays all the capabilities of a man who will always attempt to give them the chance that they need to flourish. He eagerly would protect Merriweather from being sold, his British sailors from being captured under the Impressment, of the women on his crew from not being put on equal footing, of White Wolf and the agonies that are occurring on his homeland, and a distinct intention to immerse as many cultures as he can. You could say that he collected difference, as if it was a commodity.

And Kitty, despite all the potential conflicts that she might face when being acquainted with the harshness of the world, goes to it all, no matter how ugly the scene might be. Perhaps it is because she understands the pursuit of freedom in others, because she is seeking the same thing. This leads to a dreary aspect, but a realistic one...

Facing Foes & Overcoming Obstacles

The fact is that this was a particular era in history where there was a lot of international unrest and conflict. To not write about it would be me completely ignoring history and giving a wholly unrealistic view on how the world was at the time. This led to Kitty having even more conversations where, being English, she would have to face some prejudice here and there. Again, it relates back to the idea of the pain that comes from innocence dying. She is not in a world where she is protected from these things but now must go where she has to face not being liked because of where she comes from, come to terms with her nation's history, and suffers being misunderstood. But she does not fear it, because she can empathize, while also holding her own, and trusting her own argument. That is another reason that I included such realities in the world, because it showed how Kitty is growing. All these actions show there is still great enhancement to her courage. And, if a lady is not given conflict, how do we see her strength? Kitty is becoming strong all on her own. It takes great character to see the ugly of life and still choose to see the beauty of it. She has reached that point. For those who wonder why I did not lean into the prejudices in that time in a harsher way, I admit that I preferred to do it through the use of comedy. I preferred it that way, because as Mary Poppins put it so eloquently 'a spoonful of sugar helps the medicine go down'. I'm at that stage where I look for the humor of things.

Also, there was another plus to Captain Archer's background being what he was: it gave him the chance to move about the high seas with ease. While I did not wish to fully limit myself to a particular year, this was still the time where there was tension between the USA and Britain, as well as there was a great deal of tension between Britain and other parts of Europe. Yet at this point, the USA had much trade with many parts of the world and had established friendships with other European nations. France, in particular. With Archer being Canadian, he could bring his crew to Britain with ease, and while also being from the USA, he could bring his passengers to other European nations, and they could easily be under his protection.

All Along the Watchtower

Reader, if you are familiar with the song, 'All Along the Watchtower', you might have heard the similar words being spoken by Kitty and Georgiana in one chapter. I was just having fun. Also, I liked the idea of Kitty and Georgiana saying something that, one day in the distant future, would be coincidentally used in a song. This was in connection to a quote from a play written by famous writer, Tom Stoppard, called Arcadia. There was a scene where a character named Thomasina was talking with her tutor about how she was sad that the Library of Alexandria had been burned by Julius Caesar, and all those great books there had gone up in flames, lost forever. Her tutor, Septimus Hodge, replied back with a monologue that began with the line: 'we shed as we pick up, like herders on the move'. What he implied was that when a work of a genius gets destroyed, another person comes along and has the same idea, and the world learns about it. Kitty and Georgiana are not the lead characters from 'Pride & Prejudice', so they will never be considered heroines, but in this tale, they are. And when they say that it's as if their genius dies over time, and gets recycled, turned into a song over a hundred years later. In the same way that Kitty and Georgiana's experiences are like the experiences that we have in life. We shed as we pick up...

Mr. Howard's Name Change

Yes, Reader, I had Mr. Howard request to be called by his middle name, Blake. This was not done out of any genius reason, but only nominal preferences. I've always liked the name Blake over Howard. I just do, no offense to the name 'Howard'. It's just a shallow preference. And I found myself wishing to write him as Mr. Blake instead of the name that Miss Austen gave him. So, I invented him having Blake as a middle name and being called that. But if it helps, in that time period, there were nicknames aplenty. I feel a little better, considering that historical fact.

Piracy

Yes, the novel ends with pirates attacking The Lilia. This was done so, because as I wrote, I realized that I never consider one of the common problems in that time: piracy. In all my novels, whenever a person was to travel by boat, on a voyage, they do so, and it is always safe. I had just realized that I never write about a common problem back then: pirates. When I began to write this, I realized that it would be best to show the risks a person undertook through traveling. But this catastrophe might prove to be an obstacle to make Kitty even better than she might ever be.

What of Jane, Mary, Maria Lucas, and other characters?In the next book, all will be explained, so I hope that you will still be here, ready to see these characters once more.

Friends, thank you so much for reading and I promise that I will do everything I can to make the last words in this series to be something that will hold your interest. Till the last word on the page, I will consider what works, and what ought to be attempted.

Thank you, Readers, and until the next time...

Ney Mitch

THANK YOU FOR READING

Did you enjoy this book?

We invite you to leave a review at your favorite book site, such as Goodreads, Amazon, Barnes & Noble, etc.

DID YOU KNOW THAT LEAVING A REVIEW...

- Helps other readers find books they may enjoy.
- Gives you a chance to let your voice be heard.
- Gives authors recognition for their hard work.
- Doesn't have to be long. A sentence or two about why you liked the book will do.

About the Author

Ney Mitch has been a long-standing Jane Austen enthusiast, having written forty novels that were inspired by her various works. Since stumbling on Miss Austen's books after graduating from college, she has always dabbled in Austen inspired literature, ranging from writing works for teens to adults. Originally, her desire was to adapt Jane Austen's writing in a way to help young adults connect with her, however over time, she has spread her aims to other genres and styles. Having received her BA Degree at Desales University, she is a writer, both literary and dramatic, as well as being a Historic Reenactor.

 facebook.com/courtney.mitchell.589
 x.com/CMMitchelPsyche
 pinterest.com/shebaanna

Also by Ney Mitch

WITH SATIN ROMANCE

Austen Gaskell Series

Curiosities & Contemplation

Resolved & Resigned

Triumph & Tragedy

Woes & Worries

Love & Labors Won

Economy & Ever After

~

Kitty Bennet Adventure Series

Vanities and Vexations

Forms & Fashions

Romance & Recklessness

Nuance & Novelty

Doubts & Difficulties

Follies & Forgiveness

Joys & Judgements

Happenstance & Holidays

~

Romance & Revolution Saga

The First Impression

~

The Memory Series

Moments of Moments Past

Moments of Moments Present

Moments of Moments Future

Moments of Moments Infinite

~

Pride & Prejudice Reimaginings

Rapture & Rebellion

Fortune & Misfortune

Desire & Destiny

Pride & Peace

Resolve & Revelations

Hope & Hopelessness

Faith & Family

~

Chances Series

Chances Are

Chances Come

Chances Fade

Chances End

~

Seasonal Situations

Considearations Near Christmastime

Curiosities at Christmastime

~

Novels

The Tale of Mr. & Mrs. Bennet: A Pride & Prejudice Christmas Tale

Considerations Near Christmastime

www.ingramcontent.com/pod-product-compliance
Lightning Source LLC
LaVergne TN
LVHW090557110826
845146LV00001B/162

* 9 7 9 8 8 8 6 5 3 4 9 6 2 *